the boys from Sharon

the boys
from Sharon

by Louise Field Cooper

Harper & Brothers
Publishers, New York

the boys from Sharon

I

MRS. FANNING's brother, Mr. Forrest Howe, always referred to the part of the day which fell between breakfast and luncheon as *the forenoon,* and Mrs. Fanning was apt to observe that he was the only person, besides their long-dead grandfather, she had ever heard use the word. "Grandfather, and people in the country," she amended herself by adding with the intention of being strictly fair, and in this observation of hers was lightly stuck, not at all too deeply for his notice, the implication that Mr. Howe, if content with the word *forenoon,* might have other old-fashioned tendencies.

Mr. Forrest Howe's name, itself sounding a little like an idle question, was misleading. He was quite free from curiosity. A lifetime of close association with his sister, and flanked on both sides by a consuming indifference and a disinclination to finding out things, prevented Mr. Howe ever from asking why she objected to his using the idiom of their grandparents, and he went right on saying "I may walk down to the library this forenoon," and "Seems a trifle warmer, this forenoon, doesn't it?"

This adherence to customs of his youth must not imply that he was a determined, stubborn man. It was only that change of any kind was abhorrent to him, an attitude alien to Mrs. Fanning. What was so wonderful about the *status quo*, she would have demanded. If he would take the trouble to look about him he couldn't help seeing how things need changing in this world; things need doing.

Nine o'clock one mild late-April day found them sitting in the morning room opening their mail. ("You wouldn't call it the *forenoon* room, would you?" she had once suddenly turned and asked him, her paper knife, like an often-polished silver small-sword, poised above an invitation to attend the annual meeting of a convalescent home for elderly gentlemen with alcoholic tendencies. But that had been years ago.) Now, as was their custom, right after breakfast they sat, apart but similarly occupied, in the high-ceilinged corner room against whose long windows crowded ancient green-leather-leaved rhododendrons. The whole house was set, a cube of smooth brown dressed stone, a dark Greek temple, in a crown of rhododendron. The branches pressed against every downstairs window. Secret roots must have run under the cellars and perhaps, by now, they touched.

Mrs. Fanning was erect at her desk in the bay window in the corner, at her elbow waiting her crouched, obedient telephone. Dreaded by some women, it was not by Mrs. Fanning. It was the instrument with which she was wont to pluck one-dollar bills or one-thousand-dollar checks out of a man's pocket and as good as send them sailing right over the town, through the air, into some other depository—right over streets and buildings to a quite different section of town—though sometimes the particular clinic or day nursery she had in mind was just in back of where the man lived, and then he would say how surprised he was to learn it, but gratified, naturally, gratified. Mrs. Fanning considered the telephone the blessing of the age. Now at her desk her silver knife flashed and flickered in the sun and Mr. Howe, in a plum-colored velvet chair by the hearth, wielded more modestly, more neatly and slowly, the small, pearl-handled penknife that had lived for forty years in his vest pocket.

Every morning Mr. Howe confronted the same problem: How to eke out his scant correspondence so it would take him as long to read and thereby appear to both of them to be as heavy, absorbing, and important, as hers actually was—an insoluble problem, indeed an impossible objective ever to have set himself, as she had been the first to discover, years ago when he and his daughter had come to live with her in her house on Evergreen Avenue. Her letters, catalogues, circulars, a substantial heap, were always waiting on the blotter on her desk when she walked in from the dining room and his mail ever since the day, a new widower, he had come there had been laid on the mantel a little to the left of the gold French clock whose nervous interior goings-on were visible through plate glass walls. Sometimes, as he followed his sister into the morning room, still aware of his last swallow of coffee, he was mortally afraid, so low and insignificant his pile that it didn't show from the door, that the morning had at last come, long dreaded, long imagined, when there was no mail at all beyond the gold clock. But if that day ever came wouldn't he sit down in his chair as usual, reach two fingers into his pocket for the penknife, carefully open the blade as usual in the manner he had been taught by his

[3]

father when he was a boy, and then—oh, probably that day would never come; there would always be something, it was no matter what, waiting for him to open.

Winter mornings he ostentatiously crumpled up his two or three envelopes and magazine wrappers and tossed them into the fire exactly as he would have done if, bored at such plenitude, there had been eighteen or twenty of them; and in some mysterious way this definite action mitigated their scarcity and in a few minutes he was able to pretend to himself that there had been quite a handful to tend to this morning, and that of them all he had cleverly culled and retained only the most important ones. But on a lovely warm Spring morning like this, with no fire burning in the grate and the only wastebasket in the room planted by immutable law over near the desk, thus well within his sister's domain and much too far for him to risk failure by tossing, his two envelopes could, in no way that would have occurred to Mr. Howe, be got rid of with ease.

So he sat quiet, the very portrait of an elderly man absorbed to the exclusion of everything else with his correspondence, one letter open on his knee, the other, a piece of pure white pasteboard, held between thumb and finger as if it were an invitation to a diplomatic reception of possibly quite considerable importance. He was smiling the slight smile of one who admits he is not ashamed to feel gratified at being yet again included on her list by the fashionable Duchess of Q and then, though no one at all was watching him, he frowned faintly, not as perhaps one ought because of the unfortunate scarcity of duchesses in Connecticut, but as one would who is plagued by the normal human inability to be sure whether, after all, he might not be prevented from accepting her invitation by some previous engagement he must do his best to remember. He said "H'm," but not loud enough for his sister to ask, "What's the matter?" Carefully he read the card again, every word; it was the brisk, biannual summons from his dentist's office to come next Friday at three and spend an hour with the prophylaxis assistant. No one knew better than he that he had no conflicting engagement, but the frown on his gray brow did not go away, because now he was recalling how very much he disliked having Miss Blodgett's clean stubby fingers poking about in his mouth. He loathed the brightening of her pop eyes when she found something wrong and the quiet smile that played about her lips as she picked up a red pencil to make a cruel little *x* on the printed diagram of his teeth, a diagram it was absurd to suppose bore any resemblance to the way it really was, inside his mouth. To him, the outside of his mouth was more significant, being, if small, nevertheless neat and firm, and decorated by the finest imaginable gray imperial. If people ever said the thing that is really in their minds, Mr. Howe would have said to Miss Blodgett, twice a year, in April and October, "I daresay it's seldom you are fortunate enough to work above a neat imperial such as mine, eh Miss Blodgett?" But so far he had never said this, or anything like it, and so far she had maintained the dominant position in their relationship. Nor was she likely to lose it for she stood while he had to remain not only seated but bibbed, and all the sharp little tools belonged to her.

"Well," he said now, sighing, laying aside the card, and the sigh could have applied equally well to the unpleasant zeal of Miss Blodgett or the importunity of a duchess. The other communication, as he had known from its envelope, appealed for money for a newsboys' summer camp. He was about to go up to the small desk in his bedroom to deal

[5]

with these when Mrs. Fanning, erect in her corner, extended him a temporary reprieve.

"They're coming," she said, and flicked the blue pages of a letter backward and forward.

"Coming? Who are coming?"

"The boys."

Mrs. Fanning read on in the letter which was only one of so many. When she had finished she flipped it back and forth again, picking out bits of information for her private eye. "The worst week of the whole year, for me," she said with satisfaction, for she loved the conquest of obstacles, and Mr. Howe murmured, "Boys, you said?" in an inquiring tone. He cleared his throat after the question in order to leave every faculty at its peak to receive her answer.

"I told you the other day. Cousin Mary Langdon's little boys from up in Sharon. Her father was the Fannings' first cousin, you know, way back. She, Mary, comes down for Garden Club meetings occasionally and I see her there. Well, she's had pneumonia—I *told* you all this! and her husband's taking her to Bermuda for a week. Flying. And the maid broke her wrist. Her *own* wrist," she explained firmly, having glanced up and seen the faintly bewildered look on her brother's face.

"She could take them with her to Bermuda," he suggested, really believing this Mrs. Langdon up in Sharon might not have thought of that solution and would be grateful to have it pointed out to her.

"She wants a *rest*."

"Oh, I see," he replied docilely, but as a matter of fact he couldn't have, because he himself never needed a rest from anything. There was never anything he needed a rest from. His parental responsibilities he had long ago relin-

[6]

quished to his sister, and though this had perhaps not been a conscious act, he had had no cares of any kind since that day. "*I* see. Well, of course, in that case . . . but I should think there'd be someone in Sharon who would take them in."

"So should I! But apparently not. There is a measles epidemic among their friends. She seems to think it doesn't matter if they miss a week of school . . . Actually, I don't suppose having them here will make the slightest difference. In fact I am quite sure it will make no difference at all." She laid down the letter, and deftly disemboweled with her silver small-sword an appeal from a Southern mountain school for funds to teach weaving to women in cottages.

Catherine Foley came crabwise along the narrow, dark-varnished, echoing, empty back passage bringing the list for the day's ordering. At the last minute in the kitchen she had gone back to the table and with her stumpy pencil scribbled something that might have been *currents* very quickly in between *white peper* and *cellery*, believing that this illegibility would insure a corresponding, magical laxity in Mrs. Fanning's attention. Both Catherine Foley and Anna, the second maid, drank warmed-up coffee and ate handfuls of dried currants at all hours; it was almost their only mutual satisfaction; Mrs. Fanning had been known to say she simply couldn't even imagine why she was asked to buy currants quite so often.

"They go in the gingerbread, ma'am," Catherine would answer listlessly but Mrs. Fanning would have been justified in asking, "But what gingerbread?" because when had Catherine last baked gingerbread? Years ago.

As she invariably did, Catherine approached the erect

[7]

black silk cylinder of her mistress from behind and, as if Mrs. Fanning had the eyes in the back of her head her servants credited her with, held out the curl of paper and said, "Here's the grocery list, ma'am," and instantly withdrew it. Then while she waited for Mrs. Fanning to turn to her from her letters she stood motionless, monumentally disinterested; if she had to wait more than two or three minutes she would begin, very gently and softly, unconsciously to fret the side of the neck above her uniform collar with the edge of the list. But today a long tight black silk sleeve and a white hand with delicately brown liver spots reached quickly around to her.

"Currants again? And I wouldn't say turnips; not at this time of year. I'll ask for something green . . . Oh, and Catherine, there will be two little boys staying here for a week, beginning day after tomorrow." The hurried, carefully offhand way Catherine was given this surprising bit of news was so exactly like her own slipping of currants onto the grocery list that she smiled; Mrs. Fanning mistook the smile for the well-trained servant's façade, instantly adjustable in front of annoyance. "Their mother is very, very ill," she said in a reproachful voice as if Catherine might almost have had a hand in it, "so ill she cannot have them around." (At that identical moment Mary Langdon up in Sharon was joyfully pulling her last summer's dresses from a wardrobe and tossing them about; "I'll wear *this* bicycling, and *this* sailing!" she said to her husband who passed through the room trailing seersucker suits; "I can hardly wait, can you?") "So will you please tell Anna to get two beds ready, *not* in the same room. One of the guest-room beds, and the couch in the upstairs sitting room." Mrs. Fanning was glad she had thought of separating them. Having been reared in the country they

[8]

were probably rambunctious and healthy and noisy and contentious; though of course not refugees in any real meaning of the word, perhaps she thought of them a little that way; one would have to do one's best for them, no matter how they might object; one knew best, naturally. "Yes, separate rooms." Divide and conquer, she said to herself, felicitously.

"Yes, ma'am. Do they eat with the family?"

Mrs. Fanning considered. She looked out through plate glass to her wide lawn, a line of low iron fence, and Evergreen Avenue, her hands resting at the edge of the desk, idle for the moment beside the pile of letters, the appeals to her for money, for expert advice, for guidance. In a moment she would turn on them her full attention but just now she sat motionless. For a space of time briefer than between two ticks of the clock she wished . . . she almost wished—No, no; Spring was not the time to drop everything and go outdoors and do nothing; Spring was when the clinics needed money for repainting and when the whooping-cough cases began at the day nurseries. A car with its top back for the first time that year came coasting along, carrying University students to classes; schoolgirls who must have belonged to the afternoon session at the high-school downtown, out now when they should have been home doing homework but drawn out by the Spring air, strolled aimless looking and in pairs, laughing, sometimes laughing very loudly, and raising one foot high before slapping it down to emphasize their mirth. These girls wore cotton dresses but some uncertainty that Spring could really be here, probably on the part of their mothers, had made them bring out jackets too, and these they wore as Superman wears his cloak, resting only on their shoulders; but Mrs. Fanning, who didn't know about

Superman, thought there was no reason why they couldn't have put their arms through the sleeves. Young men of the University who did not own cars or were not susceptible to Spring fever, went by on foot to the Chemistry Laboratory at the top of Evergreen Avenue, or to the Library at the foot.

"Dinners, you wouldn't want them," Catherine said. "I wouldn't think." Maybe you would though, she thought, so you could get after their table manners. "Cold cereal in the pantry at five o'clock," she suggested, helpful and dreary. Anna could perfectly well sweep up the spume of Rice Krispies from the pantry floor.

"Well, I don't know. They're about seven or eight, and twelve. I don't know if they dine with their own family at home." It had been so long since any boys had lived in that ancient house, how could anyone now living there know what boys were like? Mr. Fanning had been born there, but there he had also died, and in their intervening years together it had not occurred to Mrs. Fanning to inquire into his childhood. By the law of averages the house must once have held various children, but long ago; portraits hung here and there of little boys who had become her husband's uncles—smoothly parted hair, wide white collars and brief jackets—such demure little boys they might have belonged to a different race from the two invaders about to descend, like Goths, from the North. "They're just two perfectly healthy, *ordinary* boys," Mary Langdon had said proudly and Mrs. Fanning thought she knew what that meant.

"Rice Krispies and peanut butter samwidges?" suggested the aproned martyr.

"Oh, that doesn't seem quite right." Her eyes were on the green lawn, on the avenue filled with sunlight, but now her fingers drummed on the desk, restless to get back to sorting out the letters that justified attention today from those that could wait until tomorrow. Out on the avenue even the young men who must surely be expected to arrive at their classes at some specified and probably imminent moment were walking slowly, as if through sand, or under a spell. "What do *you* think, Forrest?" Mrs. Fanning turned away from the window to look at her brother who had been sitting all this time on the other side of the room interested, as much as he could ever be said to be so occupied, in the conversation at the desk.

"Well, I wonder."

Mrs. Fanning accorded this reply the consideration it deserved and turned back to Catherine. "They ought to have a dessert too, growing boys."

"Milk too." Catherine bent her head, falsely meek, and gazed at the Ispahan rug. It was quite an agreeable little game, this slowly bringing up points about her young guests that Mrs. Fanning herself hadn't thought of. Catherine did not care for children. "Sallid," she said.

"I suppose it would be a civilizing influence if we had them with us in the dining room. All right, Catherine. They'll eat with us."

Mr. Howe roused slightly and said oh, did she think it would be? He'd heard somewhere that modern parents let their children run absolutely wild so that they were anything *but* civilized.

"That's just what I mean! Honestly, Forrest! They'll dine with us, Catherine."

Mr. Howe, rebuffed, swept his two letters together, rose, left the morning room and mounted to his bedroom and his desk by the long straight stairs with the dark-mustard velvet stair rug and the broad mahogany hand rail that

[11]

no one had even thought of sliding down for fifty years past, or more.

Mrs. Fanning, carrying some of her letters, crossing the hall to set the front door open on the beautiful morning, encountered her niece, Forrest Howe's daughter, who, her hair smoothly brushed and her long-handled purse slung from her shoulder, was coming down the stairs. Hanging on the walls, dark with thick wall paper—ginger-brown paper embossed with navy-blue fleurs-de-lis—the big, old-fashioned mirrors would have scorned to flatter a modern young woman, but Mrs. Fanning thought: What a strong healthy big girl! and then: But then why doesn't she get herself a job?

"The little Langdon boys *are* coming," she said aloud, and reached out a heel to straighten the edge of a rug; how could the person who had caused a rug to become crooked bear to go off and leave it that way!

"Oh, they are? Too bad." Edith paused at the foot of the stairs in case she were to be told more about this most unusual divergence from their everyday way of life but her true thoughts continued flying out ahead of her impatiently, across her aunt's narrow straight black left shoulder and past her pearls, and streaming off on their own to the open door at the front of the hall, and through it, and out into the warm April day. "Awfully warm, for April," she said. She wanted nothing but to be on her way downtown to buy short white gloves; the surprisingly early Spring this year had made her long for them, though her father insisted on repeating, "It can't last," whenever anyone mentioned the mildness of the air. Now she wanted to escape from the house and walk alone along sunny sidewalks. "Too bad," she said again, with some idea of pleas-

[12]

ing her aunt by sounding womanlike and concerned and fussy; "just this week, I mean, with your culture club dinner on your hands." She thought well of herself for having so opportunely remembered the dinner; it was seldom enough that she bothered to put domestic twos and twos together and get as the sum of that addition a full-blown worry.

Mrs. Fanning had been teased by this very misgiving ever since slitting open Mary Langdon's gay, grateful note. "*Not* at all. What difference will having two little boys here make to the Recusants? They'll be in bed, quiet." Mrs. Fanning admitted no apprehension about being able to manage the boys, refractory though they might be. She had behind her twenty years of serenely directing the house committee of a home for juvenile delinquents and for an even longer period had been the chairman of the finance committee of an agency for placing orphans in private homes. "They will hardly be ruffians," she pointed out to Edith, whose intentions had been so good. "After all, Mary Langdon's father was Judge Fanning's first cousin and her uncle kept the finest horses in Litchfield County." If she had been a trifle uneasy at the anticipation of a large dinner party embedded in the very middle of a weekful of strange children staying in the house, she now tossed away that uneasiness as unworthy. She told Edith she was delighted the Langdons had decided to send her the boys, and the maids had little enough to do as it was, Heaven knew; how like Mrs. Fanning it was to assume Heaven kept particular account of her household! "If you go near Heilbroner's," she said, "go in and get some candy. Not lollipops; I don't trust the stick." Edith said she would. "I don't want any accidents while they're in *my* house. Anywhere else is their family's concern. But get

[13]

colored mints, or gumdrops. Gumdrops may be the best of all. Charge them. Get plenty."

This commission seemed almost permission to depart and Edith hitched the strap higher on her shoulder and fitted the fingers of her left glove down with the straightened forefinger of the right. Now that she was so near freedom she could afford to be not-herself for one minute longer. "It's good of you to have them," she said. "What are their names?"

Mrs. Fanning selected a blue letter from among the white sheaf in her hand and flicked it over, searching. Edith subsided onto one foot; why had she asked? She couldn't have cared less; their names would come with them. As if it mattered! Two grubby little boys! She was annoyed with herself for having given in—not that she did very often—to the nagging omnipresent realization that with so little in common with her aunt any concern that allowed them to meet on neutral ground had best be encouraged. But it should be briefly, briefly! She waited, staring without interest at Mrs. Fanning, whose appearance had not changed one whit during the years and years that Edith had lived there; the perfectly straight part divided the strong gray hair that met again in a rather high bun at the back, the silent secret pearls lay as they always had, guarding the high neck of the cylindrical smart black dress.

"M'mm," said Mrs. Fanning not caring at all that she was keeping her niece waiting; "no," and she turned back to the front page and read it to herself again.

"George and Lucius," she said at last.

Edith, an arrow released, sped straight along the hall and out the door. She ran down the sandstone steps that

[14]

looked as though sugar and some of the hardest and darkest cinnamon in the world had been squeezed and pressed and dried into blocks; under her feet they felt that way too and she always wondered if a few reluctant grains came off on the soles of shoes every time anyone went up or down.

The avenue was only two blocks long but the early town fathers had indulged a charming whim and laid it out to be most unusually wide with broad stretches of green grass, almost lawns, between the stone sidewalks and the roadway. Edith had supposed the avenue to be a park when, as a child, she had first come there to live. In each of these supernumerary lawns, in front of each spacious property, lay a scallop of tarmac where cars now, once carriages, drove in from the street and most of these shallow recurrent single parentheses had at their apex a hitching post of the nineteenth century, figures many times repainted, in red and blue and black and white, of Negro boys with one hand holding up a ring, or of patient dog heads with the ring under their chins and before some houses stood impersonal short iron posts with elaborately convoluted tops, like iron buds. Low railings, scarcely more than tokens of restraint, pressed out of iron and painted black over innumerable Springs, ran up beside the sidewalks; low and heavy, they looked as though they had been pressed from tar. Very high, parklike elms, still with only the youngest of leaves, rose, immense long-handled greenish feather dusters, over the houses—huge square dark Classic Revival houses of purple-brown cut stone with pure springing porticoes of blue-chocolate carved and painted wood—dark Greek temples. There were, too, occasional white or lemon-colored clapboard houses with white captain's walks and Ionic columns. All the Evergreen

[15]

Avenue houses were set in vast rosettes of ancient laurel and rhododendron that surrounded them like crowns, and clotted and rose up again in the corners of the vast lawns. Now a sparse froth of pansies and a few early poet's narcissus showed beneath the old bushes hiding the house foundations. Almost all the Evergreen Avenue gardeners had been caught off guard by the earliness of the Spring, and beneath many hedges mats of wet leaves still lay.

At the top and bottom of the avenue could be seen University buildings, buildings as capriciously varied in their architecture as the careers of the men who had made gifts of their money to build them. They had nothing in common with the cool classic shapes of the Evergreen Avenue houses. Oil into Gothic, Edith had thought, wheat into Byzantine complete with mosaics, railroads into 1910 English Perpendicular—all wrought by some odd alchemy.

She walked along now, tall and smooth-haired, one hand on the bag at her side. Only away from Mrs. Fanning's beautiful house did she feel herself. "Whenever I'm with Aunt Clara I feel as if I had my head in a brown paper bag," she had once cried in desperation to her roommate at college. The roommate had shrewdly inquired whose fault that was, and Edith had replied, with quick exasperation, that she didn't *know* whose. Why then had she not already escaped forever from that house by taking a job? She could not have said. Some invisible cord netted her feet. It was not that she was afraid her father would miss her; "I'm going to get a job as soon as I can," she sometimes told him defiantly and he did not demur. Perhaps if he had, she would have bestirred herself to thwart him; but it was almost impossible to thwart Mr. Howe. He wasn't vain about this distinction of his, this almost unique

[16]

trait, because he didn't know about it, but the truth is he was unthwartable, from not caring.

Probably if her aunt hadn't so often urged regular occupation upon her, Edith would have started looking seriously; putting it off gave her the sensation, rare enough with her, of having the upper hand of Mrs. Fanning.

The sun shone on her, and the eyes of the young men of Physics B3, who were moving past her in an uneven procession on their way to class. The eyes of strangers—blue, brown, green—they searched out her eyes, asking some age-old, formless, urgent question which she was not prepared to answer. She walked straight past them all, ignoring the question, in pride and fear. Dozens of young men; she pretended not to feel their living glance. "Adolescents!" she would have said, severely, herself twenty, if anyone had pointed them out to her.

2

GEORGE woke in the strange bed.

He was almost no hump in the bed at all, and what little hump he was went only a short way toward the foot of it. But he did not feel short to himself.

He lay and looked about the strange room, his glance darting; the flick of straight sandy hair at the crown of his head waved against the pillow. "George does his hair like a myrtle warbler," his father had once said, and indeed there was something very birdlike about him now, with only his pointed face showing above the linen sheet. The mahogany headboard towered above him, inset up near the top with triangles of white and blue enamel; very handsome and unusual, thought George, rolling his eyes far back. His bed at home was nothing like this; exiguous in the extreme, it was only four identical plain feet and a box spring.

It was very early, but George did not say to himself, "Good; I can go back to sleep for another hour," but only, "Well! Because I'm awake *now* has begun." He had told his friends at school: "Lucius and I are going on a hollow day," and this was the beginning of it. His fingers curled over the sheet, near his chin, like little claws and now he looked exactly like a myrtle warbler in bed. He thought he was the only person awake in the whole house, and perhaps in that whole city. The light beyond the big windows was pale gold, pristine, still cool and hanging motionless and early, laced through with the singing of birds. A band of this light, colored a secret, promising pink, lay on the white window casing—light as yet unused by the world of people. This pink is so unlike evening-pink, which contains a strong regretful tinge of yellow, the yellow of experience, and misuse. Oh, it was very early. Somewhere outside, high above the lawn, bluejays sped from elm to elm screaming down harsh admonition on the sleeping world—*"Quiet! . . . Quiet! . . . Quiet! . . ."* They sounded furious.

George rolled his eyes sideways and was amazed to see how much more of the bed there was than he was occupying. Lucius could perfectly well have spent the night there too, but the people downstairs had said No. His glance leaped across a narrow space and there—"Heavens sakes," said George—was another tremendous bed, the twin of the one he was in. But Lucius wasn't in that one either. The white counterpane, running up from the foot and over a bank of pillows, made of it an untouched Alpine meadow. George squinted and was able to imagine minute men on skis taking off from the topmost point of the pillows and having a wonderful run down. "You'll sleep better alone," Mrs. Fanning had said the night before. It had not occurred to either boy to say that sleeping badly had never been one of their problems.

A secret, dawn breeze was moving, exploring, in the room, unaware yet that George was there in the bed. He

[19]

could see it come in at the open window, stirring the white gossamer of the inner curtains, touching the plumes of the dried pampas grass bouquet, fingering inquiringly the coarse lace edge of the bureau cover. Moving on, quietly, it came over to the bed in time and very, very gently, but inquisitively, it lifted as if with one finger the jutting wisp of George's crest of hair.

What would the day bring to him? George was too young for a watch, and anyway there had always been some grownup near by who seemed more than willing to tell him it was time to do something, time to hurry up and do this, that or the other. Indeed, it would have worried George very much to be late to school or to neglect his teeth; he wouldn't have doubted that the principal would summon him in instantly to glower at him, or that his teeth, hopelessly committed to destruction by his failure to brush them, would one day all fall out in a heap. He did not know what time it was now; it felt a lot earlier than the hour he was accustomed to wake in his room at home. Then he heard, far off, in no known direction, but certainly in that strange house, a kitchen noise, the single bang of a saucepan or an oven door or a garbage pail lid, a sound unmistakably emanating from a kitchen, and he drew a little shallow breath of relief, arched his spine once, with relief, and flounced, once, under the blankets. The hour, though so early, must then be an hour within human cognizance. It had almost seemed to him to be an hour so early as to be nameless, numberless on any clock and outside daily human experience—one not worth counting, perhaps, by grownups, who have time so well harnessed and trained for their own purposes.

He hopped out of bed and over to the window. Squirrels were arabesquing in the windy trees; perhaps it was at

[20]

them the jays were screaming their exhortations to quiet; but the squirrels weren't saying a word. One, his jet eye bright with early-morning squirrel-euphoria, raced along a branch outside George's window as if pretending his life depended on it and then, at the very tip, just where new leaves were beginning to show, and just before he launched himself out into infinite space, as if suddenly overcome by Spring fever, he outdid any circus performer George had ever seen in a series of back flips and leaps—he positively danced in the air and landed right side up on a branch ten feet away and sped off. "Oh boy," George whispered, instantly convinced by the smoothness of this performance that he could do the same. He measured with his eyes the distance between sill and branch; too far. Too bad. Too far even for Lucius, who wouldn't have wanted to anyway. Lucius preferred to stroll calmly about his world with his hands in his pockets, and it exasperated George who felt that anyone lucky enough to be four years older than he was ought at least to want to do considerably more dangerous feats even than the possible ones which occurred, so constantly and fortunately, to himself.

He looked about the room. Last night he had been sure he would never shut an eye in this strange place but now he realized he must have been nearly asleep even while undressing, because he didn't remember a single thing in the room from the night before. All the furniture was very large, a great deal larger than he needed and in the plush lap of the largest chair the smaller of his two suitcases looked like a lunch box; this was his own particular case, the object of the greatest concern to him whenever he traveled; his clothes, in which he took no interest, were all in the larger one. It was in the small case that his own private treasures always went, objects inadmissible to the larger one and, indeed, too good for it. On an overnight trip the Fall before to New York he had used it to take along the engine to his electric train which hadn't, after all, turned out to be so very useful in a hotel bedroom though always nice to look at. This time he had brought his Chinese painted glass harp, from which he planned never to be separated as long as he lived.

He pounced now, and undid the catches. How *could* he have callously gone to bed without first assuring himself of the safety of this holy toy! He must have been the next thing to dead with sleep. The brass catches on the case flew up and bit his fingers, but he didn't notice. Ah, there it lay, half-hidden in a drift of Sharon grass cuttings. The narrow, green silk blades were compliantly bent under the weight of the strips of painted glass, glass so clear it appeared that the little flowers on them, red and white and pink, were the flowers of the grass itself; the glass quite disappeared as he stared and by a process of prolonged mystic not-blinking, he could see only vermilion petals, pink buds, and the bits of silver passe partout fastening together the prisms; these might have been silver flowers, to his enchanted gaze. His vision cleared and he hooked a fearful forefinger under the red string loop and slowly drew it forth. It was perfectly all right. It wasn't broken, or faded, or any less beautiful than he remembered, and the trip from Sharon had done nothing to hurt it; he released his indrawn breath of fear, a kind of fear that, as must be admitted of parental fear, often has in it an admixture of induced concern, a fear which can recur repeatedly, any number of times and without reason, and each time be so painful it is hard to imagine ever being that much worried about anything again.

He stood in his striped seersucker pajamas by the open

window and held his treasure up to the morning light, dry grass tips sprinkling down. His feet, warm from bed and sleep, grew cold on the polished floor and the breeze returned, wandering into the unbuttoned top of his pajamas He didn't notice. The breeze came up and out, lifted his hair and, with curiosity, touched the hanging glass strips of his harp and made them tinkle, a happening that never ceased to delight him. It sounded like the tips of icicles sparring, or water hurrying under snow. The casual pagoda of fragile glass and painted pale red and poison green Chinese characters and flowers precariously threaded on its pale red string and pasted with its square bits of silver paper was a magic thing to him. It had secret properties, supernatural powers, close connections with fairyland. While he possessed it he possessed powers too, undefined and mysterious. He almost believed it could grant wishes and in a way he prayed to it. The sunlight struck the swinging crystals as gently as the air had, and colored refractions leaped onto the side of the big bureau and ran around on the rug. "Hot dog," said George, tenderly, worshiping.

Lucius came in from the next room, yawning and yawning as if his heart would break. "Hi," he said, and had to bite off even this simple greeting to yawn again.

"Hi. Lookit."

Lucius came over and touched the harp with a reverent finger but George, apprehensive, swayed it out of reach. "It'll break; I know it will."

"Nuts, George," Lucius said, kindly. "Why should it? Don't werry."

"I *am* werried." The more beautiful it looked to him, the more vulnerable he believed it to be. They contemplated it together, Lucius' broad brow and sandy crest a head higher than George. They discussed where to hang it

[23]

so it should be utterly safe. To George the world was a far more complicated place than it ever appeared to Lucius— full of sudden uncertainties, inexplicable rewards, precarious joys. The exercise of free choice was hard for him; his feet caught in the hedge of doubt. Though he protested loudly against advice, and scoffed and fought, yet he would always rather be advised than not. Lucius had more faith than he in their fellow humans, but on the other hand George still believed you could obtain Heaven with the top from a box of dry cereal. He now expressed a suspicion that there might be persons, yet unknown to him, living in this house who would enjoy doing the holy toy harm but Lucius, with something unnamable that was more than his four years' age advantage, said he doubted it very much. His own private small suitcase was stuffed to bursting because there had been so many things he felt he might need —Duco cement, bits of wood with possibilities, an illustrated copy of *The Golden Dog,* the major part of his stamp collection; none of these treasures caused him the acute concern that George's harp caused him.

"Hang it on one of these bureau drawer knobs," he suggested.

"Oh, mercy, no." George tiptoed away from the very vicinity of the bureau; every time he opened a drawer for a pair of socks the harp would be in jeopardy.

"On the end of the curtain rod, then."

George squinted up to the top of the tall window draped in ginger-brown plush and masked in filmy white. An ornamental brass hanger sustained these, ending in knobs of pointed, sharply fluted, thin-brass fruit. He tiptoed toward a chair and teetered up onto it, but apprehension weakened him and he backed down again, the harp still held high in his hand. He would scarcely be able to see and

[24]

commune with it hung way up there; the prisms could never tinkle against those choking velvet folds; it would *feel neglected* way up there in the shadows; possibly he might even forget about it, so frail is human nature. "There's nowhere," he said hopelessly. "This is a horrible house."

3

EDITH HOWE, a bath towel spread around her shoulders like a damp cape, came out into the ten o'clock sunshine in the side porch. Though not yet May, it was as warm there as it would be in June. At one time—when the house had been built, something over a hundred years ago—people walking up the new development of Evergreen Avenue could look across the wide bare new lawn into this porch running along the side of the house but then someone, not long after, had planted a curve of rhododendron and lilac that now, a dense green arm, insured privacy.

Edith carried a big amber brush and comb and was running the comb through the white bristles energetically, making drops of water leap up and out. She laid the brush and comb to dry at the edge of the sloping porch and sat down on the floor boards with her knees up and her back to the yard; there was no railing. Carefully, very gently and delicately she shook her head, side to side, to make the heavy hair fall evenly and then, as carefully, nipped the very ends under with her fingers; when it was dry it would be a wig with the ends turned out of sight, defying the law of gravity. She always said she had no sympathy with girls who trailed off to hairdressers every week and sat about, prisoners for hours, beneath their insanely humming machines. This fastidiousness of hers, this unwillingness to do as the rest of her generation did, sprang from various causes and lived very strong in her. Because she had spent most of her life in a house of indubitable elegance, she was proud; because she and her father were, relatively, hangers-on there, she was ashamed. She would not spend even a part of the small allowance she had on going to a hairdresser, and by quick degrees this small abstention had grown, and became disapproval; and this disapproval spread itself over many facets of life that she knew little of. For instance, she had pretended to herself so long that it would be necessary to relinquish some part of her reserve if she found herself appealing to the young men at the University, that now she quite believed it. She said she stayed in that town, in that house, only because the right job hadn't yet presented itself; once it did, she would be off like a shot. *Never,* she said, would she have come back to Evergreen Avenue from junior college except that she had not yet found the job she wanted. At first Mrs. Fanning had urged her to go to parties, now she was home, but this very urging had alienated from her any desire or intention to go. "I'm too tall," she had said, experimentally, and Mrs. Fanning's prompt "Nonsense!" had finished the job.

She picked up the comb, hot from the hot sun, and drew its very tips once across the top of her head; she might have been dealing with floss, so meticulous was her touch. "The electric drier is the twentieth century Iron Woman, a barbarous instrument of torture," she had once said scornfully to her roommate. "Unbearable. Worse than the Iron

[27]

Woman, *because of its hot breath.*" She found it necessary to reiterate her convictions frequently for the benefit of the roommate, who backslid biannually into a permanent wave. "But *I* loathe being touched," said Edith. Probably even if she could have afforded it, she would have been antipathetic to the relaxed atmosphere of beauty shops, contemptuous of their flimsy, tattered, women's magazines. "Where's this week's *New Republic?*" she had once inquired. In beauty shops the glass ashtrays were never quite free of a deathly gray smell of tobacco ash, or the floors from a scurf of fluff and hair and hairpins. She had discovered, with shock and regret, that listening for even a few moments to exclusively women's talk made her own voice shrill and nervous; when attendants, all in her interest, approached from behind to wrap a length of oiled silk about her throat, she felt a mounting claustrophobia.

Now as she picked up the sun-warmed brush and drew it carefully backward over the crown of her head and down, her other hand following stealthily after to be sure that every hair knew its place, Anna came out onto the porch with her mop.

"God Heaven," she said amiably. "You vashed it again?"

"Oh, well." Edith went only a little way onto the defensive; Anna wasn't critical, merely interested. "Why not?"

"Vy not," Anna agreed and gave the mop a shake or two in the direction of the rhododendron barricade. "Vy not. Vy not. Costs nodding." She paused, leaned on the mop and contemplated the bent head. "Ven I voss a liddle girl, not a young lady like you are, but real liddle, oh how I used to bross and bross on my hair. Bross, bross, bross. Svediss people, we don't vash so much, ve yoost bross."

"Yes, I know." Edith had heard this before, many times, and she had by no means yet reached the state of grace, if

[28]

indeed she ever would, where she understood the urge of domestic servants to tell you the same thing over and over again. Surely, she always thought with wonder, Anna must know she's told me this at least a dozen times; twenty times! Sometimes the girl would make exactly the same reply the anecdote had elicited the previous time, hoping monotony would jolt Anna into the realization that she was repeating herself—realization, and perhaps therefore a slight, consequent remorse. Other times she would give wildly disparate, *mal à propos* answers, imagining such shock treatment would surprise Anna into recalling how recently she had told that same story. "Ah *ha!*" Edith had once replied to the oft-repeated tale of the death of Anna's aunt. But Anna had been delighted at this response, and laughed her own great hoot of laughter. "She *vass* an awful drayry old voman," she had said, agreeing unreservedly with Edith's reaction. "Alvays growlments between her and the neighbors. Vun time, I remember . . ." So Edith had been forced to an understanding that neither of her maneuvers would ever have the slightest deterrent effect on Anna; she would go right on repeating herself, week after week and year after year. She was entirely consistent, and never contradicted herself, nor said, "That vass ven I vass eleven," instead of "ven I vass thirteen," as she had said the time before, which would have enabled Edith to exclaim, in an odd sort of triumph, "But Anna! You said before you were thirteen when the cat ran away!" One of several things that Edith failed to realize about the people she lived with in that house was that Anna didn't *want* to get over her repetitiousness. The little fund of stories about herself and her childhood were, except for a navy blue silk umbrella, her dearest possessions. As another woman might linger in front of her mirror, thanking God for her nose or her eye-

[29]

lashes, Anna treasured these immutable possessions, her anecdotes. They were never added to and she never threw one away. Why tamper with perfection? She had enjoyed telling Edith for the twentieth time about the oil her mother used to put in her hair when she was a little girl fully as much as she had the first time, and she told her again now.

"Yes, I know," Edith said.

"And now, you. You vash it every two days."

"Oh no, Anna! Once a week."

Anna ran the mop along the floor and gave it a casual shake off the edge of the porch. "You going to see that young man again," she suggested. "I bet so."

"What young man?" Edith asked from beneath her bent wet-gold cap and her heart gave a single, startled skip with an unexpectedness that made her cough.

"Miller. *That's* a gloamy one! Ha! . . . Oh, vell, it might he be kine nice inside'n himself, though." She gave the mop a final, perfunctory flourish in the direction of the side yard, turned on her great slippered feet with the gnomish, inhuman bumps along the sides and, having found out everything she wanted to know as well as having said probably the kindest thing that anyone in that house was ever to say about Jacob Miller, she returned through the screen door to inarduous duties within.

The big girl on the porch sat on, and presently began, most neatly, yet unknowingly, unseeing, to lift with the fingernail of her little finger minute flakes of dried paint from the floor; they made an infinitesimal tearing sound as they were pried away. To watch her, you would have said every faculty was bent on getting up the most nearly perfect flakes possible; actually she didn't notice what she was doing. So Anna was a clairvoyant; that old, calico-

[30]

covered maid! Edith was utterly taken aback at the evidence of so much perspicacity. How on earth could the old woman have known, when she herself had scarcely thought why she was doing it, that she had washed her hair again so soon because she might conceivably—oh, probably not!—encounter Jacob Miller somewhere about the town that day? For two years he had been teaching at the University Museum and they had never met before last Tuesday; it wasn't likely she would run into him today merely by walking downtown to the post office. Yet wasn't everyone's life packed full of unforeseen meetings? Weren't almost all meetings, indeed, fortuitous? Often enough, too often, did she encounter by chance young Sylvester Wagstaff who admired her so much but whom she scorned, whether for his fat neck or his fat fortune she never bothered to decide; Mrs. Fanning had unwisely let it be known that she objected to neither. Now, surely, wishing for one needn't inevitably prevent it; scornful she might be by nature, but she wasn't superstitious. She could see why she and Jacob Miller had not met before; he was not the kind of young professor hostesses vie over; "a gloamy one," Anna had observed. "Drayry," she might well have added. He had belatedly accepted Mrs. Fanning's note of invitation to dinner and when he appeared it had been with an almost tangible reluctance; coming into the drawing room quickly around the door jamb, as if he had had to dare himself to do it; with suffering, protesting brow he had folded his dark length down into one of the drawing-room chairs; reluctantly he had unfolded himself when Anna, despite the effort of years on the part of Mrs. Fanning, had shambled to the door and murmured, "Vell," and at the table his glance from under black brows over the knives and forks and plates and flowers had been fierce, inimical, and

[31]

proud. He had picked up his silver as if he scorned it, and Edith, watching, had felt all at once that she too had always had something against it, though she didn't bother then, or now in reminiscence, to define what it might be.

". . . when our charming old friend, Mr. Packer, wrote me you were teaching here," Mrs. Fanning had said to her guest, suspending a spoonful of consommé above her plate. Mr. Packer, dean of the college in Indiana where Jacob Miller had started his teaching career, had written, "He is a brilliant young man," and Mrs. Fanning was waiting. But the Jacob Miller now at her table looked a little surprised and even offended, as if who could imagine for a minute that there was anything charming about his former dean; he had said, "Oh." Would that have been considered brilliant by their old friend, Mr. Packer, Mrs. Fanning wondered. She set herself to emit a cloud of kind words, a convenient smoke screen to mask her rising indifference to this young man. "*Oh* yes, charming," she had said again, easily. "And he wrote me such charming things about you. You know, my husband and I often met him when we traveled. In Florence especially, at a little café we knew. There he always was at noon, sipping his *Americano*. Do you know Florence, Mr. Miller?"

Jacob Miller had said he had never been to Europe. It could be no concern of hers, he thought, and he was under no obligation to mention it, that it was possible he would be sent over soon by the Museum, and that this was his greatest hope in life, his one constant longing. "I have never been to Europe." In the brevity of his reply sorrow was hidden but no one, except perhaps Edith, heard it. He had laid down his spoon as if he didn't like soup or regret Europe, but Mrs. Fanning was not the kind of hostess who admits noticing guests' vagaries.

"Of course," she had said, kindly. "You've scarcely had

[32]

time yet, or opportunity, for travel." She had rested her pointed black silk elbows on either side of her plate, lightly joining the tips of her fingers; a big sapphire slid about beneath one knuckle. "We always stayed at such a delightful hotel in Florence, I remember; quite simple but delightful, and right on the Lungarno. Do you remember it, Forrest, or weren't you ever there with us? The food was good and it was quite cheap. I can only suppose that accounted for the *simplicity* of the plumbing! You see, the elevator came right up beside the bathroom window; very curious, architecturally, wasn't it, right alongside this *interior* window, so every time one took a bath one had to hang a towel over it. Otherwise, all the passengers in the elevator—!" She had held her head back an instant and laughed, and at the other end of the table Forrest Howe had put down his roll and laughed too, promptly if briefly, but Jacob Miller had looked as if, even if he bothered to try, he would be unable to imagine the architecture of that simple little Florentine hotel, and why anyone would ever have wanted to look at Mrs. Fanning in her tub. At the table's foot Forrest Howe had shaken his head in dutiful amusement and said, "Well, well," because he knew how one must be resigned to any foible on the part of foreigners, and also quite as if the last time his sister had told that story in his hearing the setting hadn't been a simple little hotel in Edinburgh. He had always wondered whether it were not perhaps a rather daring little story, and he wondered now that she told it in the presence of a young man, but of course if she had, and she had, it must be all right; she would know.

"Oh, yes," Mrs. Fanning had murmured, exactly as she did when her anecdotes had been a success instead of a flat failure. She had turned her head slightly to see Anna coming from behind the screen with her plate for the next course and when she didn't see her had touched the bell under the carpet with the toe of her black satin shoe. "When shall we all go traveling freely again, I wonder!" she had said. "Such fun." But Edith, with lowered eyes had known that never again would she even pretend to believe the bathtub-and-elevator story. Maybe it was true and maybe it wasn't, but she knew her aunt brought it out nowadays only for unvalued guests and as for Edith, she was through with it. She resented the classification this young man had been put into; her father could go on chuckling until the end of time but as for her, she had just encountered the glance, fierce and unamused, of Jacob Miller from Fort Wayne . . . How splendid to be fierce, she thought, and unamused; so much more splendid than to retreat into sulkiness, which was her own habitual maneuver. *That's* what I really like! Several years ago at a country house party given by a cousin of Mrs. Fanning's for her daughter, a house party that had been for Edith a succession of one dull disaster after another, a self-possessed boy with a lock of black hair hanging in his eyes had asked, sadly, "Just how drippy can a girl *get?*" but not of anyone in particular, and not as if he really expected an answer— more like someone from whom an age-old plaint is wrung. "Not sharp at *all,*" he had added, and this time his glance had flicked over her in a brief, spiteful lightning. Never since then had she discovered in herself anything to warrant her having contradicted him. Now, staring across the mahogany lake that mirrored tulips and candlesticks she wondered if a fierce disdain were not superior to sharpness, the self-possessed boy with the drooping lock notwithstanding.

Lucius and George came hesitantly through the screen

[34]

door onto the porch. "Hi," they said to Edith, not calling her by name because they weren't quite sure what it was.

"Hi. Come on out. What are you two doing about missing school all this week? Won't you have an awful lot to make up?"

"Oh well." Lucius, his hands in the pockets of his corduroy slacks, kicked experimentally at a dark green wooden cupboard. "What's in here?"

"Nothing, now. It used to be some sort of outdoor storage place. They kept, oh, I don't know, potatoes in it, maybe. Or cheese."

George took his hands out of the pockets of his very short corduroy pants and they went to work on the catch. The cupboard had been painted so many times since its use had been abandoned that the latch was a mere hump, latch and wood were almost one. He hopped off the porch to a red sandstone gravel path and came up with a sharp little stone. "Here you are, Lucius, here you are—look, use this!" When they got it open they didn't seem disappointed to find only a series of very dirty shelves. "It's too far away from my room, anyway," George said, mysteriously. "It wouldn't like it." Lucius nodded with perfect comprehension, but said that otherwise it was a pretty good cupboard; useful, too, he added. Edith could see that, even as they shut the door again, tentatively, they were rapidly racking their brains to turn up some activity of their own, exclusive of whatever it was George didn't want it for, for which it might be used. They didn't quite shut the door; something might occur to them.

"Do you always have that kind of cereal?" George asked, coming over to stand beside her.

"What kind?"

[35]

"The kind we had this morning."

"What kind was that? I don't remember."

"I *don't* know its name." George sounded as if only now did he realize he had hitherto had something he should have thanked Providence for. "Rather dark gray and sandy."

"Did you hate it?"

"Oh *no*, not at *all!*" They were shocked to think anything about what George had said might have sounded rude. He went on: "Oh *no*. It was really quite good, I thought. We just don't happen to have it at our house ever, probably because it *is* rather sandy and, well, kind of horrible, you know. Don't you think so? Kind of?"

Edith, whose own childhood wasn't so far back she couldn't remember how grownups talked, said cereal was supposed to be very good for people; she said she hadn't noticed that it had been in the least horrible that morning, but George quickly pointed out that that, probably, was because she hadn't had any. "*You* just had juice and coffee and an egg," he reminded her.

Anna came back through the screen door without, this time, even the pretext of shaking a mop and, planting her great feet close to the edge of the porch, stood and drank in the sunshine.

"How are you, boyss, liddle boyss?" she inquired, her eyes shut, her face lifted to the flooding warmth. The boys were surprised; she had waited on them at breakfast only an hour or two ago; she must know they were quite well.

"We're fine, thank you," Lucius answered.

"Ah-h-h," Anna breathed, "how I love the sun!" She was a very tall old woman, and must once have been even taller, but now the upper part of her had melted down, settled between her high hips; her knees bent permanently

[36]

outward. She must once have had golden Scandinavian hair, too, but now it was a thin mere twist of gray sustained by innumerable random pins and combs; Edith believed it was not always taken down at night. She had a long face, colorless and fine-grained skin, long thin arms and very long hands that half a century of washing things had failed to coarsen. When she was at rest, as now, she would stand quite motionless, her arms like brackets at her sides, the elbows bent, the bony hands curved delicately up back, and away from her long narrow wrists. "My feet's bad," she often said. "Oh, my old bunions and scunions! But I got real good arms." Her feet had betrayed her long ago and now she wore bedroom slippers of soft leather lined with lamb's wool whenever she thought she could get away with it; if she and Mrs Fanning encountered each other before Anna had been able to bring herself to change them for the shoes that hurt, Mrs. Fanning would look at them for a second longer than one ordinarily looks at feet, significantly, silently, and then Anna would adopt one of the two maneuvers she considered adequate to cope with this disapproval: Either she would pretend she had completely forgotten she was still in the slippers she had so thoughtfully worn about the house in the early morning solely in order not to wake the family, would give her cheerful hoot of laughter and veer off as if she were at that very moment on her way up to change them or, mornings when the bunions were very bad indeed she would act as if she *hadn't got slippers on at all,* therefore had nothing she needed to be ashamed of, and she would wade right on about her work, shuffling about the downstairs rooms with her mop, like a skier with one ski pole.

"Ah, boyss," she said now, "the blessed sun. It's yoost like May Day in the old country." At these words Edith swept together her brush and comb, got up off the porch floor, shook out the bath towel and left, recognizing the gambit of an account of May Day in Småland that she had heard every warm Spring day since she was ten. But Lucius came over to Anna and said "Is it?" in such an interested voice that joy flooded all through her; she sat down in a green rocking chair and the boys went to stand at her side on the rockers, each holding on to a nut-shaped knob on the chair's high back.

"Oh yes, May Day ven I voss liddle—! The morning of the first of May music vass played all over the willage, by nice young men in vight capes." She told them the music woke up the people who got up eagerly and streamed out into their gardens for breakfast in the early light. The night before, everyone had taken tables and chairs out from their cottages and set them in the garden and now, while the merry music played up and down the town, the sun sparkled in the dew, birds sang and neighbors called greetings and blessings into each other's yards over the hedges, the coffee was poured and the rolls buttered at tables draped in white linen and decorated with fresh-picked leaves. "Then back come the music across the town, and everybody laughs!" Anna tooted through her cupped hands to show them the way it was.

"Oh, why don't *we?*" George cried and Lucius said, more slowly, with a faraway gaze, "I wish we did that."

As Anna rocked and talked they could smell the Swedish holiday breakfasts spread on the leaf-decked tables—hot coffee and wonderful rich brown crusted coffee cakes with names that sounded almost like English words but were, divertingly, just a trifle different; rich names implying more currants, fruit peel and cinnamon, and a deeper and sweeter crust. They could hear, in her account, the birds

[38]

singing their first early song, sitting, so safe and gay, up on the tops of the trees, facing the rising sun. They could hear the music played by the blond young men, with their flutes and violins, in their white capes. "Dear, dear," Anna sighed, "it voss a ducky time."

The boys hung over the arms of the rocking chair. "Then what? What did you do on May Day after breakfast?" After breakfast had been just like every other day, she said. "Yes, but what did you *do?*"

Every day Anna and her mother had worked at the loom in the kitchen weaving white fabrics with stripes and designs in red and bright blue; some they needed for themselves but most they sold, as bedspreads and curtains and tablecloths. There had been a big black cat who sat by the hour, watching the loom. "He rooned away, finally."

"But he came back," George urged.

"No, Bill, he never did."

"His name isn't Bill," Lucius told her but George, who had fallen in love with Anna said, "I don't mind if she wants to call me that." Lucius, knowing his brother's usual sharp insistence on his own individuality, looked unconvinced. He asked as politely as possible what she believed *his* name to be.

Anna laughed. "Lucy," she said, and Lucius drew back from the rocking chair in horror. He at once gave her a lesson in pronunciation but though she was amiable enough about trying she never seemed to think it mattered, and throughout the week of his visit he sensed laughter in her voice when she called him by name. "Loosis," it sounded like.

Before she left the sun and the rocking chair she told them about working in her uncle's bakery in Stockholm. That had been the happiest time of her life. "Oh, I love dough! I'd help in the kitsen and then I'd roon like mad and help in the shop. Oh, I loved it in pieces!"

Lucius asked how was it then that she had left that lovely life to come to Connecticut.

Anna gave a cheerful snort. "So to get rich," she said. Then was she? they wondered. "Yes, I was always rooning for the stairs in those days, I didn't care how much I vork if I get the money, but now my feet's bad. But I'm going back to Sveden, you bet, and have my own liddle shop and a strong girl for the rooning. I'll bake and she'll roon."

"You are?" Lucius was delighted to hear about this. "When are you?"

She slowed the motion of the chair, took a long last draught of sunshine and heaved herself up from between the chair arms. "Some day," she said confidently, and went away from them, in at the screen door.

The boys, hands again in their pockets, strayed around the porch; there was little to engage their attention—chairs, a wicker table with nothing on it, a shelf of empty flower pots turned upside down.

"Too bad about the cat," said George, who was easily capable of regretting the defection of an animal dead these fifty years or more. Too bad for Anna, he meant; she must have worried. But Lucius, with a different emphasis said, "Oh, he probably just went off for a good time and he had *such* a good time he never came back. Come on, let's go see if there's any material around this place." Wherever Lucius stayed any length of time, with whatever came to hand he built cathedrals. Sometimes they were quite large, of piled bricks or orange crates; sometimes—and this made him swear as he was a very profane little boy—he had to make do with a flimsy candy box and scissors, or even the paste-board that comes from the laundry in men's shirts. *"This*

[40]

God-damned stuff," he would say, disgusted because paste-board never bends exactly where one means it to; even scoring a guiding line, a groove, with a penknife isn't ever enough to conquer its natural irascibility; it's not to be trusted; it bends without any integrity, without coopera-tion. His room at home was a shambles of discarded or incomplete flying buttresses and campaniles, dreadfully mangled little tubes of cement that had treacherously gouted out their contents through rifts in their sides, wooden building blocks, triangular bits of lumber that would surely come in handy some day, paper clips and shingles. His mother's lost scissors could always be traced there and when she picked them up with a cry of mingled relief and rage, there would be, adhering to one of the points with a smear of strayed cement, a snippet of the bright cellophane he used for stained-glass windows. "Come on," he said now, "let's go see." George said he thought he ought to go back upstairs and look at his harp again to be sure it was safe. It had been tenderly returned to his small suitcase and still lay on the bed of tiring grass-blades. Where on earth was he going to hang it, he demanded. Lucius appreciated his concern but he managed to override him finally and they jumped off the porch to the red sand-stone path that led back past the greenhouse and a potting shed to the old faced-stone stable where Mrs. Fanning's car was.

4

MEANWHILE Edith, who had had no other hope nor intention but to hold onto her daydream by escaping from Anna, was so unlucky as to encounter her aunt in the upper hall. Forever the prey of her own abundance of energy and her unsleeping civic conscience, Mrs. Fanning in her hat and coat had already been out to a small early meeting in one of the near-by houses and was now back again. Either through the *force majeure* of her nature or perhaps merely dazed by the earliness of the hour and the airs of Spring, the house committee of the Wilhelmina Willard Nursery had, even before nine-thirty struck on all the tall grandfathers' clocks in the Evergreen Avenue houses, voted funds for the purchase of new, grade-A linoleum for the kitchen and pantry. On her latest bimonthly visit of inspection Mrs. Fanning had been unpleasantly surprised at the condition of the kitchen floor; she had seen a ragged gray weakness near the sink that was more than likely to deteriorate and betray the heel of the woman who cooked the nourishing lunches—stews liberally charged with carrots, and always on Friday mackerel because if the superintendent had found it expedient to cater to Rome still there was no need to be expensive about it—and near the pantry door an edge of old linoleum curled, listlessly, like a tired leaf. This April morning, Mrs. Fanning, so full of pure and single-minded zeal, had been able to persuade the committee to appropriate money for the pantry floor as well. "Full of holes," she had told them, "really quite dangerous, I'm afraid," and though this wasn't exactly the case, they had hurriedly voted, knowing the only other alternative to be her adjuring them to form a subcommittee right away and go and see for themselves. Each individual member thought that almost any outlay of funds was preferable, on such a lovely languorous morning, to running the risk of being popped onto such a subcommittee and they voted five hundred dollars without a single dissenting voice.

Now that Mrs. Fanning was home again, with so much accomplished so early—too early, really; she had anticipated a stimulating resistance—it came hard on her to meet Edith wandering around, idly, with a brush and comb, looking almost like a girl doing nothing more important than walking in her sleep. If it was rather too early for the committee meeting to be over yet it was certainly too late for Edith to appear not entirely awake. "What are you planning to do today?" Mrs. Fanning asked her briskly. The fact that she herself had unexpected time on her hands that morning, her appointment with the Girl Scout director not being until eleven, could not mitigate her annoyance at the aimlessness of Edith's day, of all her days. Almost a year ago she had been graduated from a junior college and what was there to show for the intervening months? Nothing. No job; no work on any committee of any charitable enterprise; no work on any specific committee of the Junior League, despite its specific rule; how had she got out of *that,* Mrs. Fanning wondered; Edith had even forgotten to go to the annual meeting, or said she had. "Don't you *care* who next year's president will be?" "I don't even know who this year's is." Looking at the big aimless creature now, in the muted light of the upper hall, Mrs. Fanning had to recognize the sorry truth that her niece probably would never be invited to carry the flag for the Colonial Dames. What was this generation coming to? . . . The generally accepted notion in the house, that Edith was in the process of waiting for the perfect job to present itself, was beginning to wear thin. Right after graduation she could have had a job selling lampshades in one of the department stores downtown but Mrs. Fanning said it was quite out of the question; those jobs must be reserved for girls who had to work for their living; what would happen to the economy of the country, precarious enough already, God knew, if girls from well-to-do families selfishly snatched up all the easy, almost menial jobs that required no thinking? She had suggested applying for work in a bookshop but Edith had cried "Oh, but that's so *obvious!* I couldn't *poss*ibly."

Now Mrs. Fanning regretfully took off her beautiful, charcoal-colored suède gloves and her hat, and pinched at the stiff horsehair ruching around the crown. "What do you suppose I heard at the meeting?" she asked. "But it's too late to do anything about it now. The Recusants have gone and taken in half a dozen of the younger men on the faculty. 'To liven things up,' they said! I wish I'd gone to the meeting of the membership committee that night instead of to the League of Women Consumers, though we *did* manage to get a committee together to

[44]

agitate for more accurate description of sizes on boxed noodles; utterly misleading, the way they're marked at present. All bachelors, fortunately, so they won't be bringing their wives here to dinner this Thursday. We do not need any new members; there are plenty of members already who do not attend regularly." She added, "That drab young man was one."

"Which?" Edith demanded, as though she could call to mind any number of young men who would qualify. "Sylvester Wagstaff?" But by the lurch of her heart she had known which, at once, and when her aunt was specific she looked boldly into her face and said, "But I don't think he *was*. I think he was . . . quite nice." The unexpectedly lame ending to her defiance infuriated her. Unconsciously she scraped the comb down the brush and Mrs. Fanning told her not to "aggravate the bristles like that. He's poor but proud; such an irritating combination, I've always felt." Then she repeated, "Nice?" and smiled. "Mr. Packer wrote me 'brilliant,' but I never encountered a more black-a-vised young man in all my life. A boor. And com*plete*ly silent." To Mrs. Fanning social silence was nothing less than a form of selfishness, and what bad manners, if nothing worse, selfishness was. "Morbidly silent," she said.

Edith scraped again at her brush and Mrs. Fanning instantly asked, "What was it you said you were going to do today?"

"Nothing." Let her think: Nothing. Let her not like it!

"Didn't you say you were mailing a package? Then will you stop by at D'Amico's for me and order carnations for Thursday? I want to be sure about the color; ask to see what they're getting in now, and insist on the darkest red. You can mail your package at the drugstore," she

[45]

added, anticipating, even as it welled up in the girl, the objection that D'Amico's was quite off her route to the post office. She couldn't bear to have Edith not busy so she invented smoothly, "I heard at the meeting this morning that D'Amico has been quite careless lately about what he sends out. You can tell him if he delivers any but the very darkest red on Thursday I shall send them right back."

Impatience, as much as anything, was what caused Mrs. Fanning to lie; lying was the quickest short-cut to insuring that people would do what she wanted them to—and surely it's essential to be quick about everything, isn't it!—and surely what she wanted would always be the right thing. Like most adroit prevaricators she could often be heard saying, "What I care terribly about is *the truth*. To me it is the *most important thing*," so that if she had been carried off untimely by some illness or accident her brother Mr. Howe would have been certain to shake his head, and say, solemnly, to condoling friends, "You know, there was one thing Clara absolutely insisted on . . ." Fortunately, this Monday morning of the week that Spring came, she was in her usual health and spirits. "Let's hope we don't have to find another florist, after all these years," she said.

Defeated, Edith passed on to her room. Where was that agreeable drowsiness now that had enveloped her on the porch, that warm daydream with Jacob Miller for its core? Perhaps if she had been allowed to dream it out, to repeat it consciously again and again as many times as she wanted to it would suffer the diminuendo all unsupported daydreams are subject to and its eventual disappearance would have been natural and final. But a single drop of the acid of Mrs. Fanning's scorn had been enough to crystallize the vague emotion in Edith's heart. Many a perfectly good, serious, honest and successful love affair must have been engendered by no more noble provocation than a daydream on a porch in the sun and fortified and consummated because of the disapproval of some near relation.

The sloping stone sill was cold under his hand when Jacob Miller tipped back in his chair and flung one long arm out sideways to rest it; his back ached from bending for hours over the desk. Under the hand that was cramped from writing the sill held the chill of eternity. Never, in all time past, had that block of stone, quarried out of the deep earth, been warm, except possibly during the negligible few days or hours while the Museum was being built. Maybe then, while the heavy, pretentious walls grew and masons in their whitish clothes clambered about with hods and trowels, the sun had lain warm for a few days on its cut surface—not long enough to mellow it. Even though he did know all that is known about Merovingian jewelry there was after all only a certain number of private offices in the Museum and other, older men, who had been there a longer time and knew all that is known about American glass and silver, and Graeco-Roman sculpture, and Greek sword-hilts and Roman bas-reliefs, were in the rooms where sun could come in. Not that he cared, Jacob had said to a similarly accommodated young instructor; one could work as well in a cell as anywhere. "This Gothic stronghold on Pine Street! Why Pine? The nearest thing to pine trees are the parking meters."

New young instructors who had taken their degrees elsewhere, promising scholars beginning their teaching careers, were always amazed at the University buildings but they were not all as promptly tactless as Jacob Miller about saying so. What attacking armies did the authorities expect would march up to its walls, that they had schemed to repel them with javelins hurled into their ranks from these narrow leaded-glass slits meagerly distributed in the thick walls? Javelins in considerable number were within, to be sure, in the Donors' Collection, second floor, gallery 3C, but there wasn't a full professor in the place who could have hurled one to any effect and all the young instructors and the assistant professors were working so hard to become assistant professors and full professors that, thus and inevitably, they were making themselves less and less capable of flinging weapons to any distance. The right arms that had learned, not long ago, to throw fire bombs, were now laid across blotters; the hands that had signaled for a landing quietly flipped over the pages, large and glossy, of illustrated books on painting and sculpture. Perhaps the guards would be expected to stand by at the narrow windows. No, not those flaccid fellows in postman blue; no, if the Goldwater Museum and Art School was ever faced with the attack of the long-bowmen it appeared to have been especially constructed to repulse, it would fall into their hands in five minutes.

Jacob Miller creaked his loose-jointed chair back and forth and flipped the ends of his pencil, a nervous little teeter-board, up and down on the printed page. His handwriting was not black and fractious like himself, like what might have been expected, but extremely neat, small and eager; rows of it hastened across the pages. On the blotter lay the photograph that was to illustrate his article. He picked it up, devouring it with his eyes for the hundredth time, as one stares at and absorbs and at the same time loses oneself in a picture of somebody one is in love with. Lines of pleasure appeared at the corners of his eyes. He somehow saw beyond the photograph; he could see the buckle from all sides, as a whole, and could feel its weight; delightedly, he knew in detail the outline and texture of the little modeled silver-gilt animal and the exact color and weight and temperature of the cloudy aquamarine enamel. He hunched himself forward again and wrote, pushing with his tired hand, "though without exuberance of ornamentation, and strictly within the limitations so characteristic of that period . . ." He crossed out "so"; why make it sound as if he wanted it to read easily! "As is the case when most of the treasures have been found in graves, we can continue to hope for yet-undiscovered examples, some perhaps even comparable to the one we are now considering." Hell, how stuffy. Who ever read the Museum bulletin anyway? No one. No one. It had a circulation of two thousand but, he was convinced, not a single reader. Maybe children sometimes looked at the pictures; not professors' children, they read comics. He had seen a copy of the April number on Mrs. Fanning's library table; it lay demurely between the *Atlantic* and *Punch,* being slightly larger than one and smaller than the other. There it would stay for exactly thirty days and its successor would fill that place for thirty-one. Mrs. Fanning believed in supporting University activities. But was it likely she would open the October number and give a glad cry to see "Some Aspects of a Late Merovingian Belt Buckle," by Jacob Miller? Would Mr. Forrest Howe stroke his querulous little goatee with glee at the news, and scheme how he might get to be the first to read it? . . . Was there anyone in that house who would read it?

He flung out of his chair and walked about the monkish cell. He thought of paying a call on the adjoining cell and suggesting to young Neidringhaus their leaving the University together and opening a hamburg stand in the desert. But young Neidringhaus knew almost all that it is possible, and desirable, to know about Roman plumbing, and maybe he liked teaching, who knows; some men did. But with any luck Jacob would be far off next Winter on a job of research; averse to prayer, he frowned very hard, and wished.

He did not leave his room. He wasn't sure what Neidringhaus thought of him, and actually, did he like Neidringhaus? He stood at the window and peered down through tiny panes to the street below; a few people walked the sidewalk; the curbs were lined with parked cars. Sometimes it seems there are more cars in the world than people. No, he wasn't sure he liked Neidringhaus much. When he got another sentence finished he would take a walk across the Green and limber up in the Spring sunshine. "Occasionally Gallo-Roman and Celtic work," he wrote, back at the desk, ". . . but we must not, therefore, jump to the conclusion . . . that . . ."

Any number of men looked like Jacob Miller from the back as Edith, carrying a small wrapped birthday present for a former roommate, walked away from Evergreen Avenue. She found it to be a matter for pondering, and for some slight surprise, that there had always been men whose backs resembled his. Naturally she had not noticed them hitherto because she had never, until so recently, observed the front of him. "Ho—black-a-vised," she repeated scornfully, with the scorn all for anyone who did not realize that black-a-vised was a fine way to be. None of the backs proved, by spurts of fast walking on her part, to be his. " 'I daren't go a-hunting, For fear of little men,' " she had sung to herself, mournfully, undressing in her room after college dances. But Jacob Miller was taller than she was. "He towers over me," she said with satisfaction, bestowing considerable grace on two inches. She felt that she was beautiful and accomplished, graceful, witty and immortal that morning and as she strode along she made bargains with God, in order that they might meet.

But the further she got from Evergreen Avenue and the environs of the University the less likely would this desirable encounter become, so she slowed her pace. Surely, she thought, with complete and mistaken simplicity, it wasn't likely that authorities on Merovingian jewelry were often, if indeed ever, to be encountered walking along ordinary, shopping streets. She forgot not only that young instructors cannot spend all their time on their only love; they have to give general survey courses and go to the dentist and write letters to their mothers; also she forgot they often buy undershirts and bicarbonate of soda like other men.

She thought: How he would disdain such surroundings; she glanced into a jeweler's, happily disdainful too. "Junk," she said. Oh, the vulgarity of diamonds! "Little as I know about Merovingian jewelry," she murmured, wonderfully able to ignore the fact that she knew nothing at all about it, "I do know it isn't at all like this."

She turned in at D'Amico's and did her aunt's trumped-up errand with dreamy incompetence, which was perhaps all the care it deserved. Out on the street again she walked so lightly she did not feel herself going, and she looked with unwonted attention at the other people out shopping that morning. Some moved fast and some moved slowly, but as for herself, she knew she had better begin to walk

[51]

more slowly; the trip through the shopping district wouldn't take long, as it was a small city, but her body had set a gay pace independent of expediency; she skimmed along the pavement. Well, I could go home by Pine Street, she thought. Oh no, no; unthinkable. She could look for him anywhere but Pine Street where the Museum stood. She could drop in at bookshops, or even pretend to be looking for someone she had an appointment with in the chintz-and-patty atmosphere of the Faculty Club but along Pine Street she could not go, though she knew herself nearly overcome with a need to turn in at the elaborate gateway and examine the remarkable collection of Merovingian remains. What a curious thing, having lived most of her life almost in its peaked shadow, she had not made the most of what the Goldwater Museum had to offer. She could have leaned on the cases for hours, other years, only straightening up, dazed but terribly well-informed, when the closing bell rang and the visitors were herded gently out by the heavy men in pale blue. How strange of me, she thought; *why* have I neglected the Museum so?

She walked more slowly. She mailed her package at the drugstore as Mrs. Fanning had suggested, and started home. Now, no one's back resembled Jacob Miller's. Within her slowly formed and floated a feeling of deprivation, and loss. Her forehead furrowed, and she felt she had been cheated though, not being omniscient, she could not possibly know that if she had not been prevented from pursuing her original plan of mailing her wrapped-up "Song of the Cold" at the main post office on the Green she would have gone the normal route by College Street and met the object of all her concern, Jacob Miller, who was even at that very moment stalking across the grass among pigeons, and that she had missed him by a hair, by a lie.

George, with the string loop of his Chinese harp hooked over his two big front teeth, stopped halfway up the tree as if his heart had been transfixed by an arrow—Mrs. Fanning had caught sight of him from the window of the morning room and her agate-colored gaze stopped him dead.

"George!" he could see her say inside the great sheet of plate glass; she tapped her finger at him on the window though she knew he saw her, and shook her head at him, brow lowered. But could he stop now, with the solution of his greatest problem so near? How could he? It was too much to expect. Dropping his lashes, swallowing with difficulty—having string around his front teeth tasted so queer—he renewed his slow climb up the straight slender trunk, up among the branches that, curving over and down, had caused it always to be known in the household as the parasol tree. No one now living in that house knew what kind of tree it was. Probably the spit he was swallowing was dyed pink from the string and he would die of poison. In that case he hoped Lucius would have the simple common sense to bury his harp with him. But at the moment he really felt extremely happy, and it didn't matter what color his spit was; the only thing that mattered was that at last he had found a safe place for his frangible treasure.

When he was about ten feet up, and not very far below the sill of his bedroom window, he stopped again and looked about him, searching for the best ultimate resting place. He would have been glad to remain in the tree for the week as custodian of the lovely thing, with food raised to him in a basket, but he knew she would consider this laughable. Some little knob, he thought, peering here and there. An upstanding twig with two pale infant leaves, hardly more than silk scraps, appealed to him; he reached up and took off the leaves, carefully tucking them in the pocket of his shorts—they might grow and obscure his darling—and there, neat, safe, and ready, was the resting place. Trembling, he unhooked the string loop from around his big second teeth so providentially isolated from their fellows by the recent falling out of the two flanking incisors. Not breathing at all he hooked the string around the twig—ah!—safe, safe. He delicately ran his hand down the hanging prisms and they sang to him, softly, briefly. He struggled up a bit higher, put his head close to the color-flecked rectangular splinters and blew, and they sang again, gaily. So they would nights, when the cool dark feline breeze ran through the leaves and touched the prisms, and in the big bed not so far away he would lie awake all night on his back with his hands beneath his head and listen to them. And the first thing in the morning he would leap up, run to his window, and see.

He sighed with relief and worked his way back down the tree, through the cage of branches that on his way up had tried, malevolently, to get him to strike the delicate glass against them.

He returned featly, jumped backward, brushed the bark from the palms of his hands, put them in his pockets and went in to face Mrs. Fanning. The sandy crest of his hair undulated gently as he marched along the hall.

"I saw you," he said instantly to her, "but I was putting up my harp."

"Oh, George," she protested uncertainly. "You didn't

have to put it up *there,* did you? Do you really think you ought to climb around in trees that way?"

"I do at home."

"Yes, I know! Of course. But with your mother and father far away in Bermuda . . ." George's glance was unrelenting. "Because you see," she said cunningly, as though it were something she had been keeping up her sleeve all along and might not, if he had been tractable, have had to pull out and confront him with instead of its being but the bright idea of that moment, "they *asked* me not to let you climb trees." That made him look up at her in surprise, as if he saw her for the first time. Surely they would have told him if they had contemplated restricting him in that unnatural way. He searched her face to see if she were fooling, but her smile was an entirely private one, blended of adult satisfaction and something he couldn't even imagine. He was baffled. "And then you nearly fell, coming down," she added contentedly.

"No!" But she seemed not to hear his protesting cry and went on to talk about her deep sense of responsibility for Lucius and himself. At that, George's eyebrows climbed. It seemed to him that he was the one with a responsibility. What else caused him to take such excellent, indeed such *painful,* care of the harp? ". . . so you see it behooves me to take the best possible care of you little boys, so that your father and mother, when they come home . . ."

"Well, I had to," he said at last, tired to death of all this insistence on false values. "There was nowhere else."

"Oh, come, in all this big house? There must be a hundred perfectly safe places for your toys. Safe for *you,* I mean, where you wouldn't get into any trouble, or danger."

But what a point of view! George, hands still in his

pockets, looked about him at the heavy, thick, eternally-stationary furniture, at the blankly gleaming windows, the faraway ceiling. His own safety was an inconsiderable trifle, after all. And why did she talk about his getting into trouble, when the only trouble he was in was what she was stirring up by talking so much?

"I have to keep it in certain *kinds* of places," he said fiercely, and would say no more except, as he was going out the door, "otherwise, I werry."

5

"Boys are not my province," Mrs. Fanning said.

Mr. Forrest Howe looked up, alarmed, and knew, viscerally, what was coming. His imploring gaze died a premature death against the narrow cylindrical upright figure of his sister in its fashionable black and its invariable choker of pearls. She was as impeccably dressed at eight in the morning as she was all day long and at eight at night. No one ever saw her in a wrapper or with her hair released from its large firm knot. Did she take off her pearls at night? No one living could say. This impeccability helped give her supreme prestige in the house and no one there would have dared to question her pronouncements.

"Boys," she said, "need the company of men. I have never brought up any boys, but that much I know." Naturally Mr. Howe was well aware of the fact of her childlessness, not having been for any appreciable length of time out of touch with his sister, but now he nodded slowly, sitting in his plum-colored velvet chair, as if what she had just said partook of the character of fresh information which he hoped he would be given adequate time to evaluate. If he yielded to a weak inclination to waylay his fate by pointing out that neither had she ever had any daughters she would instantly say "That's *quite* beside the point!" and for all he knew, it was; probably it was; it was quite a comfort to him that she was always right; it made his own life so much simpler than if he had had to work matters out for himself. He'd rather not think or plan. If he had had a coat of arms his motto would have been *Well—let's wait and see.* He didn't like to cope with people and their mystifying diverse emotions; but given the opportunity he could have taken excellent if unenterprising care of a house. But he had no work of any kind to do, nothing to take care of, so what little sense of responsibility he had been born with had long since atrophied. When he had come to live with his sister he had expressed a small but dignified desire, or willingness, to subscribe to the household expenses, but since his reason for having moved in with her was the sad scarcity of his money, there was little he could do. So they arranged it that she would let him buy the magazines for the house and this was enough to gratify him; she already knew exactly what she wanted in the way of publications, which was no more and no less than the ones she was already a subscriber to, and with the minor addition of Mr. Howe's *Nature Lore* and *Bird Watcher* the care of them was turned over to him. "I see your *Survey Graphic* has come," he would say with gratification. Months before their subscriptions ran out he would begin scrutinizing the cabalistic information in the stenciled addresses on the wrappers; he felt he wouldn't want to be caught napping if something mysteriously went wrong and *Harper's Bazaar* suddenly failed to arrive. He repudiated

[58]

with distaste the three or five year type of subscription; what would there, then, be left for him to do!

He could have enjoyed hanging around and directing the repairs most houses call for; and plumbers, he had found, were impressed with his goatee; he liked watching painters pour turpentine into buckets of paint and saying to them, "That's just about enough now, isn't it?", and his judgment in matters of small carpentry was excellent. In fact, he could have accomplished everything connected with the repairs to a house except pay for them. But Mrs. Fanning and whatever gardener-chauffeur she had were accustomed to tend to everything about the establishment and they often forgot to consult him when he might have solved some problem with the quiet words "Plastic wood."

Though without children of her own, Mrs. Fanning had sat on so many committees for various aspects of their care during the major portion of her sixty-five years—had spoon-fed so many facts into so many obdurate colleagues, conceived and reared so many day nurseries and summer camps, and ably nurtured and sustained so many groups of her fellow citizens who had, sometimes unthinkingly, committed themselves to one or another altruistic purpose— that she felt perfectly capable of caring for two small boys for one short week. She might even effect some slight improvement in them somewhere—table manners perhaps, or diction. Edith had once exclaimed to her father, in an outburst such as he was grateful she seldom indulged in, "But she never *wanted* to have children, whatever she says. Or a family, either, except to boss it around. Or friends. She's just the mother of committees, that's what she is."

This morning Mrs. Fanning was looking for a committee of one, to entertain the boys from Sharon, the young refugees. She knew herself well-fitted to be the sponsor,

[59]

kind but firm, for refugees, but it is not essential for a sponsor, indeed not advisable, to attend to every detail of their day; others can be deputized to do that.

"So?" she said now.

"Maybe they don't want to be entertained," he suggested, feebly trying to ward off his certain fate. "They might prefer to be alone." But when she told him that with her own eyes she had just seen George climb to the very top of quite a tall tree and that he had very nearly fallen on his way down, really had fallen the last part of the way, he promptly said "*Oh*-oh," as though, *that* being the case, some of his worst fears had indeed been realized, and sooner than he had expected.

"So you see."

"Yes."

But what would she want him to do for their young guests? Read aloud to them? What books? Take long walks in the wood? What wood? He cleared his throat as though begging her not to interrupt him while he made a conscientious selection from among the many merry possibilities occurring to him the one most likely to make George and Lucius happy. Perhaps if he thought fast enough he could evolve some occupation that would be less of a strain on him than any she was likely to devise. "Let-me-see." He set himself to hard and fast thinking, but, as always, urgency brought on disintegration. The keener his awareness of a state of urgency, the more floating, tenuous, and cloudily, maddeningly vague his thoughts became. He could see them drifting away out of reach, their impalpable, pale-blue fringes eluding his halfhearted grasp. A kind of domestic amnesia overcame Mr. Howe as he sat, bolt upright in his own chair in the morning room, his eyes fixed unseeing on the leg of a Santo Domingo mahogany table, all his few ideas lying in a tiny heap on the floor of his mind. Who am I, wondered Mr. Howe. . . . What am I doing here . . . oh, *must* I do something about those boys? "H'mn," he said aloud to let her know he was working on the problem, and then again, valiantly, "Let-me-see . . ." He might show them his stamp collection, but good Heavens, not letting them hold the book or touch anything! What if they wanted to touch one! A spasm of fright killed this solution to his quandary at birth. They might even ask him for some, and that would be simply unbearable. "H'mn," he said again, judicially, not an idea in his head.

"Oh, just go talk to them," his sister relieved him by saying, and then plunged him right back into misery by adding, "and find out what *they'd* like to do. I have to balance the Ear Dispensary's checkbook and I don't want them in here bothering me."

So that was why Mr. Forrest Howe put his gray felt hat level on his head at half past ten in the morning of Monday and ventured out to the side yard where the visitors, against a background of ancient high rhododendron, were happily absorbed in a game of catch.

"Playing ball, I see," he said. They paused and said yes, they were. "M'mn. George is a good bit smaller than you are," Mr. Howe pointed out to Lucius. He had picked up somewhere in his journey through life the fantastic notion that no opportunity to admonish children ought to be neglected by those unfortunate enough to have to be with them. "You must make it easy for him."

Lucius laughed, missed the ball which George launched with fierce accuracy and went off to pick it up from the rhododendron border, calling back across his shoulder, "I would, only he's better than me."

[61]

George, eager and happy, crouching like a veteran, crying, "Here y'are, Lucius. Come on, Lucius. Come on now,
let's have it," didn't want to stop playing but Lucius,
though he had no way of knowing he was supposed to act
like a grateful refugee receiving alms knew what would be
considered the normally polite thing to do, and presently
all three were sitting in a bored and idle row on a green
garden bench against the hedge. Mr. Howe did not lean
back; no one had sat on the bench or washed it off all
Winter, nor yet so far this Spring, and the wooden slats had
a blue patina of city dust that was sure to rub off on the
back of his coat—a patina of long-dried snow and rain, of
time itself.

"Well, well. Now, how old are you, George? Ten?"

"Eight," said George, grinding his teeth with shame,
"almost."

"Oh. Then *you're* ten," he coaxed, turning his gray-
hatted head in Lucius' direction; he was sure his sister had
said one of them was ten.

"Twelve," said Lucius.

Mr. Howe, who wouldn't have been able to say how old
the boys were if anyone asked him an hour later, made the
acquiescent sound that comes halfway between *ah-ha* and
m'hmn and implies: Well, then, that's nicely settled once
and for all, and he went on to ask them how they liked
visiting on Evergreen Avenue. He wondered if it were true,
as his sister kept insisting, that having them there was to
make no difference at all.

Lucius said they liked it very much. His eyes roamed
the lawn, so vast and well kept and empty, and he wondered if they did like it very much, really. Of course he had
to say they did, but staying there a whole week was taking
quite a piece out of their lives. If their mother and father

[62]

had only known a family in Sharon whose children were not having measles or in a state of quarantine, he wouldn't have had to miss the Scout picnic at Kent Falls. Mr. Buongiorno, the Scoutmaster, was a much more interesting man than this old man Howe. Mr. Buongiorno could tie two half hitches in three seconds but Lucius bet to himself it took this Mr. Howe a good five minutes just to tie his necktie.

"Now let's see," said Mr. Howe unexpectedly loudly from above the tie, above the goatee, "is there anything special you boys would like to have me do with you today?"

George immediately fell into a brown study, swinging his legs, turning the baseball about absent-mindedly in his small, dirty hands, trying sincerely to think what entertainment could be devised that would please Mr. Howe as well as themselves; but Lucius looked sidelong at Mr. Howe's goatee and scoffed in his soul. Mr. Buongiorno wouldn't be seen dead wearing a thing like that. "Have you ever been to Sharon, where we live?" he asked, doubting it.

"Oh, yes indeed. That is, in the course of my life I suppose I must have been in most of the small towns of Connecticut. I've gone through Sharon several times, I believe, but I'm not quite sure where my sister told me your house was. But quite possibly I have seen it on one of my trips through. Can you describe it to me?" He relaxed and crossed his legs, and forgetting the dust, leaned back; this was easy; this was pleasantly sedentary; if *this* kind of thing was all that was expected of him . . .

"Well, it's a big white house, long and wooden, with a red front door," Lucius said.

"Ah. I wonder if perhaps I haven't seen it. It sounds very familiar." Mr. Howe looked thoughtful, summoning up such a house. "How do you go, to get to it? I've probably gone right past it."

"Did you go along a very bumpy road for quite a long way first?"

"Yes. Yes, I believe I did."

"And then did you come to a turning and go along beside a brook?" Lucius, sitting on the very edge of the bench, turned an eager face to Mr. Howe and Mr. Howe thought: What a pleasant little fellow and fond of his home, and so, though he really could remember almost nothing about the town of Sharon and its geography he said yes, he believed that then he had driven along beside a brook, and Lucius beamed.

"Well, then, did you cross over a stone bridge?" and Mr. Howe, shamelessly abandoning the last vestiges of his integrity said yes indeed, then he had crossed over that bridge. A beautiful clear light of triumph dawned in Lucius' eyes and he cried with delight:

"*Well!* That was the wrong way!"

"Who's that guy watching us?" George demanded that afternoon and Lucius, his back to the avenue, just about to throw the ball to George, turned on his heel and confronted a tall dark man with one black shoe up on the fence. What an awfully low fence it is, Lucius thought; most people who decide to lean on fences to watch things happening can lean with both elbows but with this kind of fence you have to lean with your foot, with only one foot indeed, and it must be far less comfortable.

"Hello," he said to the stranger, and George wandered up.

"Hello." The man didn't look very pleasant, but he had a deep voice that Lucius admired. "Do you fellows live

[64]

here? Are there any children in this house?" He would have sounded no more dubious if he had said tigers instead of children.

"There aren't. We're just parked here so our mother and father can go to Bermuda. I and George wish there *were*."

"We're having a hollow day," George said, hollowly.

"Do you know the people who do live here?" Lucius asked.

"M'mn. Scarcely."

"So do we."

"Know them scarcely?"

The boys nodded and produced a few further explanations, of their mother's pneumonia, the surprising incidence of measles among their friends, and the remote family connections between the Langdons and the Fannings, but not very interesting ones apparently as the man kept looking over their heads toward the house. "I see," was about all he said but with only this slight encouragement Lucius, who enjoyed many, many things in this world and perhaps most of them all the sound of his own voice, launched into a balanced comparison of his home in Sharon and the house on Evergreen Avenue. He also gave more than a hint of his feelings at having to miss the Boy Scout Outing and Cook-out and a brief but very flattering character sketch of Mr. Buongiorno. "I see," the young man kept saying, sometimes changing feet on the low railing as though he appeared to be brooding on some problem of his own, something quite different from Mr. Buongiorno's dexterity with knives and ropes; the fact that he had put his briefcase down on the grass encouraged Lucius to believe he was in no hurry. George, however, was bored, and getting the ball away from his brother without his noticing he began an intricate game of tossing it from

[65]

his left hand to his right through adjacent interstices of the grillwork fence, in a sort of perpendicular hopscotch. He was just too young to be even a Cub Scout and had not yet come under Mr. Buongiorno's spell though, as Lucius never let slip an opportunity to assure him, he would be helpless to resist it when that wonderful day came.

"But at least I'm missing a history test," Lucius confided to the inattentive Jacob Miller. "That's one good thing that has come out of all this. All about the causes of the American Revolution."

Jacob pulled his gaze away from the brown Greek temple, through whose large windows no face had appeared to look out upon the lawn. "But you know what they were, I suppose?"

"Oh I know, all right." Lucius wagged his head. He had a large head and a deep brow that looked packed with all sorts of good solid information; like his personal suitcase, it was full to bursting. "I couldn't *not* know them, the way the teacher dins them in to us. You don't want to hear them, do you?"

"God forbid. If you insist I'll feel I'd be justified in putting you straight about the migrations of the Goths, Visigoths, Ostrogoths, Franks, Burgundians *and* the Langobards."

"Well, don't bother. I don't need to know that yet. Well, and next week after we get back to Sharon comes the math test and the French test and the Latin test. Pugh! I absolutely hate the pluperfect."

"Then I guess that means you'll have to do some studying this week?"

But Lucius pushed a heel slowly into the soft Spring turf, removed his foot and gazed down into the deep dent. "I may not have time," he said dreamily, "visiting, like this."

Slowly, slowly but perceptibly, the languor of the waxing Spring came settling down over him, over his shoulders like a cape—a lovely lethargy dropping down through the blue air, from above the high fledgling-green elms. The new but growing warmth of the sun inhibited action and he had hardly strength to push a companion dent in the turf with his other heel. "It's terribly queer, visiting," he confided. "All these people belong in the house except George and me. There's Mrs. Fanning and an old man with a kind of a sharp beard and another woman and a gardener and a lot of maids and things."

"Yes. Yes, I do know her. Is she home now?"

"Who?"

Jacob smiled down at him, his forbidding sulky face lighting up. "The other woman. But she's only a girl, really, you know."

"She's pretty darned big for a girl. I only hope she isn't *still* growing." He scrutinized Jacob for the first time and a suspicion was born in him. This man, all along, had been harboring other interests than hearing Lucius talk; and all those encouraging "I sees" and "Yes, indeeds" had come out of him without his being aware of them. Lucius was less annoyed than interested. Here was the first person he had ever met who was nicer when he was not paying attention than when he was. "Was that what you stopped for?" But Jacob Miller was not willing, or perhaps only not yet ready, to admit that, not even to himself, and said, "Oh, no," very offhand. "I was just passing by." George looked up from his game with the baseball and the holes of the fence. The things people said! Passing by! He'd been standing stock still for ten minutes, with his big foot planted on the railing. "Passing by on one foot, I suppose," George whispered to himself, scathingly, their game of

[67]

catch ruined forever. Why couldn't there be less talk and more play around there?

"If she is in, perhaps I . . . might . . ." Jacob, not bothering to finish, or explain, put a dark-trousered leg over the fence. "Run and find out for me, will you?"

Anna and her duster chased the boys from the morning room whither they had wandered in search of occupation. They had already read, twice, the first of the highly-colored post cards of specific scenes in Bermuda which had arrived by air, which would continue to arrive throughout their stay there and even afterward, and these last ones Mrs. Fanning would scrupulously remail to Sharon, though the loving parental loneliness that had dispatched them in the first place had been entirely dissipated, and forgotten, in the resumption of the normal, on the spot, loves and irritations of family life.

"There isn't anything to do around here," George complained and Lucius who was very much afraid his brother was right said, "Shut up, you damned fool." Side by side they strayed out to the hall and across into the dining room. There seemed indeed to be very little to take up their time; what a terribly long time a week was. They had never before had so much time and so little use for it. "Whenever we even start to have a good catch," George went on, relentlessly, "some man comes along and stops it. I wish I knew how to get rid of them." Lucius repeated his previous advice.

But they had disposed of Mr. Howe's induced concern for them better than they knew, and once and for all. Directly after their encounter in the side yard he had retired, worsted and trembling, to his own room and there tried to restore his self-esteem. He had settled himself at

[68]

his desk murmuring, "Now I *must* get things tended to." He had rearranged his papers, opened and shut his single-checked checkbook several times, hemmed and humphed, frowning portentously, sharpened a pencil to screaming point. He had fiddled with his fountain pen, ascertaining by causing a drop of ink to run out and down the nib its willingness to serve him at any time, in the most sudden emergency, and in the end, after preparations that could well have forebode the drafting of documents that were to merge two great corporations, he renewed his subscription to *Nature Lore*. . . . Jacob Miller, shortly before this, had seen a smooth cap of hair pass behind a hedge of rhododendron and had pursued it with long steps over the lawn.

"How much *can* we play around here? What is there to do, Lucius? Lucius, what fun are we going to have?"

"Oh, shut *up*, George. Probally none."

There was little enough in the dining room to detain them until, glancing up, they caught sight of a row, eight feet long, of framed, much-larger-than-life-sized engravings of dog faces. This work of art hung above the sideboard and the noble faces gazed thoughtfully about them, some forever out the window, some into the lower reaches of the chandelier, some down on the boys. "What good, old-fashioned-looking dogs," Lucius said with enthusiasm. The larger section of the frame, the center, was occupied by a group of four, long-eared, large-eyed, and at either end a single face was set off by narrow strips of golden oak. Were these two perhaps the parents of the four in the middle? In one corner a line of print, quite small, said *"La Meute de M. le Comte de Barral."* Lucius went up and leaned his stomach against the front of the sideboard and read off the names engraved under each immensely sad and noble face

[69]

"Calypso, Margano, Sereno, Lentenor, Nicanor and Barbaro. Which do you like best?"

"Lentenor. I'll take him."

"No, I like him best. I'll take him. I read the names to you."

"No, because you *ast* me which I liked best. You take Barbaro."

"I don't like Barbaro— Oh, yes, I do! Yes. O.K. I'll take him.

George darted a searching look at Barbaro's aristocratic muzzle and eyes, and liked him too. "Well . . ." he said, doubtfully, "well, now . . ." As so often happened in his dealings with his older brother he was confused rather than consoled by Lucius' good-natured capitulation to his own more intensely expressed feelings. Lucius never betrayed his own real desires but he didn't enjoy fighting; incorruptible and kind, he sometimes exasperated George to the verge of hatred. It wasn't that Lucius gave in because George was younger, though George sometimes suspected him of such foul play, and it wasn't at all from a lack of conviction or a weakness. Lucius was, quite simply, a man who was able to change his mind without feeling he was losing his integrity and without embarrassment, and a man of peace, and when this combination became altogether too much for George to endure he would flail his arms around, unavailingly, and stamp and weep. Though Lucius adhered stoutly to his own high standards for himself, with others he was often more than lenient and naturally George wrongly attributed this to disinterest. "I've *taken* Barbaro," Lucius said calmly, and they sauntered out of the room, the specters of two huge hounds now loping at their heels.

"Let's get them up into the attic and brush their fur," George suggested, but what was their amazement to be able to find no attic stairs. They opened every door on the second floor several times, racing faster and faster from room to room, from the front hall to the back hall as their surprise grew. Finally they clattered down the back stairs, bumping into Catherine coming up, and out a side door to the lawn and there were able to verify their astonishment. With their mouths open, they stood and stared up at the dark Greek cornice, the classic cyma recta and ovolo moldings that, like a long bar of dipped chocolate, ran primly around the abrupt top of the brownstone box that was Mrs. Fanning's house. Innocent and empty and serene, the pale blue sky rose directly above this; *no* attic.

"Then where does she put all her old stuff?" George demanded, remembering the attic at home, so wonderfully impassable with marble-topped commodes that smelled acridly of the turn of the century, with chests, trunks, chairs with weak backs and innumerable random square hard sofa pillows covered in Oriental rugging. Lucius asked if George hadn't noticed some of Mrs. Fanning's old stuff still down in the living room. George said that some of it was in the bedrooms. "I've got lots in mine; in fact, it *all* is. Come on, let's race the dogs. Lentenor and I'll race you and Barbaro to the stable and back. Lentenor's a wonderful runner. He's a racing-runner, really; that's the name of the kind of dog he is," George asserted, discounting without a qualm the years and years of careful breeding on the part of M. de Barral and his kennelman, and of numerous other French gentlemen and their servants, to make of Lentenor and his breed the finest possible *chiens à la chasse*.

But Lucius had caught sight of two people standing near the back of the house by the rhododendron hedge. He watched them a minute and though they did not seem to be saying much, some private absorption had settled down

[71]

over them like a big glass bell. He felt he didn't want to go whooping past them just then, accompanied by Barbaro who would probably be barking madly. "Not now," he said.

". . . if there's anything else you ought to be doing."

Though the formula was immemorially polite, awkwardness made it sound as though Jacob wished some other occupation would indeed call her away then and there, leaving him free. The chip on Jacob Miller's shoulder had lain there so long we must assume he had been born with it, as some few other, happier creatures are born with little pale blue wings of angelicness. The shoulder padding has not yet been contrived by human tailor that can hide these attributes. Edith, glancing up into the flat, dark face with its hook nose jutting out so disapprovingly, said earnestly, "Oh, no, there's nothing I ought to be doing." Now that they were face to face his voice and his expression were so dark and cold she felt that after all she probably disliked him, even very much, and that her warm dream on the porch had been concerned with someone quite imaginary, nonexistent, made up out of whole cloth and her need to love. She was not too young but she was too inexperienced to see that his coldness was only the thin, shrinking skin of diffidence. How could she know the only quilt this man had to pull over his painful uncertainty, all there was between himself and what he imagined the world was thinking of him, was this brittle integument of rudeness?

"Oh, no, nothing at all," she said, failing to sound convincing; she sounded as though there were many things she would have to attend to, the minute he left. She had been poking damp mats of dead leaves from among the green fans of iris leaves when he had come stalking menacingly at her over the lawn; she still held the stick she had

[72]

been using. "I don't know why *I* bother to do this," she
said in a sudden ill-considered attempt to be airy, and she
threw away the stick. "Tom, the gardener, is supposed . . .
Oh!" For the stick had landed and skidded, and mowed
over a clump of daffodils. They hastened to the scene of
the damage and bent above it. She felt she had done a
murder. Already bright silver viscous drops crept from the
snapped green flesh. "Oh dear," she said and knelt, her
knees uncomfortably pressed against the brick edging of
the garden.

"Too bad"; and though he was really sorry to see so
much beauty broken in mud the little monitor within him
that gave him so much and such constant bad advice made
him sound only bored.

"Oh, it doesn't matter. Only," she held out the draggled
bunch, "what can anybody do with four daffodils? They'd
look silly in any of Aunt Clara's vases. Two dozen of everything or none, is her motto." She lurched to her feet, her
knees mortified forever by contact with the cold sharp
bricks, and walked toward the back of the house; out here
in the bare muddy sunny garden she felt vulnerable. Her
aunt, moving through the upper hall, might glance from
a back window and be surprised to see them standing out
there; he might become aware of the inimical glance, and
leave; to be close under the wall of the house almost insured safety from scrutiny. But why do I care whether you
go, she thought; you're so surly—only, don't go, don't go!

She fiddled with the flowers, while he watched seriously.
Since almost the beginning of time couples, a man and a
woman, have stood together in gardens; there is something
eternally lovely then, but *what was there to talk about,* they
wondered with mounting discomfort. Deeply disappointed
because this almost-silence was so unlike the imagined con-

[73]

versations each had been having with the other ever since Tuesday, they avoided each other's eyes. They both supposed it was important to be saying something, anything, making some sound. She could have felicitated him on becoming a member of that very special little group, the Recusants; it would never have occurred to her; he could have said anything, no matter how banal; but he would not. The voices of the boys on the side lawn came to them and they looked quickly and hopefully in that direction, but the boys did not appear from around the corner of the house and Edith, with the desperate and disagreeable expression of someone taking a step she knows all too well to be irrevocable, said in a rush, "Well, we might sit down, I suppose. Standing around like this . . . I mean, there's a bench over there against the wall."

Often, at such a time, awkwardness becomes manifest by two people starting in to speak simultaneously; in spite of their fervent wish to the contrary this happens to them repeatedly and at last their very awkwardness becomes a helpful joke. With Jacob and Edith it was their silences which corresponded and though, if they had only known, this could have served as a fine basis for comradeship, they were both so naïve that they waited for each recurrent silence with helpless dread; they peered into each chasm of muteness with horror and flung themselves backward, away from emptiness, only to fall and flounder in the bordering thickets of superfluous speech.

Yet, they were happy; that is they slowly became happy, sitting there. At first she went on resenting his uncouthness that had forced her to be the one to suggest sitting down; he was annoyed at himself for not having thought of it. But seated, they need not face each other; they could look out over the garden where stands of daffodils rose miraculously from the still chill brown earth; or they could scrutinize the friendly sky and observe the flight of town birds. At some few courageous instants their converging gaze lay on the four battered daffodils and the four bladelike leaves in her lap.

"You had a perfectly horrible time the other night, here at dinner."

"Oh, no."

"Yes, you did."

"Why should I have had?"

"You looked so . . . glum. Were you thinking about how much better those far off Merovingian times were than now?" She feared she might be overbold, saying this.

"But they weren't."

"Well, you looked as though you thought they were, or something." She arranged the daffodils meticulously straight. "I just wondered."

"I used to think that," he said thoughtfully. "Back in Indiana when I was, oh, fifteen or sixteen, and I had begun to be interested in studying, but no one else, there, could understand *that*. They thought I was either lazy, or a fool and maybe I was. They thought . . ." She leaned back at last, closing her eyes as she listened, letting light pry at the lids. What he said was less important than the fact of his confiding; she felt all at once happy and wise. Liking herself better, she liked him again, with a warm rush of feeling. If it is a fact that they spent only twenty minutes on the bench, yet it must be admitted that the gauge is as yet uninvented that could measure the real elapsed time, which amounted to the passage of several years of companionship and understanding. She heard about the dissatisfactions of his early life and when she could manage it, she slid in explanations of her own..

[75]

"But you've had everything," he objected, screwing around to look at her, her calm exterior of smooth brow and quiet tweeds.

"I *haven't*. I certainly haven't. . . . Oh, good food and lodging, yes. . . . Then what did you do? Did you get the scholarship, after all?"

Perhaps only looking back, days after, years after, was it the idyl they believed it to be.

When the boys, utterly unable to restrain their racing-runner dogs for another single minute, finally slipped the leashes and all four of them barking at the top of their voices tore for the stable door, Jacob, though on his feet by now, was still talking about himself. When he left he carried the four daffodils out in front of him, carefully, rather as though they were a chalice, some rare ancient chalice, of silver-gilt and enamels.

6

"A LADY I vork for vunce, she keep a dairy."

"Is that so; I suppose you helped with it."

"Vy sood I?"

"Well, I don't know," Mrs. Fanning said coolly, not too coolly; she was on the point of breaking it to the maids that they were giving a large dinner party Thursday, unaware that Anna read the engagement pad on the morning-room desk as regularly as Catherine said her "Hail Mary," and with more interest. Anna, folding napkins, knew perfectly well what was in the mind of her employer; she recognized the slight stiffening of manner that presaged the all-too-casual announcement that extra work was in store. Anna didn't mind the extra work; parties were a blessed change in her monotonous life. She enjoyed looking at the people sitting so straight around the dining-room table, man, woman; man, woman; man, woman. She liked to look at the women's colored party dresses and to hear the silly way they talked. She had been looking forward to the Recusant dinner party ever since the day the memorandum had first appeared on the engagement pad, but there wasn't any reason to make it easy for Mrs. Fanning to tell her about it; if Mrs. Fanning felt the maids perhaps had a grievance, she wasn't going to be the one to disabuse her. Mrs. Fanning, running the end of one finger along the shelf where the cook books stood, thought she must remember, after Thursday, to speak about dust. Now was not the moment. Now was the moment for a cool, firm friendliness, when hurry or criticism would be inadvisable but laxness fatal. "I thought perhaps the dairy might have been part of your work. Was this in Sweden?"

"Vest Hartford. God Heaven, no, I voss the vaitress only. But it keep her busy for a liddle vile every morning; m'mn; vun solid hour, sometimes. Right after breakfast she get it out and she open it up and she write, write, write, everything vot hod hoppen the day before. Ha! Yoost imagine!"

"Oh, I *see,*" Mrs. Fanning had never bothered to memorize the vagaries of Anna's vocabulary; it must be admitted that neither had Anna ever felt any necessity to study Mrs. Fanning's speech; she merely, presumably with admiration, referred to it as "high English," and let it go at that. Words she didn't know might as well have been nonexistent. "I see. Now, let's see—today's Tuesday, I'm out for luncheon today, we'll all be in for dinner. Thursday there will be a meeting of my club here, the Recusants, and I think if you have any free time today I'd do the silver instead of waiting until the end of the week."

"Yoost the teaspoons?" Anna suggested, knowing as well as Mrs. Fanning that what was in store for them all was a full-fledged dinner party. "The silver teapot, or the shina—I guess probably the shina's good enough. You want liddle teena-weena sandwiches?"

Mrs. Fanning eyed her sharply. Surely after fifteen years Anna knew that the Recusants always sat down and were given a four-course dinner. Imagine old Professor Benda, the greatest living authority on the life of the common wasp, having to stand up for any length of time or balance a cup! Even sitting down, one trembled for the china. And Mme. Pelletier, and the Master of Scoville College; one had to be careful with such people. Mrs. Fanning sighed; Anna was proving more stubborn than usual. It was one of her domestic crosses, a very old cross now, fifteen years old, that Anna always continued her work while Mrs. Fanning talked to her. Earlier in their association she had sometimes suggested that Anna pause for a time, but Anna had gone right on with her work, saying, amiably, "I hear. I listen." Now, as she bent over a pile of clean napkins she continued to peer closely at hems and monograms through her inefficient, wobbly spectacles. Mrs. Fanning had the impression that Anna never quite took in what she said or noticed when she went away, and perhaps had been talking to herself when she had brought up the subject of her long-ago employer with the laughable habit of recording all her yesterdays.

Anna often talked out loud to herself. On particularly gay days she sang over and over the only song she knew, a wordless song, a wordless trumpeting of euphoria that resounded in the back halls and bounced up the back stairs. Contrary to most maids, she was always happiest the day after her day out, and Fridays the house rang with her gay hoots. Days off were a worry to her because then she had nothing to do. She pushed herself around downtown on her painful feet, but without anywhere to go.

[79]

Except for a friend in California and a sister-in-law in Brooklyn she was without emotional entanglements; nor was she interested in movies; and to have spent money in a shop for something she didn't need was unthinkable. At Christmas and for birthdays she bought doilies or handkerchiefs and sent them off to Sacramento and Brooklyn. "Oh but the prices is vicked!" she would report to Catherine. "Turrable! Next year I crochet it myself." The only thing she looked forward to on Thursdays was coffee and a piece of pastry in a drugstore at four o'clock. The coffee was good but she was deeply scornful of the pastry, and sitting alone at a little square plastic-topped table, drinking slowly, gazing at counters of pink powder-puffs and impersonal stacks of boxes of Band-aid—she whose naïve nose was always shiny, who had no children to fall and suffer small cuts—in the glare of neon bands, with crowds about her of people she did not know, drinking slowly, she remembered Småland, and the innocent sweet day of her youth. She could remember prettier china than this, and better coffee; instead of the prescription department she saw a small sunny room, her mother moving about in it, and sun lying in the road outside. What impulse had led her, years and years ago, to leave, treacherously, its bright simplicity and cross the sea? Why had she ever left home? "Oh, I come a long vay, a long vay," she sometimes said aloud to herself in a little bewildered voice; where was that young girl now, with everything she owned in a suitcase—cotton shirtwaists, cotton handkerchiefs, memories of home? "Oh, it voss a blessed time," she would say. "Yes—Yes, it voss."

Often, long before she had to, a tall figure came sailing slowly up Evergreen Avenue in the dusk past the dark Greek temples of houses and turned in at the low iron

[80]

gate—Anna coming home from her day off, and glad of it. . . . Catherine, on the other hand, always scuttled in, breathless, at the last possible moment. Some nights, the lights left for her on the back porch and in the back hall burned so late that Mrs. Fanning, wakeful, thought: Now it has come at last, the day off when she is *not* coming in. No one knew where Catherine went on Thursdays and Sundays; only to Anna did she vouchsafe an occasional glimpse into her private life. "M'married daughter and kids" . . . "M'first husband who drank." She had a current husband and also a current friend who was a brakeman on the New York, New Haven and Hartford railroad. "Him," she said, not meaning her husband. The liaison seemed to give her but little joy, conditioned as it was by the cruel rigidity of the train schedule. Anna, at once fastidious and derisive, veered away from her ill-tempered confidences.

"All the flat silver," said Mrs. Fanning now, erect and inflexible by the swinging door. "It will be a dinner, as it always is. Oh, not the oyster forks, of course," she added, as if not having to shine them naturally cut down the work by half.

"Vell, today's only Tuesday." Anna peered at a tiny monogram that refused to divulge to her which side was its face.

"I know. But there will be other things to do, nearer the time. You'd better get after whatever large serving dishes we're likely to need, and the flat silver, and I'll get the Recusants' épergne from the bank. It will probably need only a touching up." Her two maids were the only people living whom Mrs. Fanning was afraid of but when Anna said, "I might vould vait and shine all the silver at vunce," she stood firm, prevailed, and when George and Lucius

[81]

came out to the side porch a little later they found Anna sitting on a bench resignedly humming and rubbing with all the Fanning platters and bowls and pitchers spread around her ankles in a tumultuous silver sea.

"Hello," they said, and paused.

Mrs. Fanning, victorious, buttoning her long, many-buttoned coat, appeared at an open window. "Don't bother Anna, will you, boys? She is very anxious to get all the silver done this morning."

Anna smiled into a bowl and said not too ambiguously, "*They* don't bother."

Mrs. Fanning, preferring to ignore the implication lying curled up like a snake beneath the innocent surface of this remark, appeared now in the doorway, working at the fingers of her beautiful suède gloves that were as black as charcoal and as soft as a butterfly's body. "*Is* it going to rain, do you think? I just saw a cloud come by. Or isn't it?" She spoke pleasantly, wanting, as all good employers want, to leave behind her when she went out the quiet atmosphere, the contented relationship that obtains between a good housewife and a good servant, each firmly established in her predestined place. But not patient enough to wait for Anna to speak her part in her role, she answered her own question. "No, I don't believe it is." She encountered a mature look in Lucius' eyes and, George and Anna being but children, it was to him she said, "You know, I always believe that if I think of a thing first, then it won't happen; it's a kind of insurance, do you see?" Her smile invited his indulgence for this uncharacteristic whimsey.

After she had gone the boys slumped off the porch and down the path, hands in pockets, without occupation or desires.

[82]

"She must think she's awfully important."

"Why, Lucius? Why does she?"

"I mean, if she thinks she can work things happening just by her *thinking of them first.* Who's she," he demanded, waxing indignant, "stopping the rain off just because she thinks of it! Why didn't she think of Mother's pneumonia then, if she's so smart!"

"I don't get you. Well, she *is* important, isn't she?"

But Lucius shook his head, baffled by his own perceptions. "Let's go back on the porch; she's gone by now."

The spread-out silver glittered and winked, heliographing cheerful irrational messages with the sun's rays. Anna's old, sheep-lined slippers were planted among unrolled gray flannel cases where dozens of knives, forks and spoons, like silver mice not one of whom was managing entirely successfully to hide himself, dug at their burrows; despite their efforts their initialled rear ends protruded. There was an odd dozen spoons with bunches of grapes on their handles in *haut relief* and Anna, who would have been instantly and sternly forbidden to do any such thing had Mrs. Fanning suspected her of the practice, had undone the enameled daisy pin from her dress and was picking with the point at a stubborn black deposit between grapes. An open jar of wantonly pink stuff stood on the bench, its smell sharp and sarcastic on the mild Spring air.

"Can I do some?" George asked eagerly. Anything, anything rather than these aimless days of nothing-to-do. At home he would have fled the house for hours, if a maid had suggested he help her with so much as a single salt spoon but here, in this land-locked idleness, he looked with real hope on a black-smudged rag and a pot of pink.

"Vy not?"

They sat cross-legged on the warm board floor, each

with an immense piece of silverware in what they probably thought of as their laps and discovered with pleasure how pink can very quickly become black. The smell curled up into their noses and made them sneeze. They drew designs with their fingers in the rapidly drying paste film and played tick tack toe on the flat bottom of a chop plate. George lost.

"Oh well," he said, and returned to his agreeable labors, rubbing away hard on a ladle, and presently he remarked that he felt useful.

"It's better than nothing," Lucius admitted.

"Ven I voss liddle ve had four spoons," Anna said. "It voss a plenty." She threw a scornful Swedish glance over all the extravagance spread about her feet. "Spoons for coffee fife or six times a day, coffee all day long. That's the vay we do in Trekarten. Ven I go back to Trekarten I'm going to have a liddle bakery, a *lid-dle* bakery yoost my own." Her eyes behind the askew spectacles narrowed with tenderness and amusement at her own delicious future. "I'll set the dough. Oh, I love dough! I'll do the baking, and there'll be a young girl for the rooning."

"Oh, Anna, *when?*"

"Ven I go."

"Yes, but *when* are you going?" George liked plans definite. True, he tolerated and even relished a certain amount of worrying, but how much that certain amount was, who could say—and once over and beyond the indefinable line of its limit he demanded certainty, and now he suddenly, with utter clarity, saw the little bakery and Anna in it, slapping up great coffee rings as big as the wheels of his bicycle.

"Next year," she said, smiling as though it were a secret she knew in greatest detail, forgetting she had said "next

[84]

year, next year" ever since her early middle age and that
here she still was and shining the Fanning silver for the
seven hundredth and fortieth time. "I vant to collect up
yoost a liddle – more – money."

Oh, why doesn't she start right away! George wondered.
Why delay at all what you want so very much, as he could
see she wanted to be standing in her own bakery, beside
her own stove. It troubled him; he urged her to get going.
There being never anything at all to prevent grownups
from doing whatever they liked, at once, he couldn't understand why she wasn't already there.

"Liddle blue curtains at the vindows," she said, nearly
breaking his heart.

"What are you waiting for!" he cried.

Placidly she heaved up and took two handfuls of silver
into the pantry; they could hear her put it in the sink,
twist the metal stopper and run hot water to make a big
square puddle. She sailed back and stood at the edge of
the porch, looking off across the lawn, over the hedge,
her hands and arms brackets above her cotton-print hips,
her wide-apart long-fingered hands curved delicately back
from the bony wrists where blue veins ran. George, his
black rag suspended, gazed anxiously up at her.

"I am going," she said.

But would she, ever? It is hard to say. Would she one
day indeed pin on the high-crowned black hat with the
single purple-red rose in the very center of the front,
stuff the last lumpy mysterious newspaper-wrapped parcel
into her suitcase, click the catches shut and leave Evergreen Avenue forever? It is beyond human prophecy to
say. Could she conceivably straighten the edge of the rug
by the closet door in her room for the last time, shut the
drawer in her bureau, leaving her closet, her bed, and the

smell that was compounded of the starch in aprons and collars and the oil she used in her hair, the liniment she put in hot water for soaking her feet, the scent of the violet talcum powder Mrs. Fanning had given her for Christmas and of a perpetual bag of licorice drops and the ink of *Svea,* her Swedish newspaper? Is it possible to believe that she will leave all that forever, and with a new passport in her old black handbag, go clanking down the back stairs with her suitcase and navy blue silk umbrella?

"I am going," she said again.

"Think how *old* you are," George reminded her tenderly, and Lucius kicked him.

"*Ho,*" said Anna, "*I'm* not old." She hooted out a few notes from her trumpeting song, waded back through silver to the bench and picked up the rag and the coffee tray. "*Ho!* Ho, ho!" she sang loudly, polishing with wild circular sweeps, but George, folded up at her feet, wiped away two tears with his soot-black rag, two tears that had sprung up—but whether because of the pain where Lucius had kicked him on the ankle or because he was in mortal fear for the little blue-curtained bakery, he couldn't have told.

7

EDITH shepherded her young victims into the drug store, finding it not an easy thing to do because the boys were so well brought up that all three of them became entangled in a quite useless politeness; they were accustomed to trail behind their mother in shop doorways and Edith was accustomed to trail behind her aunt. Finally the boys managed, by saying "No, no," repeatedly, and clinging like limpets to the door jamb, to get her through first but then something suddenly occurred to Lucius and he booted George, slightly, in the rear; being the next oldest he must insure his being next in.

"Now!" Edith said, with every evidence of satisfaction at having got them into the shop and of vicarious pleasure at the pleasure she was about to bestow on them. Contemplating treachery, she yet was able to pretend out loud that she had only their happiness in mind, whereas she really owed them the deepest debt of gratitude for furnishing her with an excuse for her afternoon's schemes. What *is* it that metamorphoses the candid young, so shamelessly, so

quietly, into the scheming grownup? Is it simply years—
the mere passage of time, days and hours? But years are
kind, really, laden with gifts of delight. Is it self-interest?
But George, for instance, who was a positive monument to
self-interest would never have done to her what she was
planning, under guise of friendliness, to do to him. She
herded them up onto revolving stools. "What will you
have? Sodas? Sundaes? . . . What flavors are there?" she
asked the white-jacketed adolescent lounging behind his
battery of silver spigots, a negligent magician, able to turn
out miracles with two or three flicks of the wrist. He
pointed over his shoulder at a list posted on the glass
behind him; couldn't she read? But she was not bad-
looking, if severe and bigger than he liked, so he unbent
enough to say, "Them."

The boys drooped against the chill marble. It was only
quarter past two and they were full of chicken and rice
and stewed apricots. "Well, now," they said listlessly, wishing they didn't have to cram in anything more on top of
the apricot layer.

"Order whatever you like; I'm not having anything."
She went on to the back of the store to buy a toothbrush.

Lucius, catching sight in the mirror of the look of extreme indifference on his brother's face, pointed out that
she probably thought she was being nice.

"I know it." George languished against the counter and
wondered why she couldn't have suggested this treat some
other time, any other time. There had already been innumerable moments in his one and a half days on Evergreen Avenue when he would have welcomed a trip to the
drugstore. "Double chocolate sundae with hot fudge sauce
and nuts," he said, dispiritedly. He had the air of a man
who knows what is expected of him, does his duty, and does

[88]

not skimp. Strong New England instincts drove him to make the most of this unwelcome but free offer and he would eat it to the last sickening tan smear, but it *was* a pity she couldn't have thought of it some other time. Lucius ordered a glass of orangeade and George wanly told him he was a fool.

"Probally," Lucius agreed, cheerful and cool; he gazed about him alertly. Maybe he and George might run a drugstore when they grew up; of course it would be a lot harder than being an architect, which was one of his present plans, but he felt himself to be one who would not flinch from difficulties.

Edith had objected to the color of the drug clerk's first suggestion in the way of a toothbrush, and she waited by the counter at the back of the store. "This one's more on the white, like," said the clerk and handed her for her consideration a purely white toothbrush, white as a bare bone long exposed to desert sun.

"So I see." She pulled her shoulder bag around to pay for it, but there was no money in it, nothing but a lipstick and a handkerchief. She flushed. Her "So I see" had held a little mockery at obviousness and at his common speech, but here was she now, confronting him with an empty purse, a superior person at a loss. Her mockery withered; she was left as bare of accomplishment as he was and so, curiously, she began to employ the words, phrases, mistakes and intonations native and natural to him. Her voice changed to one resembling his and though before she spoke aloud the words moved through her mind in preparation, she was shocked to hear herself say, flatly, "How about if I charge it?"

"Yep," he agreed. He whisked the toothbrush into a small triangle of paper.

"Hadden I better sign your slip or something?"

"Nope." He flicked open his book. "Name'n'address?"

Dignity returned to her as inexplicably as it had abandoned her. "It's my aunt's charge account. Mrs. Fanning on Evergreen Avenue. But don't you want me to sign?"

He was supremely uninterested and almost without watching the pencil, jotted down even less information than she had given him. "It won't be necessary, thank you," he answered, all at once suave, and she came away from the counter, disconcerted, thinking how sad it was that she must look that much, that unmistakably, a lady; never, never to be suspected of little peccadilloes in shops was almost humiliating.

"Where are you taking us to play?" George asked her.

"Oh." She clicked shut the clasp to her empty bag and faced them, no longer able to postpone perfidy. "Well, I thought you'd probably like to go to the Museum and look around." She spoke calmly, but just saying it out loud to two little boys made her blush.

"Animals?"

"Art."

It was the boys' turn to say, "Oh." When she had offered to take the boys off somewhere for the afternoon Mrs. Fanning, though accepting promptly, had been naturally surprised at such an evidence of consideration coming from a quarter whence she was more used to encountering either apathy or resistance. She had said it wasn't at all necessary but that it would be very nice indeed, and for some minutes she had continued to look mystified, back and forth from Edith to the boys as though she wondered if they were in collusion about something. But the boys had been as ignorant as she of what was in store for them and now it appeared that Edith's idea of a fun afternoon was to drag them around on marble floors. George had expected an afternoon outdoors in a green field somewhere, perhaps with other boys, certainly with a ball or a bicycle or apparatus of some kind. He would have welcomed even a babyish park playground, if it had swings and a slide.

"I see; *I* see," he said, hollowly. And with slow meticulous strokes he drew the drugstore spoon through the shallow tan puddle that was the last of his sundae. A museum! . . . Certainly there wasn't any hurry, then.

"Mercy," said Lucius, mildly.

To Edith's much-too-quickly-expressed surprise, Jacob Miller had materialized from nowhere, had joined them, and was now the most important member of the group at pause in the entrance hall of the Museum before a more than life-sized rendering in enduring bronze of Romulus, Remus, their foster mother and a healthy scattering of little lupine foster brothers and sisters. George was being told their story by Edith though he already knew it and kept saying "Yeah, I *know*," to make her stop, but though she could see he had heard it before she didn't know how to stop herself and continued to bend educationally above him until she had recounted all she remembered of the legend. Without the boys for a pretext she would not have been able to visit the Museum with impunity so soon after the meeting with Jacob in her aunt's yard. The casual observer seeing two little boys in jerseys and blue corduroy pants would never have known them for what they were—chaperons. Nor did they themselves know their own true function that afternoon. She had assured Jacob, during an aberrant moment in the garden, that she was perfectly familiar with the Museum because of frequent visits; she had been unwilling to have him think she was not, and now she was regretting her insouciance with the truth. What had it been, that implication that she often strayed about the great halls, renewing friendships with the contents, but a lamentable case of showing off? George, kicking at the marble base of the heavy group, privately thought that he and Lucius in their present circumstances had a lot in common with those two long-gone Roman boys; both pairs of brothers were condemned to an existence removed from their native haunts and the facial resemblance of the mature wolf to Mrs. Fanning seemed to him striking. He regretted sincerely that there were no corresponding young cubs to be played with on Evergreen Avenue; maybe they could have been taught to retrieve balls, a thing Lentenor and Barbaro declined to do.

"Is this a very famous statue?" Lucius inquired after they had stood in front of it for so long that, even though it was the very first work of art they had come to, it seemed they were never going to move on. He sounded as though he doubted it, as if indeed it would surprise him very much to be told that it was, and that he would find himself forced to wonder at the judgment of anyone making such an assertion. They all looked at Edith, who surely didn't know. Jacob was smiling, to himself. She thought it was cruel of him, and finally, seeing he wasn't going to help her she said to him in exasperation, "Well! Is it?"

Apparently it wasn't. Apparently it was a contribution from the rich man who had given his money and his surname to the building, and though deplored by everyone who had the Museum's best interests at heart, it had to stand where it was, the mother wolf's bronze teeth permanently bared in a terrifying welcoming smile to every visitor, man, woman or child who ventured in at the door.

"Even if I was supposed to like it, I couldn't," Lucius

said, but George shot him a troubled look and murmured "Maybe some people don't mind it."

"I'm not some people, and I'm glad I amn't. I think it stinks. . . . Shut up, George," he was forced to add, to forestall argument.

Edith was looking at Jacob out of the corner of her eye, speculatively, wondering if the way she had been remembering him since eleven o'clock yesterday, somber and exciting, was the way he actually was. She was almost as tall as he; she could see into his ear; she stared earnestly but the convolutions of the little cavern told her nothing and transferring her gaze to the flat cheek, the dark, averted eye, the mouth, she felt she was struggling in a state of total ignorance. His suit was dark; his tie was dark and secret . . . who had given it to him? . . . and at last she wondered if it had been worth the trouble of pretending to Aunt Clara that she thought the boys might get in the way in the house that was experiencing the first slow upheaving throes of a house that is to be got ready for a dinner party. She thought: It would be much better if the boys would go off by themselves and look at things but I can't very well suggest it to them; it would sound as though I wanted to be alone with him. "Come back!" she cried as George and Lucius suddenly broke away and achieved a long slide across the marble floor. A uniformed attendant stepped from behind a bust of Pompey and said, "Here, now!" They returned, practicing very short slides. There must be some way to get rid of them, safely, for a little while, the exasperated girl thought.

Together they straggled along to the next display, a dingy, priceless rug hanging limply between two dull swords—gift of a rich man who had endowed the Museum with funds for an expedition. No one had any illusion that it was necessary to admire this group; they passed in front of it with brief and wordless sidelong glances and soon clotted up again, the boys stepping on the heels of their elders, before a thirteenth century bas-relief in marble of a row of saints.

"*This* is quite nice," George offered to the void. "What big heads they have. They look like the comics."

Jacob, sounding distracted, asked why the boys didn't run off and look at things for themselves; he assured them they would have a lot more fun.

"What things?"

"In the basement, for instance. Miss Howe says she's been here so often there's no sense in her trailing around with you. She's seen everything." He paid no attention to her quick, "Oh, well, maybe I—" "You'd have a lot more fun by yourselves I should think."

Fun was something George had given up all idea of for that afternoon and he experienced the confusion of one asked to relinquish abnegation. "We don't know where the stairs are," he objected. Jacob pointed, his dark-clad arm as long as George himself.

"O. K.," said George. The boys disappeared like rabbits down a burrow and two abnormally silent people were left to walk with aimless steps down the long gallery. I am the host here, he thought; it's up to me to say something.

Mistaking her large, smoothly finished exterior, her calm cold look, for a maturity she had by no means yet achieved, he supposed her requirements of him would be considerable; he had no way of knowing that her sophistication was all external. He could discover instantly the minutest crack in an ancient enamel, but he had no trained eye for the hiatus in Edith between her present partial state of development and her potentialities. He took too much for granted;

rather, he took the wrong things; when she had said how familiar she was with the contents of the Museum, he had not recognized it for a simple, scared boast which she would have done much to recall. They strayed together down the endless hall, only just not bumping their shoulders together. He liked her clubbed-off, turned-under hair and the big bag that swung above one hip. He would never have suspected the emptiness of that bag; she looked to him like someone in a tapestry, a boy traveling with, in the bag, a loaf of bread for the journey, or a roll of messages to be delivered to a king.

Time to say something now; overtime. What he burst out with was, characteristically, an accusation: "Now don't say 'I think it must be very interesting to work in a museum!' " and trembled for her with compassion, because he knew instantly from her too-quick denial that that was actually the very thing she had been about to say. From her stricken eyes and mouth he knew that to have been the one, the only idea that had, painfully, just detached itself from the floor of her mind and begun to float slowly up, a frail marine weed, to the surface where, in another minute, she would have gratefully caught at it and offered it to him. He stopped and irritably adjusted a card on a case of Roman glass fragments, knowing he was hard to talk to. He knew his face closed against people; he could always feel the special muscles at work that did it, making him safe against the world, and against the words and feelings of others, whom he didn't understand and didn't want to understand. Those muscles had started their protective functioning years ago, back in Indiana. His father had expected him to go to work in the family drugstore and his mother had said, when he showed her pictures in his history books of old swords, old belts and buckles and cups,

"I think they're all horrid." The intervening hard years had brought him a large measure of competence but withheld the gift of ease. He felt now, walking along the gallery side, that he looked sullen and that she might be wishing she had gone with the little boys.

"Do you . . ." they turned and cried to each other in desperation.

"No, no," he protested. "You started. Do I what?"

"Do you—well, have other things you ought to be doing?"

"That wasn't what you were going to say."

Her eyes withdrew. "I know. But won't it do? I'm not exactly sure *what* I was going to say."

"I have a thousand things I ought to do. Each more useless than the thing before. Life in a museum is a living hell, I'd have you know."

She muttered that she wondered, if that were the case, why he worked in one.

"Because I love it!"

They paced narrow polished boards in an inner gallery, pausing with consistent un-sight before statue groups and glass cases of tiny, and partial, objects. They leaned on the cases, staring down as though they leaned above small ponds and stared at meaningless pebbles on the bottom. He gave no indication of leaving her to go and make a beginning on his one thousand useless jobs. She pointed to an open door in one hall. "I've forgotten, what's in there?"

"Never go that way. That way lies madness. Ceramics."

"Oh, yes, of course."

He was becoming sorry for her, seeing she couldn't support her assertion of familiarity with the contents of the Museum; he could now see quite clearly it had been nothing but a pretense, but at the same time he held all pre-

[96]

tense in contempt and would do nothing to help her out of her hole. "Since you've *seen* all this stuff—" he began, but then professional enthusiasm overcame meanness. "Oh, we've got one new thing on the top floor. A Venetian marriage chest. I'll show you."

How very much happier they were right away with an objective! They found they could breathe easier all at once and when the boys appeared from a side door they greeted them with affection.

"Hi. How was the cellar?"

"Fine. We've done it," George told them.

"Then go look in that room over there."

"We've done that room."

"How about the gallery with armor?"

"We've done it."

Jacob asked if they had seen the collection of Roman coins and set their feet in the right way but they were back almost at once, even before Edith and Jacob had reached the elevator. "You didn't examine them very carefully," he complained, but they said they had.

"As well as we could," George amended, "with only one side showing. Where are you going?"

"Up. Want to come?"

The boys did and, though scowled on by Edith who should have been so grateful to them because their mere existence had allowed her to visit the Museum with impunity, they all crammed themselves into the small elevator. Many budding love affairs have had less to contend with than George and Lucius. The elevator, which had been installed for the very few distinguished arthritic ancients who came to evening receptions, gave an affronted lurch and began to rise with majestic, protesting slowness and so slow was their progress that on the way Jacob had

[97]

an idea. "Second floor!" he sang out and clanging open
the door with one hand he held Edith back with the other
and neatly, inexorably bunted the boys out with a knee.
He shut the door and pushed the button for the top floor.
"How's that?" he asked her and they laughed in each
other's eyes at his resourcefulness.

Released from tension, they wandered through the gal-
laries of the top floor. It was almost as though they strayed
through a blossoming wood hand in hand. The Venetian
marriage chest could wait. He showed her his own exhi-
bition, a small collection in a small case. She didn't feel
any more that she had to pretend to have seen everything.
They leaned long and gazed deep. "I see. Yes, I see," she
breathed as he pointed out fine points of his treasures.
He confided his hopes for a scholarship next Fall to go to
Europe for further study, and though her heart gave a
sickening dip to hear it, she said she did hope he got it.
But he wouldn't go off, would he, her heart inquired of
her, not soon, not right away?

Meanwhile George and Lucius were making a rapid
survey of what the second floor had to offer. They moved
very fast up and down the galleries, almost running from
one exhibit to the next, earning and ignoring stern glances
from uniformed guards who stood, hands behind their
backs, with swiveling eyes and swinging holsters. The boys
sped on.

"Isn't that horrible?"

"Yes. But *that's* a handy-looking thing."

"Yes, it is. What is it?"

"I don't know."

Taking a quick turn around a door jamb they found
themselves facing a small but full-sized reconstructed
Syrian chapel. It looked as though it had been molded,

carelessly, by some giant's preschool baby out of great masses of kindergarten clay. There were steps which George mounted, his sneakered feet making no sound. "Come on, Lucius, there aren't any of those blue guys around here." They tiptoed about under the clay canopy painted with stars and symbols, wondering what game could be devised that would utilize this unusual and pleasant structure.

"It's not like a boat exactly; we couldn't really pretend it's a boat."

"No. It might be a cave. No, it's too open for a cave. It *isn't* much use, is it, though it's the best thing we've seen so far. What's this part, do you suppose?" They descended into a square, hollowed-out place and called each other's attention to what a serviceable bathtub it could be, or even a very small swimming pool. "I'm afraid it wouldn't hold water very well," Lucius said, picking at the plaster with his fingernail. "See, it isn't very good material."

But George was not to be diverted from the pleasing idea of a pool. "The water could start pouring from up there, and come *swishing* down onto you. It would be kind of a magic bath-pool."

"You'd drown."

"No, you'd only partly drown and they'd come and haul you off to the hospital in an ambulinch and you'd be holy and magic forever after . . . What's that!"

They crouched low, holding their breath, as slow, official-sounding footsteps approached from the long gallery, turned in at the door, and paused near by. There was a long, nerve-destroying silence and George began breathing through his mouth; this made rather more sound than if he had used the customary apertures. The footsteps

[99]

moved a little, as though the owner of the big feet were peering around with a suspicion of something untoward going on; the feet moved on, but not far on, not enough. Then they returned, very near, and George rolled his eyes in an agony—he would sneeze any minute now—he would burst—he would scream in spite of himself. Then, with a sound like doom, louder than any sound George could possibly have made, the guard blew his nose. The toot reverberated through the little room, bounded back from the walls of the tomb and nearly toppled the altar; surely never in ancient times had the little structure been subjected to such atmospheric pressure, never since, perhaps, long long ago when ceremonial trumpet blasts may have been sounded near by. Then the guard coughed, a curiously anticlimactic effort, realigned his great feet and slowly, slowly went away.

"Great jumping God!" Lucius breathed. "Was I scared!" They scrambled out, their sneaker eyelets scoring the ancient clay, tumbled down the altar steps and were away.

"The Venetian chest is in the Jones Wing," Jacob said and waited, as though for her to make the start in the right direction. How undependable he is, she thought; I thought he had forgotten or forgiven. Surely he knows by now I don't really know my way around and I'm not going to pretend any more that I do. Just when I thought he was all smoothed out, here he has crinkled up again. "*Oh,* well," he said, as though it simply wasn't worth his while to show up her duplicity any further. He strode on ahead. The boys appeared quickly from behind a statue. "You!" he said.

"Oh, *we've* been up here for *hours.*" They were negligent and carefree, and perhaps only their mother would have thought them a little red in the face.

[100]

The great painted chest stood against the wall. It was long and high and heavy, covered with pictures of processions of festive men and women winding under flowering fruit trees, all wearing colored clothes, all carrying gifts to a wedding. "Venetian marriage chest, late fifteenth century," he recited, in the manner of one of his colleagues he particularly disapproved of. "Perfectly beautiful thing and rare as Hell. Well . . . almost." He suddenly flung open the cover and in his own voice, made gentle by love and admiration, said, "And here's the girl who owned it."

"Oh!" George was one who never feared to state the obvious. "She's bare."

There on the inside of the lid, painted full-size and gayer than life was the reclining figure of a young girl. Wearing nothing at all but a necklace and a bracelet, here and there a feathery spray of flowers crossed the white body. Her little face framed in feathers of pale gold stared out insolently at Edith. "Just look at you!" she seemed to say to her. "So *much* too tall and clumping around in that thick cloth, all *covered up!* How unpleasant. What ugly shoes. Are your jewels at home? I believe you have no jewels."

Jacob, holding the cover open, looked from one girl to the other and smiled at the living one at last. "Don't mind her," he said comfortingly, loving the big, discomfited one. Neatly and silently he closed down the lid. "She's a silly little bitch. Come on. Where have the boys gone to now?"

But George and Lucius had walked right out of the room. Propelled by horror and self-consciousness they walked right down the middle of a long gallery, looking neither to right nor to left, still seeing the startling naked figure. What, Lucius couldn't help wondering, would Mr. Buongiorno have made of that?

[101]

8

FARAWAY, yellow and dim, seeming ready to extinguish themselves at a breath, a few night lights burned against the ceilings where one gallery crossed another. Not bright enough to read by and not obscure enough so that anyone could creep in and make off with a painting or a javelin, they stayed on all night. If the night guards wanted to read *The Daily Mirror* they had to go into an office and switch on the desk lamp, but then when they had to emerge to walk their rounds the rest of the Museum was disagreeably shadowy. They had their pistols, of course, and no one ever had broken in at night; the nearest approach to a crisis that had ever occurred was once when a new young guard had whipped his pistol out and leveled it at a suspicious figure in the gloom; the figure had neither answered nor run away when challenged, and cautious further scrutiny had showed it to be Apollo, smiling.

Jacob had stayed late in his office after Edith and the boys left and he was still there when the night guards came on duty. Foregoing dinner he had been sitting at his desk writing a letter, trying to write it, rewriting and throwing away. His long bones ached from hours of concentrated bending over his blotter and the result, now, at ten o'clock, was a page and a half of cold neat script. "Sorry not to have written lately," he had said in one draft and eliminated it from the final copy because it wasn't particularly true. "Reno," he had written distastefully, and that was true. The address on the envelope was a boarding house in Fort Wayne.

By now, he thought, he should have become accustomed to frustration in his personal relationships, but the way he had seized the first chance to escape from Fort Wayne proved he never would be. He sat, solitary, his under lip thrust out, probably more than a little hungry, teetering his pen up and down on the desk, and upbraided himself for his own naïveté which he recognized extended to a degree that was surprising even to himself. "I should have stayed and had it out with her, once and for all," he said. "Why did I act so young and stupid? Because I *was* young, and damned stupid." Not a great deal older, even now, he trembled with uneasiness at himself and what he might do to his own life. . . . Sitting there, in his cave of shadows, he looks mature, but how could we dare assume that because he looks like a grownup and is so knowledgeable about the ways enamels are applied to metal that he also understands the human heart, his or another's?

He straightened up, sore and tired, and switched off the desk lamp. In the long gallery he saw a guard's back slowly turn a corner and disappear. This was the way Jacob liked the Museum—empty, silent, and therefore his own. This was now his temple and his toy-closet. Now, at this hour, he could forget all the meretricious objects, second, third and fourth rate, that clot up any museum, and his love

[103]

dwelt only on the worthy. In the half-dark, the really beautiful things rested in their cases or on their pedestals, their existence of a more precious quality than during the day. They were simply themselves now, and Jacob their only worshiper. Their integrity would have been the same without him; he often thought this, and it kept him humble. Days, these immortal fragments had to endure the sticky gaze of crocodiles of school children on tour and the insultingly candid admiration of art students pointing out to each other what they thought they had discovered— "This plane," they would say, gesturing; "The values of this mass against that. . . ." Jacob's informed gaze flowed over them in delicacy and tenderness, a tenderness such as he had never felt yet for any human creature.

This was the way he liked it. He stalked down the long high gallery lighted only by the bulb in the hall at the far end and by the gauzy glow from the street filtering in between motionless statues through the terribly high, grilled windows at their backs. He was so alone that he felt he could see himself going, taller and thinner than life-size— a rigid white envelope, holding his pride folded up thin inside it, swinging in the hand at his side. His legs, straight and scissorslike, moved without his willing them to and yet at the same time he had the impression that, as in dreams, he wasn't moving at all and could never arrive anywhere. Perhaps this was because the gallery was so long at night. Godlike and aloof, Apollo and Marsyas and Ceres watched his passage, smiling their sarcastic, archaic smiles to see how little, in the intervening centuries since Athens, men had learned about the management of their lives. In the entrance hall he caught the eye of the wolf-mother; time her large family of young was asleep, he thought, but she stared him down with her bold, bronze eye.

[104]

Earlier that same evening George had laid down his fork and looked at Mrs. Fanning. "Do I have to eat this if I don't like it? I don't like it." She opened her mouth but he had made his own reply and now confronted his hostess with a bland gaze. So she too shared that fantastic adult conviction that the more you ate the happier you'd be? After only eight years of personal experience he could have told her that this wasn't so. He knew that almost all grown-up people subscribed to this belief but he had dared to hope that, having no children of her own, she might not have heard of it. . . . But why should he have hoped? While she ran on about finishing everything on one's plate because think of all the little boys in the world who would have been delighted with corn pudding and getting to be a big boy and his surely *wanting* to be big and strong, didn't he, he picked up the fork again, nearer the tines this time in desperation, and set to upon his dinner. But he was unable to refrain from murmuring, "But I'm stuffed."

"How could you be, possibly." There was no question mark in her voice; the words were only assertion's twin sister.

"I am, though."

"But we've hardly begun. Now if you want to be a big boy, and I'm sure you do . . ."

He looked over meaningfully at Edith, who had halted the boys on the sidewalk halfway up Evergreen Avenue and impressed on them, most solemnly and fiercely, but without giving them a ray of reason, that they must not say anything to anybody about the excursion to the Museum. Did that mean they mustn't mention the stop at the drug-store either, or the chocolate fudge sundae? He hiccuped softly; it was a genuine hiccup and Edith rose to it and came to his assistance, as he felt it was only right and fair she should.

"I'm afraid it's my fault if he isn't hungry, Aunt Clara. I took them to the drugstore and they had ice cream." Not wise enough to leave pretty-well alone, she added, "I thought you'd want the house free, getting it ready for the dinner party tomorrow night—"

"Not tomorrow!"

"*Not* tomorrow? —and you'd want them out of your way," she ran on with mechanical fluency because these words were part of what she had planned to say before Mrs. Fanning's interruption, disconcerting her, had thrown her off schedule. She had expected contradiction but was unprepared for interruption. "Not tomorrow? I thought of *course* it was tomorrow." She sat very straight, her guilty cheeks burning. Lying ought to come easier, in a good cause like this one. How mean it was of Aunt Clara not to be grateful to her for having pretended she thought she had been taking the care of the boys onto her shoulders for the afternoon. Unrighteous indignation, always so much brighter than the other kind, overlay for the moment all her genuine satisfactions underneath—her exultation that she had managed in the morning to persuade herself that in the boys' entertainment she had a perfectly valid excuse for going to the Museum, and relief that later in the day she had been brave enough to build up her pretext into something viable, successful, and solid. The only flaw in the afternoon had been unforeseeable and had had nothing to do with the boys from Sharon or with her aunt—the Venetian bride; she had hated the look of her and been afraid of Jacob's amusement which might well be admiration; she wished she looked just like her, or could have her life. She sat erect at the table, proudly wronged, her eyes

[106]

ranging over her stable of two well-instructed boys who, she was sure after George's stoic reticence in the matter of the fudge sundae, would not give her away. She felt only a little, momentary twinge of pity for him, battling away there with his corn pudding. Her own concerns absorbed her and she slid easily into complaisance; it was *good* for little boys to eat a lot; it made them big and strong—not that she cared.

"Corn," said Mr. Forrest Howe at the very moment the subject would have so much better been dropped, "corn has been used by man since earliest times, they say."

Mrs. Fanning frowned at him and moved her shoulders in a gesture that meant: Oh, for Heaven's sake, let's drop it. But George, committed now to suffering, said, "Yeah. I suppose even those two Roman boys had to eat it, way back then."

"Roman boys?" Mr. Howe inquired.

"Romulus and Remus." What a consolation it was to George to see Lucius' face dodging at him from the other side of a silver épergne; he must be trying to flash warnings; George didn't feel inclined to send him a reassuring glance. "Oh, just a story I read once," he said, very offhand, as if he had only happened to recall those infant prototypes of Tarzan, as if, too, his mind were packed full of similar interesting bits of information, mere general knowledge to be sure, but often found to be apropos in social intercourse. He ate away at what little was left of his pudding, one soft repulsive kernel at a time. Far away across the shining table, the salt cellars, the lace and linen, he could feel his brother relax. Mr. Howe, miffed, kept quiet. He said to himself he had supposed the only reason they had to have the visiting boys at the dinner table was so they might have the benefit of adult conversation. Mr. Howe had always assumed that any grownup was automatically wiser than any child. Wisdom happened, he supposed; and since he confused wisdom with information, it is easy to see how he came by this belief; some grownups probably had accumulated more of it than other grownups, but it would be tiresome to go into the subject of why. "Ah, well," he said, seeing Clara at the opposite end of the table frowning at him; willingly he let drop, at once and forever, any project of improving the minds of their young visitors.

Mrs. Fanning, however, who was unable to forget her responsibilities for very long, sat erect and smiled at the boys over her choker of pearls. When George had quite finished his corn she would reward him with some improving nugget. She waited—she knew she would not have to wait long—for something edifying to occur to her. But George forestalled her.

"In the Museum," he began and Lucius in the same instant cried, *"George!"* from beyond the épergne. "In the Natural History Museum in New *York,"* said George, evenly and blandly, "they've got this perfectly enormous whale."

"Oh, mercy"—Edith's voice was weak, and fretful because he had frightened her—"is that thing still there!"

"Oh, yes—hic, yes, I mean." His hiccups were coming regularly now but he managed to space his words and keep his hold on the conversation. "Enormous—hic. . . . It's the best—hic . . . thing they've got. And that's the best . . . best museum I was ever—hic . . . in."

"Well, that's not very polite," Lucius said. If George would only shut up dinner would be got through much sooner and far more safely. Mrs. Fanning asked why that wasn't polite and Lucius could only mutter that he just thought it wasn't; George was exasperating him. Mrs. Fanning, too, sighed, and wished dinner were done. The kindly impulse which had led her to take in these two little refugees of a week had become dissipated. They were to be on Evergreen Avenue for such a short time it wasn't worth her while to try to change them in any large way, and indeed she admitted there was nothing fundamentally the matter with them. "Just a pair of average boys, rather boring, I'm afraid," their mother had said, her wide smile betraying how little her heart agreed with her words. Mrs. Fanning was inclined to believe the words. Of course if they had been going to live there for a year or so there were a thousand tiny improvements she would feel justified in making —hands out of pockets, flannel trousers instead of corduroy, less slouching, more eating, shorter haircuts and longer fingernails. "Call me Aunt Clara," she had suggested the day they came, in the flurry of affability that accompanies arrival, but both boys had replied, "All right, Mrs. Fanning," and probably it was for the best.

"Hic . . ." went George in his chair, softly and continuously. "Hic. . . ."

Mr. Howe, really good and kind, rousing, persuaded himself not to nurse sulkiness about his earlier rebuff and he suggested to George that he try a pinch of salt on his tongue. Out to a truly astounding extent shot George's narrow pink tongue; it quivered, shrank and grew, and shrank, and blindly he reached out to the silver and Bristol glass salt cellar and scooped up a tiny spoonful and deposited it on the quivering tip. Everyone, suspending eating, watched and waited for the miracle.

"Hic!" went George louder than ever; the tongue shot in like a snake's and he nearly strangled on the salt. "No good," he pointed out as soon as he could speak.

Edith, who would be intensely grateful if attention had

[109]

at last been drawn away from the delicately dangerous subject of museums, suggested drinking from a glass from its far side. George said that didn't work, he'd often tried it, and that anyway he didn't mind having hiccups and never had minded. Edith was beginning to like the boys and though she could see how Mrs. Fanning's patience, that gossamer rag, was wearing thinner and thinner and might have blown away altogether by the end of the week of the boys' exile—even now her eyebrows said: That I should have to put up with such performances in the dining room!—offered, "I'll show you what I mean," and she demonstrated with her own goblet of water. George's glass had milk in it and the end result of his imitation was a mopping up with napkins. Mrs. Fanning's narrow black-silk shoulders moved again, and she could hardly bear it when Mr. Howe solemnly tipped his glass as in some reverse toasting ceremony or prandial Black Mass communion and lapped at his water.

"Really!" she cried.

He looked up from his glass. "It *doesn't* seem to work very well, does it?"

"But *you* haven't *got* hiccups!"

"Oh, so I haven't." He was nettled, wiped his lips and his damp imperial and spoke no more.

Chocolate blanc mange followed and the boys gave each other long steady looks, looks to remind each other and themselves of the vows of politeness extracted by their mother on the eve of her departure for Bermuda. As far as possible they averted their eyes from the nasty smooth thing; long ago they had clarified and asserted their position in respect to desserts in their own home: Anything you could poke a finger into and have the impress remain, was intolerable.

But when you went visiting, then, sometimes, even the intolerable must be borne. This their mother had warned them of, adding, "It won't kill you, for once."

"I wonder," Mrs. Fanning looked thoughtfully at the brown dome in the silver bowl. "I wonder, George dear, if I ought to let you eat dessert tonight."

"Oh?"

"I'm sorry, but I don't — believe — I would if I were you. I always think hiccups are an indication of too much sweet stuff." George instantly cast down his delighted eyes and tried not to grin.

"O.K.," he said, and "No, thank you," piously to Anna at his elbow.

Then Lucius became really angry. It wasn't fair. Why should George be let off blanc mange because he had stuffed himself like a pig at the drugstore while he, the philosopher, who had only orange juice must now endure blanc mange. Philosophy deserted him. Inexorably, its contents shaking, the silver bowl approached him around the table. "You dope!" he cried to his brother. "If you hadn't run and slid around like crazy full of fudge on all those marble floors you wouldn't have *had* hiccups!" George's lifted shocked eyes and Edith's quick indrawn hiss of doom told him what he had done. His heart completely stopped beating, and when it began again it pumped madly.

"Marble floors?" Mrs. Fanning murmured and at that Lucius turned upon her eyes of such enormous innocence that she at once knew all. All she had said was, "Marble floors?" and in spite of its upturned tones it was not a question. She did not look to Lucius for an answer. Her dark glance, level, sardonic and smiling, was upon Edith; she knew what marble floors. "Well, well," she murmured.

[111]

She picked up her dessert spoon and slid a chocolate bite in through her continuing smile.

Edith caught up with Lucius on the stairs and grasped his shoulder.

"I know, I know!"

"I *asked* you not to!"

"I know." He was aghast at himself and couldn't understand how he had been led into betraying her. "I didn't mean to. I didn't *say* we'd been to—been there. Not actually."

"You didn't need to say it." All her gratitude had been nebulized in the wind of her rage.

He searched her face for some indication, not of forgiveness which he knew he did not deserve, but of understanding of his own horror at himself. She slapped him on the shoulder; she would have loved to hit him hard in the face, or push him down the velvet-covered stairs. She thought: The Venetian girl would have known some way, sharp and catlike and terrible, to punish him! How could he have ignored her request, ruined her lovely secret afternoon, ruined her life? By his thoughtless words she had been treacherously delivered over, bound, to Mrs. Fanning. Never before had she slapped anybody and there was no satisfaction in the blow on the thin-clad small knobby shoulder. The fact he didn't resent it added to her despair. She longed to convey somehow to the perfidious child what destruction he had wrought. She felt that every secret she had ever had, and they had not been many, had just been ripped open to the view. He was whispering that he was sorry. For a moment she looked into his miserable square face and pitied him and then, as her own first anguish began, inevitably, to wear thinner, she said, "But how *could* you!"—a dishonest, tear-jerking "but" and putting into her voice that heart-rending quaver that comes so readily to the service of diddled women, sometimes rending the heart only of the women themselves. But in this case Lucius was a ripe victim. He looked like somebody caught robbing a bank. He had no excuse to give, except that he had been as surprised as she was to hear himself speak out to George.

"Do you usually not know what you're going to say when you open your mouth? Oh, not that it's at *all* important," she sobbed, and hurried past him up the mustard-colored stairs to her room.

Lucius went on up more slowly, mystified and sad; though he had begun to understand the real reason they had been taken to the Museum, he bore her no rancor. What he could not understand was why anyone should go through such involved maneuvers just to see Jacob Miller. The comforting words, "She's nuts, isn't she?" which were ready on the end of his tongue were never spoken because when he went to the guest room to deliver himself of them to George, there was no one there. This was because George, having realized suddenly that he hadn't paid homage to his harp since noon—an unwontedly long and unjustifiable abstention from worship—had darted through the pantry after dinner, up the back stairs to his room, leaned briefly from the window into the damp Spring darkness and *not* heard the voice of his treasure; not a tinkle, not even a reassuring crystal whisper, came to him from the dark. Terrified, he had raced back downstairs and had had the ill luck to be caught by his hostess on his way out the side door.

"But I have to go see if my harp is all right!" He was as agitated as a thwarted wasp.

[113]

"Of course it is all right. What could happen to it? And I have told you you're not to climb. You should never have put it up there in the first place, you know. And certainly you are not going climbing trees at night." Then she smiled, falling back on the happy invention of Monday. "Your mother is very worried about your habit of climbing," she said. The exigency of the moment, which she seemed not to recognize at all, prevented him from untangling this melancholy statement from dim but actual recollections he had of his mother occasionally murmuring, automatically, "I do hope you have enough sense not to break your neck." But he knew that if his mother hadn't wanted him to climb trees at all while she was in Bermuda, he was the person she would have told; she would never have gone, whining and fearing, behind his back to this tall black column of a woman.

"I've got to!"

"I'm afraid I shall have to say no. So you won't, will you?" When she said to the board members of a settlement house, "You won't further the welfare of the birth control committee at the expense of the layette, *will you?*" they never did and now, standing by the side door she could not feel the urgent night breezes calling him, and she naturally assumed complaisance to her will on the part of George. No one but he could have told her how mistaken she was but, for one thing, he hadn't time to. He had to mumble equivocally, back off and go the tiresomely longer way around by the back hall, the kitchen and the kitchen door. He had just laid both hands on the bark of the parasol tree when, high up, sweet and clear as the morning voice of a bird, he heard his harp speak to him. "Here I am, here I am," it said, tender and impersonal. Then it was still, but he didn't have to worry any more. He sighed; his hands

[114]

dropped to his sides. He knew how the air, moving through the young silk leaves, plucking them aside, had come to the magic prisms and touched, barely, their cool surfaces. "Yea!" he whispered, relieved.

He stepped away over the wet grass, passing on his way to the kitchen door the lighted windows of the morning room. Through a rather wide crack in the drawn curtains he saw Mrs. Fanning in spectacles, writing a list on a slip of paper. Ordinarily she didn't wear glasses, though in the course of the day when she needed to read something she flicked open a lorgnette hanging from a fine black ribbon around her neck, a ribbon longer than her string of pearls but nearly invisible, black against black. George admired this adroit flicking motion very much, placing it on a par with practical gun-handling in Western movies and he had decided to wear a lorgnette himself when he grew up. He paused now, one eye to the crack. What could she be writing? A list of his and Lucius' sins to be mailed to their family? Just so would Romulus' and Remus' foster parent have looked, reporting to whatever surviving relatives the Roman boys might have had that they played too roughly with her baby cubs. He softly withdrew, having wronged her fearfully—she was writing only a list of what she thought the Recusants would like to eat on Thursday—and made his way past the shadowy greenhouse, into the back hall and up the back stairs to Anna's room.

"Vell, hello, Bill," she said, delighted to have a visitor. "Come in and be pleased to take a shair."

How really nice it was in Anna's room; there was none of that heavy, octagonal, spice-colored plush that cluttered up the rest of the house. She had tossed back the curtains from the sides of the window and they hung ungainly, one draped over an electric light fixture, the other caught be-

[115]

hind a calendar for year before last; the window space, thus enlarged, let in mysterious airs of the Spring night, whispers that could not, need not, be accounted for, and the last sleepy fluting of a bird. Peepers' voices came shrill and exciting from some lawn with a pool, or from some stagnant spot beyond a converted stable. Anna had rolled back her rug too, in a fit of elimination of earthly worries and the bare floor looked as though she prepared for a ball, a ball with not more than two couples, who would revolve between the bureau and the door, the bed and the chair. She was sitting on the side of the bed, sagging it down, soaking her feet in hot water in a big white china washbowl with a gold and royal blue rim, the brilliant sophisticated blue of Victorian enamel-and-diamond jewelry. "My old bunions and scunions," she said, and poured in Epsom salts from a pasteboard box. "Ven I voss yoong I was always rooning for the stairs, up and down, up and down all day, never tired. Not-a-bit." She shifted the big feet in the big bowl. "I still got vonderful strong arms," she said.

George came over and looked down with interest into the bowl. She certainly had very knobby feet. They didn't track the way Lucius' and his feet did, but turned far out and her knees turned out too, and when she moved about the house with mop and duster she looked as though she had only just that moment hurriedly risen from a sitting position and had not yet quite straightened herself up. He watched the steam waver over the water and the salts dissolving when she threw in another handful. They had a comfortable discussion about feet that soothed him, still somewhat wrought up by his concern for his harp and the useless encounter with Mrs. Fanning. She was interested in what he had to say but she didn't make him feel watched,

[116]

the way other people in that house did, and every now and then her attention wandered away from him, she answered only, "M'hm," and he found that soothing, too. She was interested when he told her he had heard somewhere you could tell how tall one would eventually be by the size of one's feet when young. "Mine are *quite* long for my age." He hopefully displayed his neat blue sneakers.

"Them liddle tings!" she said and they both laughed.

He wandered around the small square room. A sweetish smell pervaded everything, the paper on the walls, the bedclothes, the maroon wrapper hung by its neck on the closet door. He idled by the bureau, looking at the scroll-shaped china pin-tray of pins, a peppermint Life Saver, a couple of curled-up dry 3-cent stamps. A tannish-gray hairnet, like a dead family of many daddy-long-leg spiders, lay on the bureau scarf, speared through and through by their death weapon, a wire hairpin. There were small brown oval photographs of very blond, straight-haired people. One was a tall thin young girl in a flounced dress who stood with herself from the waist down turned to display a truly astounding behind, *en profile,* with the top half of her front-face and smiling; she seemed to be saying to the surprised and admiring observer, "Look what I can do to myself!"

"Who's that?"

"Me," said Anna complacently. "Tin, vossn't I? Yes, I voss. I guess all my relations at home, they're pretty tin too, these days. No sugger, no sveet stuff, no yam." She sighed a conventional sigh and when George said but she could send them sugar to make jam, part of her retreated from him and she said in a voice that implied he had brought up a matter she preferred not to discuss just then, if ever, "Vell, maybe they don't got the fruit, either," as if that would be a solution for them, and even, almost, a relief.

"Maybe not." George knew he sounded as though he agreed with her but he felt there was some fallacy here, only he couldn't quite put his finger on it. He opened his mouth to ask, but not in time.

"Oh, my old bunions and scunions, honest and truly," murmured the woman on the bed. The subject of the post-war privations of her relatives was closed.

"When you go back to Sweden and open your bakery—tell me about that." He came to rest on the only chair. She told him all over again about the big white stove and the girl who would be so glad to do all the running and the blue curtains and the wonderfully twisted and frosted breads she would make. She was an artist planning out her future masterpieces. "Currants and reasons and nuts," she said, as a painter might say he must get ultramarine, Chinese white and vermilion. "Some with ceenamon," she said, "and some not." She described the two window boxes of purple petunias and pink geraniums that she would have on the front of the shop and how her bedroom might be upstairs above the kitchen. She talked to him as though he were exactly her own age, or she his, and perhaps by some true chronometer they were indeed of an age. Her endless repetitiveness didn't annoy him in the least as it did the other occupants of the Evergreen Avenue house; it soothed him and pleased him; it augured a certain layer of stability in what he was on the verge of suspecting might prove to be a shifting, sliding world. Really dependable iteration was an island, a safeness. He enjoyed hearing the same thing over and over, and waited for known details with delight.

"When will you go?"

"Oh—ven." She removed her feet, now terrifically pink, from the bowl, and wiped them carefully. "Ven. Ven. Ven I collect up a liddle more money." She would never have told him of the more than sufficient thousands of dollars accumulated during thirty-eight thrifty years in Connecticut, thirty-eight years of nickel rides on trolleys, nickel cups of coffee, a new hat like a black, blunt but decorated chimney pot bought only very, very rarely. These thousands lay in the bank and were steadily added to by an Anna who did not work for love. Indeed, what was she waiting for; what kept her? It was not a devotion to Mrs. Fanning that she could not bring herself to tear that kept her mopping and dusting; Mrs. Fanning was only the slot machine from which popped a sizable weekly check. "Yoost a liddle more money, so ven I go, I go in style. I motch up the boardwalk onto the boat like a good vun. I don't vant to have to be a stealaway." She laughed her boisterous short laugh and dried between her extraordinary toes. George asked what a stealaway was. "He's a person takes a ride on a boat without he pays. Not me," she assured him. It didn't seem to trouble her that the plans to consummate her splendid dream were not immediate, but it troubled George. He watched her solemnly as she creaked off the side of the bed and thrust her assuaged feet into soft slippers. He wished he knew some way to get her started home. What if she never— "Roon along now, Bill," she said. "I'm going to get out of my turrable old cosset. See you in the morning."

9

A DARK wind carrying rain on its back prowled the town, searching for the best place to cast its burden; it came to the foot of Evergreen Avenue, apparently just what it had been waiting for, and raced up, shouting, tossing the rain over its shoulder and down, and it was the sudden clatter of drops on the broad stiff leaves of the rhododendron under her window that woke Mrs. Fanning.

Her bed was a solitary coracle, canopied in white ninon, revolving in the darkness of Tuesday night. She stretched out an anchoring hand to the bedside table and switched on the little pink-china lamp; it was Wednesday. It was much later than she would have guessed; the hair-thin hands of the gold French clock, twin to the one on the morning room mantel, pointed to five o'clock; she switched off the light. Never having been able to endure for a waking instant not to know what time it was, and even now when there was nothing else to do but lie in bed, it relieved her to have consulted her clock because now she knew absolutely that she was quite through with Tuesday and that the challenge that would be Wednesday was coming up. The reason it was so dark was the approaching storm. Ordinarily, at this time of year, it would have begun to be light outside at five, birds would be calling from lawn to lawn and she would be still asleep, accreting strength for the problems of the day to come.

"So I must go back to sleep now," she said.

But she continued to lie wide awake in the dark under the pleated mushroom of the canopy, staring at nothing, seeing as yet no early dim outlines of the other furniture. She heard the busy wind traveling past the house and up the avenue, and then a growl of thunder from not very far away. She turned on her side and stared at the wall toward the street and soon windows were briefly, hectically, adumbrated by weak lightning. Was the rain coming in, she wondered; but it was only a soft pattering, a fresh, cool suggestion of rain, not long, wet, driving spears. Naturally, nothing was near the open windows in her room but she wondered about her young guests; more than likely they had left clothes, toys, books, on the window sill. Pity she couldn't be the person who had brought them up; no clothes on the floor in that case, one may be sure. "I wonder—had I better get up and see?" Maybe, too, they were afraid of storms, but probably not, because modern children surely knew enough not to be. If she got up and went in to pick up the clothes she could so clearly imagine lying in small heaps below the sills, and found them awake in their beds she could say, kindly, "But big boys are never afraid of thunderstorms, you know." *If* she got up . . .

She sighed. Why was it always and only she who took the care and the responsibility in that house? Dragon and nurse, mistress, slave, slave-driver and queen, no one ever contradicted her and no one ever helped. It is terribly tiring to be always right; no one knows what a burden it is. She was the one who planned the days of all the others, chose the colors to repaint the bathrooms and would have named the cat if they had had one. She was forced constantly to adjure and admonish. But for her who would have seen to it that all telephone messages were written down at once because, often, apparently minor messages have major import; it was she who had to remind Anna to keep full aspirin bottles in everyone's bathroom cabinet, for what is more discouraging than to wake in the night and, knowing an aspirin imperative, to grope to the shelf and find no bottle or, worse, an empty one? It was she who had to be sure the green vegetables were cooked without soda because it isn't *necessary;* Mrs. Fanning yielded to no one in her insistence on bright green spinach, but briskly boiling salted water will do it; upon how many, many cooks had she had to impress that simple fact! The leaves of the ivy must be washed weekly to make them shine. There must be plenty of pins in the sewing room when little Miss Handel came to sew . . . oh, the reserve boxes of Roger and Gallet soap on the linen closet shelves . . . the pleats on the Summer slip covers . . . the knots between pearls! A thousand, thousand little matters of equal urgency. Not only in her own home was her fearful adequacy relied on; almost before calling the plumber to the day nursery the matron telephoned Mrs. Fanning when dusky little Serafina Langousti threw her psychiatrically-approved-of plastic doll into the toilet.

And now, just as she began to relish the flat softness and solitude of her bed, must it again be she who had to get up, instruct her feet to find the slippers on the floor, walk across its chilliness, and grope her way along the unlighted hall to reassure two visiting children, who were probably fast asleep anyway? Lying there, her imagination readily did all this for her. It was all almost, if not quite, as though she were indeed making this effort—she felt it in her muscles—and a moment later she said "Oh!" startled to find that she was still flat in bed, not merely back in bed after an expedition, and drowsy, and she went through it all again, even more reluctantly this time—the cold slippers, the cold door knob; "Big boys never are afraid," she had said, no, *must* say, kindly. Nights, the hall was always chill. She yawned in her bed, night floors were always chilly. She mustn't catch cold from that cold floor. She reached out an arm, down along the bed, and pulled up over her the soft pink basket-weave blanket that, cunningly pleated for just such an emergency, waited below her feet. Now her feet would be warm again and she could sleep.

But she did not go back to sleep. The rain had begun to drum more loudly on the leaves outside and on the roof of the portico, and the wind poured through the tree tops. . . . Twenty-three Recusants for dinner Thursday. Twenty-five, counting Forrest and Edith, who were not members; Forrest, in spite of the rather clever look his imperial gave him, not being eminent in any way at all and Edith being merely a young girl of some physical distinction but no intellectual attainments, past, present or likely. But she could perfectly well marry Sylvester Wagstaff by half-trying. "But no domestic ability either, even," Mrs. Fanning murmured, and sighed and murmured again that she wondered what on earth Edith intended to make of herself. The child had been given what is known as every advantage since the day she first set foot in the house on Evergreen Avenue. She had attended good schools and

Mrs. Fanning had gone over her report cards carefully each term, with exhortations, if indicated, for further work on French irregular verbs and praise for B-plus in History, if deserved. On Monday afternoons, Winter after Winter, Edith had stepped into a series of increasingly longer black patent leather slippers and attended a class in dancing at the Tennis Club, given by an ageless, nimble spinster in chiffon, and there revolved and glided as directed until collected and brought home by Anna. In any given school-age dancing class the girls are taller than the boys; Edith was taller even than the girls. Mrs. Fanning had had more urgent ways of spending that hour than joining the rows of mothers in little gold chairs who, under the tinkling from the piano and the cries of the teacher, kept up a steady, relentless murmuring, a susurration, as of bees . . . "now that Gracie's teeth are such a problem" . . . "now that we are trying to rent a place in Maine for the Summer" . . . "well, now that Gracie seems to *want* to wear stockings" . . . "but there isn't a house to rent in the whole of Maine, or so it would appear" . . . "since I must always consider Sylvester's hay fever" . . . under waltz and conga, under polka and foxtrot, murmur, murmur, murmur. "I should get claustrophobia," Mrs. Fanning had asserted after one experience, and gone marching off and never gone back. Edith had been just as glad and, as it turned out, had never cared much for dancing anyway, nor for music lessons either, though a good many half-hours of her childhood had been spent swinging numb legs from a piano bench.

There she lies—Mrs. Fanning, the central being of that house, under the soft blanket she has certainly earned by a life of doing the right thing. One must give her great credit for never sparing herself nor shirking a job however tiresome, and perhaps one should give compassion, too, for anyone trapped by such a fierce and humorless integrity as hers. One must give her credit for never pretending to herself nor to anyone else that she has been a mother to Edith; she has not; she has tried to be a very good aunt and even that is not easy; nor is it her fault that Forrest Howe conducts himself toward his own child as though he were her not-too-interested uncle. If his natural paternal instincts have never developed, that is not a sister's fault. . . . Perhaps, once or twice, she has said, "Please let me handle this, Forrest; after all, I am a woman and women know about young girls." He is not a man of strong feelings; perhaps his only strong feeling is his disinclination to accept responsibility so the whole burden of his child's bringing-up had devolved upon her, and she had not flinched from it. "I have nothing to reproach myself with," came now in a strong voice from beneath the perfection of pleats.

The rain was drumming softly and steadily on the lead covering of the portico. It should have sent her comfortably off to sleep, but she remained wide-awake in the darkness. She thought that maybe her body had rested enough, and she was not to go back to sleep that night. Time gained, then, for thinking. She habitually made the natural, not rare, mistake of confusing planning with thinking, probably because there was never any end to the planning for one thing or another that her own life demanded of her; always there were *arrangements* to be made. Now was a good time to decide the final minutiae of the dinner party—whether buttered asparagus on toast or broccoli with Hollandaise sauce would better accord with Professor Winding's paper on agricultural practices and animal husbandry of early Welsh farmers. "Not *too*

[125]

early," he had assured her gaily over the telephone, "not a minute before 1300." She had said it sounded extraordinarily interesting and at that he had made a pleased, almost shy, guttural little grunt at the other end of the wire. But when she had told Forrest of the treat in store he had said, "Oh?" and looked more apprehensive than glad, and then exasperated her further by asking, "Am I coming?"

"Of course you're coming!" she had cried. "Right here in the house!" Such an opportunity, she might well have added; Professor Winding was the world authority on Welsh agriculture. He always looked as though he were being propelled from behind, against his will, by some force, some great wind of intellect superior to his little physical strength; his pink face pleated up beside his nose and mouth in little folds of protest, the wind at his back was so strong; his speech was one long lisp of information; oh, he was very eminent indeed. It was to him Mrs. Fanning owed her membership in the Recusants, though she did not know it. At a meeting ten or twelve years before, Professor Winding then younger and considered by some to be something of a hothead, stimulated by one of his colleague's papers—"The Place of the Edible Fungi in World Economy," it had been—had startled all the other members by saying he wondered if they ought not to climb down a little way from their ivory tower, perhaps not climb down exactly but anyway lean over the edge a bit, and take in some local person who was not connected with the University but had an established position in the town's civic life. He never knew how to account for this impulse of his; it could scarcely have been the subject matter of the evening's learned paper because mushrooms had poisoned him since a child, and cries of "No, no," and

"Certainly not," had greeted the wild suggestion, but Professor Winding could be very persuasive when the whim took him, and after he had made a speech about new blood and the way the world was moving and present-day realities and the desirability of having one's feet on the ground, there were other faint cries, not cries at all, really, but murmurings of "Well, perhaps," from the partially convinced. Mrs. Fanning was by far the most civic-minded person any of them could think of, and also she had a large house easily thrown open for entertaining. Then as now she sat on more committees and boards than any other five women in town, made and unmade policies of nursing associations and summer camps and alcoholic missions as readily as less or differently gifted women can snap twigs. It may well be pointed out to her further credit that after joining them she kept her capable hands off the Recusants' business. "Heaven knows I have enough else to do," she sometimes said to her brother.

Probably it was because the Recusants weren't committed to accomplishing anything that she left them to run their own affairs in their own way; there was nothing concrete to be achieved if she did take a hand. Her singularly effective blend of municipal farsightedness and exasperated common sense was laid aside the fourth Thursday in every month; all the little adjurations, predictions and mendacities with which she was wont to prod fellow committee members to the doing of God's work were out of place in that esoteric gathering. Not that her methods nor even her motives mattered to the innumerable citizens whose lot, by dint of uncounted committee meetings, she had improved. Perhaps she was all the more effective, her heart having no part in her work; it could in no way matter to the little Italian girls who lived on Harbor

[127]

Street that despotism rather than warmth of heart was to be thanked for their mid-morning milk; they were pounds the better off for that restless despotism. The milk was Grade-A, even if not of human kindness but merely cow, and their teeth improved very much. Probably they were asleep now, all those little Italian girls, in their narrow lumpy beds and their wide lumpy beds, away across the dark city. Only Mrs. Fanning, the benefactress, lay awake.

Her arms and legs stirred under the covers, she turned over, and something about changing her position had a clarifying effect on her current problem; she knew the answer, and "Asparagus," she said aloud, with decision. If she only had a pad and a pencil handy she could work out the seating arrangement. Professor Winding would be on her right, naturally; then the shyest male member must be on her left. There were several candidates. Actually, the guest with the least to offer would be Forrest Howe without question, but it would hardly do to take him under her protection at dinner. It was so many years since she had propped him up in the place at table opposite to hers that now he belonged there by right of eminent domain. Years ago when she had taken him and his daughter in, when his fortunes, never so very promising and gay, had reached their permanent low tide, she had said to herself, "Now I shall never regret this, *because* one never does regret doing the right thing," but there had been times during the subsequent years when she felt she could scarcely bear either of them. It wasn't their activities she objected to; it was their constant state of unactivity. Nor did she expect them to dwell in a condition of perpetual gratitude to her, but it would have been nice if they had taken a normal interest in what she was most concerned with, or if they had

[128]

projects of their own in which she could have, would have, mingled. Naturally one does not expect rising votes of thanks from indigent, rescued relatives, nor a sustained testimonial-dinner mood to prevail in the home, but gratitude should be there all the same, lively though hidden, constantly lurking and felt, though unexpressed.

"No more initiative than a bump on a log," she said aloud in her bed. She lay and marveled for the ten thousandth time—but perhaps her marveling couldn't be divided into separate times and this was only the latest layer in an infinitely laminated structure of vexation—how her brother and herself could have turned out to be so different. With exactly the same background and ancestors! More than the darkness of the Spring thunderstorm kept her from seeing, on the wall by the dressing table, the photographs of their father and mother, who faced each other in gold frames forever, as they had faced each other if not quite forever, across their dinner table and their hearth rug. The pictures had hung there so long she never saw them any more; only if they had disappeared, blown down, slipped behind the table, would she have noticed a not-thereness; habitualness, too, prevented her *seeing* the plump complacent cheeks, the deceptive tininess of her mother's determined chin, the deceptive languor of her father's decoratively down-brushed hair. Both Clara Fanning and Forrest Howe were the not surprising result of these two *en face* in their narrow frames—Clara who had had to fight to establish individuality in spite of them, and Forrest whose vitality had been siphoned off by these parents and this more vigorous sister, years and years ago; its reservoir had suffered too severe and constant a draining; never since had it filled up. It would have surprised him very much if he had been told he might better have

[129]

been deprived, early, of a leg. A delayed marriage had given him a few years of self-importance but his wife had soon fooled him by contracting pneumonia and dying.

It was his sister who, many years before, had suggested he grow an imperial. "A goatee, you mean?" he had asked, to which her firm reply had been, "An imperial. It would fill out your chin." She considered she was employing restraint when she did not add, "You must know your chin is tiny, don't you, like Mama's?" Fortunately he was pleased with the suggestion and set to to implement it. The result was most satisfactory, and he never knew how close she came once or twice to referring to it as "my imperial." He nurtured it through the years; it became in time his chief pride, and his bulwark against a confusingly brisk world. He would have looked well, with it, behind a desk in a bank, Mrs. Fanning sometimes thought; but Heavens, what bank!

The thunderstorm was almost done with Evergreen Avenue; she could see the shapes of the windows now, and the white ninon canopy floating mosque-like above her head, though its million minute folds were still not apparent. The weak lightning was soon routed by a vigorous dawn which grew and spread from beyond the stable-garage. The rain diminished as she lay and listened, but ponderous drops still fell, slowly, from the cornices. A fortitudinous robin called once, his voice clear, immortal, heartbreaking. A fresh shower, heavy and brief, the last before the storm's withdrawal, swept over the tree tops and, lulled by its drowsy iteration, Mrs. Fanning at last fell asleep.

George always rode out thunderstorms in his mother's bed. There was never any question about it, no hearty

[130]

adult *"You* aren't afraid of thunderstorms! A great big boy like *you!"* Nobody at home pretended, for their own purposes, to think he was big; they agreed he would be, one day, but for the present years he had his neck and ears inspected daily by some competent and taller member of the household, was not allowed to eat more than one macaroon at a time nor crab meat at all, and by as firm-established a custom, enjoyed certain privileges which Time had snatched from his elders—he did not yet have to wash out the tub after a bath and, at the first menace of thunder in the night, he could crawl in beside his mother's silk back.

He got quickly out of bed in Mrs. Fanning's house and stumbled, not along the hall to her room, to her silk back, but next door to the upstairs sitting room where Lucius slept. By the fitful lightning he found the couch; Lucius possessed it utterly. His square brow was in the very middle of the pillow, arms and legs were tossed freely in several directions, leaving no room for a visitor. "Move over," George said and then again, more sharply as lightning maliciously played over them, "Move over, you pig." He pushed at Lucius' near arm; in sleep it weighed a hundred pounds; it was an arm of lead. George managed to lift the forearm from the elbow but it fell back again with a thump. He tried pushing at Lucius' body but though when awake no one was more pliable, agreeable and co-operative than his brother, asleep he only snarled, swallowed loudly and rapidly three or four times as if he had an oversupply of something in his mouth, groaned, moved his head once, and then his whole body settled deeper into the comfort of his still solely-possessed mattress. He was not a large boy, but a sleeping hippopotamus would have been no more impervious to George's efforts. George drew a sad, quavering breath, waited for the help of a little lightning in order to see where to punch him, punched him, and stumbled back to the guest room. He went deep under his covers where no thunder or lightning could get at him and there he lay in the fusty dark, afraid, but not as afraid as he would have been with his head out, and slowly, voluptuously, began to pick sock-fuzz from between his toes. "Calypso, Margano, Sereno, Lentenor, Nicanor and *Bar*baro," he whispered, over and over again in a chant, a spell, an incantation against storms. "Calypso, Margano, Sereno, Lentenor,"— He had carefully shut Lentenor in the cellar for the night; now he wished he had brought him into bed with him; he might just as well have. A pity; but nothing could now be done about it. You don't un-pretend, or re-pretend, with a dog like Lentenor; a dog of such nobility and integrity can't be pretended fast and loose with—"Lentenor, Nicanor and *Bar*baro."

Suddenly he started back up the bed, working his way beneath the covers like a mole possessed. He scrambled out and ran to the window, lighter now with the coming morning. He leaned far out and listened; he painfully stretched his senses, fear for his treasure stronger than the fear of himself being struck by lightning. No tinkle, no glass song, not even a whispering reproach.

The wind and the rain were fighting in the parasol tree, tossing the branches and slapping at the thin little leaves. But the harp, his harp—there was no sound of it. He capered with terror by the open window. It was dead of course, broken. He had put it out there and now it was dead because he had. Its own magic qualities had somehow failed to preserve it. He ran and threw himself back into bed in despair, buried his face in the pillow and vowed vigilance and repentance until it should get to be light enough to go out and see. See what? In his heart he could already see the tangle of wet red strings holding only shattered shards, bits broken off, sharp and dangling . . .

He woke again about six o'clock and with fatalistic calm rose, pulled on the damp clothes that had lain all night in a heap beneath the window sill, tiptoed downstairs and eluding Catherine who was moving about in the back part of the house, ran out of doors. For a minute he peered up among the leaves and then, just by chance, before starting the sad climb, he glanced down and there in the soft turf, he saw a dozen separate prisms. Fragile but whole, they sparkled in the early, slant sunlight. Not one was broken. The painted Chinese designs on the inch-wide strips were fresh with water. During the wild night each strip had slowly, slowly, the glue of its tiny square of silver paper dissolving, slowly and with due care for its own rare value released itself from its parent piece of glass and slid down a shaft of rain into the green cushion of grass. "Oh, my!" said George, profoundly moved. He kneeled and plucked the glass flowers. A minute later he was up in the tree painstakingly detaching the loop of string that still held an inverted crown of short prisms. He carried everything to the upstairs sitting room.

Lucius lay in bed blinking up at nothing.

"Look, Lucius."

"What?" He rolled over and out, so easily no one would have believed that an hour earlier he had been a boy of lead. "Oh, George," he said sympathetically, seeing the small, wet, collapsed heap of glass and string, and George, who had been sustained thus far by fear and surprise and relief, began to cry. Together they examined the mess and Lucius discovered two broken pieces.

They ran away after breakfast. No one saw them go. Perhaps Lucius was actually too old at twelve to be considered a runaway and George, in an older brother's company, would probably not be considered errant, but the fact remains that they were careful not to say good-by, and no one saw them go.

They had the harp in a disemboweled egg box, bedded on a great quantity of rumpled-up guest-room Kleenexes, and they made their way without a hitch through the downtown streets to the Museum. They didn't know Jacob Miller's last name but miraculously, as they stood in the entrance hall saying to each other "Well, how *shall* we find him?" "Well, I thought *you* knew!" they saw far down a corridor his figure pass from one office door to another.

He laid the pieces of glass, discouragingly haphazard looking now, on his blotter and considered them carefully. "I see," he said. "H'mn. You want a job of restoration done on this or is it something you're bequeathing to the Museum?"

"Do you think you can fix it?" George pressed his stomach anxiously against the desk.

Jacob fitted the broken pieces together and straightened out the tangle of string. "I should have thought two smart boys like you could have done this themselves. If I had children the very first thing I'd teach them would be the technique of the glue pot, which is far and away man's most important tool."

"Well, you couldn't," George reminded him. "You have to be married before you have children. I know."

"Must be nice to know so much. As a matter of fact, I am married. My advice would be, stick to glass harps." How impatient, and yet careful, his fingers were, sorting the splinters. "Why didn't you do this at Mrs. Fanning's?"

Lucius answered. "Oh, not there. We could have at home of course, but we couldn't find any Duco at Mrs. Fanning's and regular glue's so yellow and we couldn't ask anybody because she had told George not to go up in the tree with it anyway. She said, 'I shouldn't if I were you.'" His amused glance invited Jacob to share his enjoyment of the absurd, imagined picture of Mrs. Fanning, in narrow black dress and gold lorgnette, shinnying up a parasol tree.

"Edith?"

"Oh, Edith's mad at us."

None of them even considered Mr. Howe worth mentioning as a possible possessor of a decent variety of glue.

"She is, is she? What for?"

The boys looked at each other and then away. "Oh, well, no special reason," George said gallantly, with false and futile politeness, but Lucius sternly confessed and Jacob laughed out loud. Laughing changed his whole face, breaking up the scowl. He went rapidly to work assembling the harp and though George was instantly grateful and now had nothing further to ask of life, Lucius couldn't repress a feeling that here was a man who was amused at not intrinsically funny things, like Mrs. Fanning climbing trees. "She was especially mad at *me*," he said, and waited, but Jacob only laughed again, as though much pleased, and Lucius could only infer that the odd fellow had taken an inexplicable dislike to him.

So he left them bent over the delicate restoration of George's talisman and wandered to the open Gothic window and leaned out; the cold rectangle of the slanting stone sill came just below his chest and felt, after he had leaned there for a minute, like an iron band inside his

[135]

jersey. He pressed harder, to make it feel worse. A wave of discouragement swept over him. How could he ever get to understand how adults were inside before the time came when he had to become one himself? A tragic disparity might occur in his case. Why should Jacob Miller laugh because Edith had been angry because the boys, by mistake, had let Mrs. Fanning know they had all visited the Museum? Was he vindictive? To do him credit he hadn't laughed as though it were a joke on the boys, but as though from some sudden, secret, grownup access of happiness. How could a boy of twelve ever assume he would understand? . . . I suppose I'll understand only when I've forgotten how I feel now, like canceling out equivalent fractions, and am all grown up, he said to himself, but that prospect brought no comfort because who could want to be a grownup, at such cost? In that moment he dreaded the trap of the future, which he saw to have a big, square, hungrily open, avid mouth and insanely rapidly converging walls inside.

Young men in gray flannel pants and varied jackets walked in the street below. From his high point of vantage Lucius contemplated them; some looked very young; their hair looked young; he wondered whether, in their feelings, they were boys or men; of course, he assumed, they were either exactly one or exactly the other. For the first time in his life he knew *it wouldn't be long now.* Any day now *he* would be that old, and dressed in the negligent universal gray pants, the tweed jacket. His eye darted over the strolling figures, half expecting to see himself, there already, one of them. Maybe he was there; had he, he wondered, already left Sharon and joined the grown-up young men, left Sharon and George? If so, would he be able to recognize himself from above? In a panic he reared

[136]

up his chest away from the cold sill and hurried back to the desk. George was still there, his straw-colored head bent over Jacob's moving fingers. "Ho!" said Lucius, relieved, safe for the moment and therefore scornful. "You're *still* working on that old thing!"

Even though they slid into the Evergreen Avenue house by the back way they were caught. They needn't have been, but Catherine betrayed them.

"Here they are, ma'am!" she yelled along the brown passage from the kitchen to the front hall, in her voice as much relish as if she had bad news, and with a black susurration Mrs. Fanning's erect figure bore down on them through this tunnel.

George always used the tactics, so admired by military historians, of attacking first; however successful this maneuver at Waterloo and Pearl Harbor, it failed on Evergreen Avenue. He drew from the open egg box his expertly mended glass harp, lifted it toward her for inspection and launched into a lively account of his naturally harassed feelings when, because there had been no fit place to install it in her house, he had been forced to hang it in a tree, at the mercy of all the elements and it had therefore been broken—well, kind of broken, he amended, and would have gone on to give her, reproachfully, an exact account of the damage done—"*George!*" she interrupted, and George quickly took the holy object back unto himself again; she looked as though she might dash it from his hands. To do her justice, the furious look on her face came not so much from anger at their two-hour absence as from a quite reasonable fear that something might have happened to them in a strange city. They might have become lost and wandered about for the whole day;

busses might have mown them down. "What do *you* know about traffic?"

"We've been to New York," they reminded her.

"That makes no difference! You were entrusted to my care for this week; for this week you are my responsibility. It isn't at all as if you had been brought up in a city. You've no idea how worried I've been all morning. I haven't been able to sit down or tend to anything, since you left. I saw you go, of course, and called after you, but you didn't answer." When they said they rode their bikes all over Sharon all the time she said again that made no difference.

It was an unequal battle, there in the kitchen, because the boys held no ammunition; the combatants were grouped around the center table, two against one, but with the one possessed of intangible advantages. Here it was, only Wednesday, and yet how far the boys had moved from their polite casual acceptance of the week and the Fanning-Howe family toward disenchantment and arguing. They had started off trustful and easy but now they could observe themselves, with surprise, growing to trust less as they were trusted less. They didn't understand how this state of affairs had come about, but the fact was that their only-natural boys' ways had cooled the first self-congratulatory glow of Mrs. Fanning's hospitality. One always forgets, when arranging to harbor refugees, that it won't be merely a matter of plenty of food for them, and new clothes; one is never prepared to take into account their unreasonable attachment for glass harps.

Catherine at the sink, scraping carrots, cast a pleased, inimical glance around at them. Was there no one in that house who liked them? She seemed happy to hear Mrs. Fanning upbraid them. Mrs. Fanning rose without smil-

[138]

ing and swept away, suddenly ignoring them and all their gradually accumulated sins, saying to Catherine from the entrance to the brown tunnel, over her shoulder, "And don't forget four pints of extra cream for the *crème brûlée.*"

The boys went out to the side porch, sulky and bored, and there they found Edith surrounded by jars and jugs of water and flowers.

"Hi!" she greeted them, with the most astounding affability.

But they were wary. "Hi," they said. George turned away and eased his fragile burden down on the wicker table.

"Did he do a good job?" she asked, in a singing, smiling voice. Lucius asked how *she* knew where they had been; did she employ spies? "Oh, he telephoned." Her attempt to sound casual, as if he telephoned all the time, every day, several times a day, was unsuccessful in her own ears, so she said it again. "He telephoned me." The words absolutely refused to lie down and sound flat, or ordinary. It seemed that particular combination of words had a gay life of its own, and she smiled. Popping daffodils in and out of jugs, apparently she couldn't stop smiling. Lucius even thought she looked foolish. "Well, *we* got Hell," he informed her, his wide brow still unappeased, and at that the strange, unpredictable creature burst out laughing.

"Oh, you mustn't mind her," she said all too airily, all too unconcerned for their trouble. "She'll be in a terrible flap from now on, getting ready for the dinner party tomorrow and she's tired. She spent most of the morning writing letters to congressmen about G.I. housing. She didn't even know you weren't here until Catherine told her ten minutes ago. So you see, everything's lovely!" She

[139]

sprang up and playfully snapped the jaws of the garden shears at him and Lucius ducked, not because he was afraid of her scissors but because she looked exactly as though she might be going to kiss him.

"Come on, George; let's play." Anything to get away from women, he thought and led the way well around the corner of the house. He had no plans for amusing himself and his brother but he thought he couldn't stand the sight of another woman just now, not even Anna who was so much the nicest person in that house. In the back garden they encountered Mr. Howe gazing solemnly up into an elm where he had some reason to believe a chewink was hiding from him; the boys were pleased to come up with a male creature and they gave him their habitual greeting, and Lucius added that he knew a funny story. Mr. Howe politely lowered his bird watcher's glasses as a guarantee that he would listen.

"Well, there was this American soldier down on an island in the South Seas and he was talking to this South Sea Islander he was trying to teach English to. See?" Mr. Howe said yes indeed; quite a job, he should imagine. "Well, this American soldier pointed at a tree and he said, 'What's that?' and the South Sea Islander said, 'Tree,' so the American said, 'Good,' and he pointed to a hut and said, 'What's that?' and the South Sea Islander said, 'Hut,' and the American soldier said, 'Good,' and he pointed up at a plane and said, 'What's that?' and the South Sea Islander said, 'Well, I can't quite see from here whether it's a B-24 or a P-38.' " There was a momentary silence and then Lucius asked anxiously, "Do you get it, or *not?*"

"I don't believe I do."

"Well," Lucius' voice held a slight strain of discouragement. "I'll tell you again." He repeated the point of the story with painstaking clarity and this time Mr. Howe laughed pleasantly and said, "I see. The American wanted the South Sea Islander to say, 'Plane.' Very amusing. I guess perhaps I wasn't listening very carefully the first time."

Anna came skiing across the kitchen floor with the mop handle in one hand and in the other, held high like a votive offering on its way templeward, a full dust bin. "Better ve vait to Friday for our afternoon off, she says."

This was not news; they had known since Monday that their day off would have to be switched that week; Mrs. Fanning had discussed it with them, expressing regret and at the same time pointing out how seldom she, unlike many mistresses, disturbed their routine. Contentment had hummed inside Anna ever since; it was so cosy knowing she didn't have to put on shoes and go downtown, to be gone hours, with nothing to do. Catherine had been doubly furious at having her day switched—first, because she had a grievance and second, a far more serious concern: What would the brakeman think if she were not waiting for him, according to their long-established sweet custom, Thursday at three, beside the rack of comics in the station waiting room?

Anna skied slowly back from her trip to the ashcan. "Better ve vait, she says," she repeated mildly, beaming because she knew the rearrangement bothered Catherine.

Catherine threw down the carrot she was scraping for luncheon and the knife she was scraping it with. They bounced and clattered in the sink. "I will not!" she cried, but not about her work on the carrot. "I don't care!"

She yanked off her apron and threw it toward a chair. Then, so strong is habit, she pulled down her sleeves and neatly, if very angrily, buttoned the cuffs before marching out of the kitchen along the passage and into the morning room to give notice.

"Not another minute!" she said to Mrs. Fanning who was at last at work on the seating plan and now, half-turned from her desk, was unable to take in what blow Fate had struck her from behind. "Them two boys upsetting everybody and everything for a whole week, racing up and down the back stairs all hours—why can't they use the front?—and oatmeal cooked, and a great big dinner party and all the extra work, and all!"

"Catherine! Having the boys here is making absolutely no difference whatsoever. You know I told you it wouldn't. What could they have done to trouble you, two *little* boys?"

"Yah!" said Catherine, to whom they had done nothing.

"And you've known about the dinner party all week, and you know we give the Recusants a dinner every year. And Nellie is coming in to help."

"It's Anna she helps; she don't have nothing to do with me except eat up all the food I cook. Cream bruley!" she said, fierce with self-pity. "I never see such a dessert before I come here. 'Scatter with brown sugar,' it says and if I don't scatter it thick enough I get complaints there's no crust so it's no good and if I scatter it too thick it all sinks down, into the soup, like. Enough to drive me crazy." Silent at last but seething still, she stood with her under lip thrust far out in front and her self behind.

For a moment or two Mrs. Fanning tried talking to her, soothing, cajoling, but it was useless; she knew it from the beginning; Catherine would leave. Sometimes a maid giving notice is perched on a fence of indecision even while she delivers, smoothly, without a hitch, the leave-taking

[142]

formula, and a practiced employer senses this and sometimes is able by a judicious word of praise or affection, or
hearty-sounding disbelief that there is any real grievance,
to give the maid a tiny but definite push so that the confused creature, with a squawk and a flurry of apron strings,
flaps down on the right side of the fence, back into the
reservation, and for days thereafter an unnatural peace
and amity reign in that household. But though, in times
past, Mrs. Fanning had occasionally accomplished this
small domestic miracle, this morning she knew from the start
that she was beaten. There was a look in Catherine's eye
that had nothing to do with visiting boys nor large dinner
parties, not even with the switched afternoon off. Catherine had been telephoned the evening before by a friend
who told her that her lover the brakeman had been seen
two nights running in the company of a spirited young red-
haired milliner, once at a pizzeria in Harbor Street and the
next night at a roller-skating rink. Who could keep her hand
steady for the meticulous sprinkling of brown sugar when
pictures danced before the inward eye of these wicked two
romantically sharing a hot tomato pie or, hand in hand
and shoulder to shoulder through a long evening, sweeping around a rink on skates while music inflamed them?
Though she couldn't identify it, what Mrs. Fanning saw
in Catherine's face was the look of a woman who had
revenges to plot and to take, and she was right to abandon
any attempt to keep her in a kitchen. Mrs. Fanning had
never in her life had as urgent a personal trouble as the
one now confronting Catherine but she recognized desperation when she saw it. How silly to be desperate, she
thought—strange, unpredictable creatures that they are—
desperate and unable to stand the addition to the household for a week of two little boys; unbalanced, she rather

[143]

suspected, all of them, even the best of them. Ordinarily, when Catherine had a grievance against her it only enhanced her servility; this time was different.

"Very well, Catherine. Though I cannot understand you doing this to me, and naturally I shall have to think twice about what references I can give you."

"Think once, think twice," muttered the harassed woman. The words meant nothing at all to her, and nothing to Mrs. Fanning, but they sounded so surly they had the instantaneous effect of making Mrs. Fanning decide not to give any references at all, even guarded ones, even qualified ones, which are such fun to write and sometimes almost compensate for desertion.

She turned back to her desk and Catherine stumped away forever, shaking in her soul because now she was free to deal with a lovely young milliner and she didn't in the least know how.

Mrs. Fanning dialed the better of two employment agencies. "Oh my no," was the burden of the manager's reply. "Nothing; nothing at all."

"Someone merely temporary, then," Mrs. Fanning pleaded. "Just to see me through this dinner I am committed to giving."

But there was no one—well, there was a very young girl, completely inexperienced, who had been in to the agency and said she might like to be a cook; the manager couldn't keep from her voice a merry implication that the sanity of any such girl must surely be open to question.

The other agency had no one. "But next Fall, maybe; try us again, won't you?" they replied cordially before Mrs. Fanning hung up.

Edith came in and was told of the disaster. "How perfectly horrible!" She stood stock-still and looked out the

[144]

window, as if to summon up by staring up the street an immediate replacement for the perfidious Catherine; as though she had been shipwrecked but believed she could, by taking thought, make a sail appear. "But there must be *some*one!" Like most girls, legend to the contrary, she had a deep and healthy distaste for housework; left to herself she would never have lifted a finger but eaten crackers out of a box and drunk from a milk bottle. The over-zeal that attacks the married woman may be in some sort compensation for this early distaste. Edith saw the dinner party, bearing Jacob Miller on its crest, disappearing backward from her. Up till now it had been inconceivable that at some time during the evening they shouldn't have had moments of contact. Maybe now there would be no evening. "*Some*one?" she repeated.

Mrs. Fanning reluctantly called the first agency again and said she would be willing to interview the inexperienced girl but in the intervening five minutes that desirable young creature had been snapped up by a nimble housewife in New Canaan.

"Maybe Nellie, isn't that her name, I mean the extra waitress, can cook," Edith suggested.

"Oh, no. No; she's wonderful in the dining room but nothing on earth could get her out of that scalloped apron of hers and into a real job of work in a kitchen."

"She might have a friend."

Mrs. Fanning, as though it could scarcely be worth the effort of dialing, telephoned Nellie. Nellie *had* a friend. "In fact she's me sister," came quacking miraculously through the receiver. "Delia Mahoney by name."

"*Well!* Thank God!" said both women in the Evergreen Avenue morning room and they turned and smiled warmly at each other as though together, by quick work,

[145]

they had averted a threat of war in Europe. They radiated good will. They were friends, conquerors. Oh, if there were only, more often, disasters to be overcome, what good friends they would always be! In a rush of love and family affection Edith asked Mrs. Fanning if she liked her new blouse. Mrs. Fanning's lorgnette flipped obligingly open, she stared through it for an instant and said yes, she did very much; she thought it was very, very becoming.

10

"THE Count de Frontenac is hopelessly drunk," muttered Lucius who was lying reading, in a position likely to make any good oculist wring his hands, behind the enormous olive-green plush sofa that cut off a corner of the drawing room. It was such a big sofa that to be behind it was as good, the boys had discovered, as being in a separate room; a long window lighted this lovely spot, though the good oculist would never have agreed that it admitted light enough, at this hour of early evening, to read by. Thick, falling folds of velvet poured down the window side, so much velvet that some of it lay in a pool on the floor and in the unlikely but desired event that they heard anyone approaching this secret place it would have been but a moment's work to conceal themselves behind this mossy green cascade. Here was a secret, triangular little room they believed no one else knew about, one wall the green Spring evening beyond the window—the fresh lawn, robin-sprinkled, stretching to the hedge, the trees springing up, tenderly and proudly shooting their new infant leaves into the crystal sky. George would have transferred the Chinese harp from its precarious station in the tree to this safe place except that by so doing he might appear to be deferring to Mrs. Fanning. Lucius turned a page and propped his sagging chin on his other hand, the opposite elbow having gone numb for the time being. George was playing quietly with small, ten-cent-store cars, nipping up the very edge of the rug to make Quonset hut garages, flattening it down to make rough going for the car which was a police car in pursuit of an escaping gangster.

Like a gong waiting to be struck the big house, swept and polished, waited for the voices of people who were soon to come. There was silence all about the boys and over their heads. The maids had long since finished getting the dining room ready and it waited now, in partial dusk. A single wall bracket near the pantry door was on, but five minutes before the filing in of the hungry Recusants, matches would be applied to the white candles and the wall bracket discreetly snapped off; candlelight could be counted on to blur and soften the deep-graven lines of wit and worry on the faces of these men and women whose whole lives had been spent in the pursuit of truth hiding behind its many and varied veils—a pursuit amusing, and undeniably exhausting. The dining room without occupants waited, as smooth and impersonal and perfect as a full-page colored advertisement in a magazine of house decoration. "Gracious Living" would have been printed beneath the picture in flowing script, and then in smaller, but upright letters: "*You too* can have the atmosphere of luxury that comes only from Lus-Tro-Glo, the NEW furniture polish." On the long table down the center of Mrs. Fanning's dining room and on a smaller square one set up in the bay window each knife was in line; the Recusants' own silver épergne rising in the middle of the room, appeared to float, pure and empty; in Venetian glass cornucopias each Talisman rose, each anemone, bowed from the waist; at the corners of the tables each little pepper grinder, proper, and proudly erect, stood close beside the eternal object of all its protection and affection—its wife, the docile salt celler.

Accommodation for twenty-two alien coats waited, upstairs and down—empty hangers in the hall closet, the white bed and the chintz chaise longue in Mrs. Fanning's bedroom; any other week in the year but this week—"Having the boys here is not in the least inconvenient," Mrs. Fanning still insisted—the women would have trouped into the guest room to cast their coats on the two big beds with the dark blue and white enamel insets in the headboards, and made themselves at home in its impersonal air for five minutes, just long enough to tend to their hair and shoulder straps, but this week George was so palpably in residence there that Mrs. Fanning had admitted it would be better to use her room where no running jumps had wrinkled the bedspread and no small almost invisible cars waited on the floor to upset the unsuspecting poetry editor of the University journal or the authority on labor laws for women in industry.

The house brooded, benignant, smelling of wax and roses, expectant yet not too expectant, having harbored other dinner parties before this without the world having been noticeably altered for better or worse. But there is of course always the possibility that a spark may be struck off during the coming three hours, a magic word said, an old word suddenly made new, or two words that have never met before brought into galvanic alliance. Constantly, everywhere at this hour, in every city and town and in

[149]

country houses on illogical small dirt roads that are hard to find, this is happening; this state of suspension and hope exists in houses that have been swept and garnished ready for invaders, guests, dear strangers. Tonight may be the night when the perfect stranger will appear. "Oh, *may* I bring John Robinson, who will be visiting us at the time?" "Oh yes, yes; do bring him," the hostess has answered, in her heart the beginning of a prayer, or an impious wish— hard to tell which—and now all day she has been flying about, not ceasing to extend her love to her husband and children, but picturing to herself all the time the wonderful tall stooped man who will come at eight o'clock and be struck dumb by her, by something in her no one else has ever noticed. . . . Will it be John Robinson who is to be the father of the incandescent word? There is nothing to prevent between the soup and the shad the birth of that phrase which is going to kindle the earth. It has happened. It will happen again; perhaps tonight. . . . Therefore, all the curtains must hang perfectly straight and shut out the sweet disturbing unorganized air of evening, making a safe and lighted inside place for the birth of the world-shaking word, the little great phrase. Napkins must be folded so carefully, so perfectly, that no one will be disturbed by seeing even one silky monogram off-center; there is no telling what small flaws inhibit miracles; the flowers must all be full-open and attentive, leaning toward the guests. Then, with all these preparations, this hush and anticipation, if the word isn't coming from some one of all these people, where *is* it ever coming from?

"Oh!" cried Edith in her square bedroom, slamming open and shut the drawers of her dressing table. She sat on the very edge of the bench and her open dressing gown kept sliding from her shoulders as she searched for a pair of stockings sheerer than any she possessed. It would have been no use pointing out to her that under a long dress she could wear woolen stockings, for all he could see; she was overcome with a need to know herself beautifully and thinly dressed. Slowly she drew on the best pair she had; that they were not the right color had to be ignored, but they should have been thinner, thinner.

Mrs. Fanning lay on the chaise longue with cotton and witch-hazel pads fitted into the brown hollows of her eye sockets. "I must relax," she said, but unless she forcibly stopped it, one hand kept smoothing at the chintz, and her teeth clenched together from lifelong habit, and her tongue clove to the roof of her mouth. Would that dark horse Delia Mahoney know enough to cut the lemons for the shad lengthwise? Would Anna remember to draw the drawing-room curtains while they were at the dessert? Sometimes, exhilarated by a party, Anna would forget to do the perfectly simple tasks she automatically performed every other night of her life; sometimes, inexplicably, though on ordinary nights she not infrequently forgot to turn down Mrs. Fanning's bed, party nights she would push aside the piled coats and meticulously prepare the bed for sleeping. Would Delia Mahoney dry the lettuce carefully? If there was one thing Mrs. Fanning disliked more than a lazy committee member it was a wet lettuce leaf. Would Nellie remember where the extra coffee cups were?

In his room Mr. Howe, lips pursed above his smart goatee, eyes steady if vacant, ran a selecting hand over the ranked accumulation of forty-five years of bow ties; when the selection was made and the tie tied, he looked to himself in the mirror so like a college professor the resemblance alone was enough to satisfy him. Clever fellows, professors. He smiled gravely at his professorial aspect; he was an eminent historian, he felt, or perhaps an eminent physicist.

For a long moment he stood before the mirror regarding this admirable character who, though required to be the sole support of a daughter, the comforter and confidant of a busy sister and, this week, trusty mentor to a rabble of visiting children, yet was able to maintain the serenity, the poise of the true scholar. "Very fine," he murmured to the mirror. "Oh, very fine indeed."

"The Count de Frontenac," Lucius said to George, "he—" but even as he spoke his whole-hearted concern plunged him back into the printed story and he could not go on.

"Z-z-z-z, z-z-z-z," murmured George, guiding one of his little cars over a route of breakneck intensity suggested by the pattern of the rug. "Calling police car 8-2-8-2. There's a murdered body at number 1-2-3-4 Abercrombie and Fitch Street. Proceed there immediately and—" He looked up quickly and his hand slowed the car. Someone had come in to the empty drawing room. The car came to a silent stop and he poked Lucius in warning—should they hide behind the curtain?—but Lucius, in no condition to notice, was reading, *Are you mad, Deschenaux? You knew she was his sister, and how he worships her! Retract the toast, it was inopportune!*

"We might sit down," said a voice somewhat like Edith's, but not altogether like hers, and to George's mingled concern and amusement he heard the plushy sofa give forth a plushy, flatulent expiration as a person, or it must be persons, sank onto it; he glanced at his brother to see if he shared this amusement but Lucius was reading, *He walked across the drawing room to one of the gorgeous panels that decorated the wall and touched a hidden spring. A door flew open, disclosing a stair heavily carpeted that led down*

[152]

to the huge vaulted foundations of the Chateau. . . . He
descended the stair with hasty though unsteady steps. . . .

"Sorry I'm early," came Jacob Miller's vexed voice and
George heard Edith quickly reply that he wasn't, and anyway, luckily, she was just that minute dressed. There was a
momentary silence and then her voice, mournfully low,
"Oh, that was a lie. I'm getting as bad as Aunt Clara. I
knew you'd be coming early and I've been dressed for
ages."

There was a quick relieved laugh from beyond the green
velvet barricade and Jacob said, "Well, thank God, an
honest woman at last."

There followed inquiries about whether he had been
searching very long for any such legendary creature and
replies about wasn't everyone always, that may have
sounded witty to their perpetrators but which finally made
George, hiding behind the sofa, sigh deeply; this was the
very kind of conversation that, having no meaning whatsoever, yet might go on indefinitely the participants not
knowing, naturally, when it had come to a normal end,
and perhaps there *was* no normal end. In George's opinion,
it should never have been begun. He bent his head and
silently revolved the tiny rubber wheels of the gangster's
car with a careful finger; the wheels did not squeak; perhaps the game could go on at quarter speed and in silence.

Edith, watching Jacob's face, said slowly, "No, I don't
believe there is any such constant search going on because
if there were, if even only you were, there would be more
honest women in the world than there are, to meet the
demand. Don't I remember something to this effect from
my economics course?"

"Edith . . ." he said, and stopped. What had he been
going to say? What was he going to tell her? But she knew

[153]

he had decided against telling her whatever it was when he went on, too offhand, to assure her that the laws of supply and demand weren't necessarily true. Not sounding much like himself, he said, "If you just look at the shamefully scanty supply of beautiful women, for instance, and yet, *surely*, the *demand* . . . !"

She laughed, not at the way he spoke, but because she could feel implicit in his words the realization he thought she was beautiful. I am, too, she thought, in my large, standoffish way. She leaned back against the sofa, sighing with happiness; she felt as though little gold flowers, or bells, were blossoming downward from the lobes of her ears, and as though there might be a coronet of them springing up out of her smooth hair. It felt too as though her lashes had all at once grown to be an inch long; they were heavy and it was an effort, though a delightful rewarding one, to have to lift them when she looked at him. She looked down often into her lap all for the pleasure of making the sweet effort needful to prize up her lashes for the instant when she gave him her glance. His regard was steady. Presently he suggested they might manage to sit next each other at dinner.

"Oh, Jacob. There'll be place cards."

"Oh. Well . . ."

"Sylvester Wagstaff for me, I suppose. And they'll all be coming soon," she murmured.

"Don't say so." His voice commanded her and she nearly said, meekly, "All right, I won't." Instead she smiled at him with her new-feeling smile. His taking her hand had the amusing effect of making sprout from her finger tips more little bells and flowers. "They'll come all too soon," he said, and she answered in a voice drowsy with love, "I hate them, Jacob, don't you?"

How they wasted their time, gazing at one another! They should have been plotting, leaguing themselves together to circumvent fate, and their own awkward natures, and Mrs. Fanning. They ought to have known they needed to; at any rate Edith should have known, having lived so long in that house, but she was so simple! She forgot how, with Mrs. Fanning, aversion to something or to someone led soon to plots and schemes for their undoing.

Lucius hadn't needed to turn a page for some minutes because the print was so fine—how the good oculist would have shaken his head; the light from the green lawn outside scarcely came in now between the green curtains but was all gathered up in the remote crystal sky; the robins had gone home—but now it was imperative for him to find out what Le Gardeur would answer to the seemingly careless question of the bravest man in New France, *seemingly, for in truth, it was vital in the last degree to his happiness, and he knew it.* Lucius lifted his head, his eyes too far out of focus to see George, his cars, the window or the sofa-wall, but he became aware for the first time that the sofa was tenanted. Now that he knew it, he was afraid to turn a page so he lifted the book to the level of his face and with the softest breath imaginable, blew the page over. George watched this maneuver and grinned approval. They both believed themselves to be narrowly escaping detection, having no way of knowing about the sweet, peculiar deafness that had descended on the occupants of the olive-green sofa, nor would they have understood how, when summoned by a look from Mrs. Fanning in the hall to come out and mingle with the first rush of guests, Sylvester Wagstaff's fat face gleaming among them, Jacob and Edith, reluctantly rising, found to their surprise how the legs of the newly-in-love are almost no good to them, no real support whatever; they wobble; they don't begin to be able to hold up all the wonder.

Because no one concerned himself that festive evening about George and his bedtime, his teeth or neck or ears, he stayed up far later than usual. Finally he faced the disagreeable truth that no one was going to argue with him about anything so, yawning with disappointment at this boring state of affairs, he had dragged himself off upstairs, so sleepy he shut his eyes as he brushed his teeth and, after whispering, "Good night. Sleep tight," out the window to his harp, hanging and invisible, out there, safe, holy—he had neatly nipped up the tree during a fortunate moment when Mrs. Fanning was talking to the maids on the other side of the house—he fell into bed murmuring his new cabalistic spell against any evil contingent on darkness and solitude. "Calypso, Margano, Sereno, Lentenor, Nicanor and *Bar*baro, Calypso, Margano, Sereno . . ." But Lucius, a willing prey to Spring fever, prowled the dark lawn.

The Recusants were arriving in force. Cars came into the tarmac scallop in the grass between the avenue and the iron fence, decanted one or two, sometimes even three, learned persons, and were driven off, sometimes to be parked for the evening on the avenue itself, sometimes sent quite away and not required to return until eleven. Lucius, his hands in his pockets, like a bit of watchful statuary, lurked in the shrubbery near the front door. He had been told that each of these individuals was almost perilously eminent; he scrutinized them carefully, trying to make out from the brief glimpse he had in the porch light which was the man who had discovered and dug up a totally unsuspected temple in Greece, which was the man who knew all about atomic energy, which the bold editor of the University monthly. He picked a hearty, broad-shouldered old man for the archaeologist; those shoulders, he thought, had been the ones to bend to the shovel; and he never even saw the actual antiquary, a tiny wispy gray little fellow who blew in at the gate on a gust of Spring wind, almost as though by chance, and up the walk and in at the door like a leaf. Once two cars arrived simultaneously, but nose to nose, at the high point of the tarmac curve and there was much laughter from all concerned. The speaker of the evening was one of the last to come and he scurried up the steps out of the darkness with a flurry of papers in his hand and his black coat tails following after. Lucius had kept count of the arrivals and was about to give up numbers twenty-one and twenty-two when a sedan whirled into the scallop and out sprang two women in colored capes who, gathering up their long, flowered skirts, bending, sped up the walk and the sandstone steps, wasting their breath in mutual exhortations to hurry, hurry.

Lucius wandered out of the rhododendrons, pleased with what he had just observed—one of those terribly nice men looked just like the piano tuner at home and one like the proprietor of the Sharon bicycle shop; put him in overalls and give him a wrench and no one would have known the difference. Thinking of Sharon as he strolled a little way up Evergreen Avenue brought a twinge of visceral sorrow and apprehension; next week, in Sharon, he would have to take his Latin examination. He frowned; the dative and ablative singular of the second declension are alike and are formed by replacing the ending $\bar{\imath}$ of the gentive singular by $\bar{o}$ . . . ah, nuts! And he strolled back having bravely decided to put it all quite out of his mind. Wednesday would come soon enough. He rambled out the back path to the courtyard where nowadays no horses ever stood, backed into carriage or sleigh. Nowadays the big cobbled enclosure was used by Tom on sunny days to wash the cars or sift the loam for the greenhouse but at this moment, at this timeless night moment, it held only a high tide of moonlight. Lucius walked over the blunted stones to the corner where, the day before, he had started construction on an immense cathedral. He had discovered a pile of bricks and brickbats beyond the stable and little by little a Gothic temple, now fully three feet high at the crossing, was rising in the corner least likely to be disturbed by Tom backing cars out.

Lucius bent, selected a good clean brick and added it carefully to a wall; this was to be a church to end all churches. Drawings of fantastically ambitious cathedrals filled the margins of his French grammar and his bedroom desk at home was so littered with splinters of the balsa wood intended by toy manufacturers to be used for boys to make model airplanes, with jars of paste and glue-sticky tools, that he was forced to do his school homework on the floor.

"Well, well," friends of his family would say when they encountered finished results of his obsession, "so you're going to be an architect when you grow up?" They would beam approvingly.

"I don't know as I am," Lucius would reply with his incurable integrity, incurable and sometimes inconvenient; he couldn't bear to think he was misleading anyone and he had no reason to suppose he would always want to build cathedrals. He simply happened to love to, now. He had felt exactly the same way last summer about collecting grasshoppers and keeping them in hot holes in the ground with pieces of glass over them. It had been his passion. "I think, maybe, I'm really more interested in reading adventure books."

"Ha! Not much money in *that!*" the family friends would say, wagging admonishing forefingers. To that no good answer had occurred to Lucius, nor had he made much of an effort to find one. His future, except perhaps for the faintly troubling, imminent Latin examination, stretched calm for him; he knew he didn't have to know yet what he would become. The moonlight washing down over his fine face revealed no doubts, no troubles. Unlike George, who often teetered apprehensively on the sharp, shiny blade that rises between possible alternatives, he strolled about his world with relaxed hands in his pockets, viewing whatever he encountered with kindness and amusement. More polite than George, who cared so terribly for a good opinion that sometimes he gave the impression of heedlessness or anger, Lucius trusted himself almost as much as he trusted other people, and went his own way.

Now in the cold Spring moonlight he leveled off an unfinished place on the brickbat wall. The shadow on the cobbles was the shadow of a real, full-sized cathedral; enchanting. So must the shadows lie, this very night, bent stiffly out from the bases of real cathedrals in France. He worked for some time, a giant, and then left it abruptly because it would be too bad to get it done before the end of the week, before Tuesday morning when he would be going home.

He made his way back over the damp lawn and circling about the house tried to see in; though he pressed in among the rhododendron and azaleas, close to the bay windows of the dining room, the curtains had been too carefully pulled. A diffused glow came through the dark red

[159]

fabric and he could hear the party talking to itself in there in a high monotonous hum; infrequently, a high quick laugh thrust up through the hum, like a fountain. He would never know the cause of this laughter.

He moved along to the back wing where the shades were not pulled and each window was a *tableau vivant* of the bright, warm, animated life of the kitchen. Lights blazed down from the ceiling on a gay confusion of bouncing pot lids, darting women, towels cast down in a heap and caught up again, piles of used plates teetering on tables, piles of virgin plates waiting demurely. Steam shot in nervous spurts from the spout of the coffeepot. Delia Mahoney was slipping a spoon into a pan of sauce and transferring it into her wide cheerful mouth; she licked it, and then dipped it back into the sauce; she liked it; it must be good.

Anna, a formidable figure in her best black uniform, excited by the party, all at once began dancing. The Recusants must be safely launched on the long shad course. She broke into a gay *pas seul* down the middle of the kitchen floor, doing a wild, wonderful, stamping dance on her big, turned-out feet that shook the dishes on the tables. Delia and Nellie ran out of her way, and began clapping their hands in time to Anna's prancing, and screamed with laughter. Her apron strings flew out and from her long, uplifted, bracket arms a towel flew like a pennon; her long fine fingers held a wine bottle to her mouth. Was she drinking? Was she pretending to blow a horn? The watcher at the window pressed his forehead against the cold glass and watched her with delight; he laughed out loud, he the perennial connoisseur, the adult, at Anna, the real child and merrymaker. She made a deep, extravagant bow to the icebox, then one to the electric dish-washer, then back she came up the room and now through the glass he could hear that she was singing a loud, booming, presumably Swedish song, interspersing the phrases with toots and hootings; she held the empty bottle high, bottom up, the mouth close to her mouth, and tipped her gray head this way and that, opposite to whichever great foot was lifted in the air. She anticked up to the other two maids who were leaning on each other's shoulders and sobbing with joy; she paused, bowed and scraped, backed and filled before these two who were by now helpless with tears streaming down their faces and their mouths working but giving out no sound. Then she veered away, still amply gesturing, and capered slowly off, a more-than-life-sized figure, toward the back pantry and the shadowy back hall. Outside, among the rhododendrons, Lucius laughed again, a clear solitary high laugh in the cool Spring night.

The last philosopher in black tie and pumps, the last vigorous mistress of the arts in satin so tight that when, in farewell, she shook hands before, she bounced tautly up and down behind, the last member of the History Department and the speaker of the evening and his notes and the visiting Provost from Oxford—all of them had gone; even Jacob had gone when he had quite run out of pretexts for staying, pretexts that withered untimely under Mrs. Fanning's glance. Lights still blazed though the rooms were empty; the laps of chairs and couches still were concave from all the wit and wisdom they had held that evening.

"Oh *really*, that young man makes me very tired," said the hostess when the door had shut on Jacob's final backward look. She said she wouldn't have been surprised to learn that he was walking backward down Evergreen Avenue, his enchanted gaze still fixed on her house. "Very tired," repeated Mrs. Fanning whose fatigue was actually the normal exhaustion following on the giving of large dinner parties.

Edith flushed, or had been flushed all evening. She needed to say something incisive and adult. "I don't see why," she said only, and sounded like a child who has been told candy is bad for the teeth. Where now was the agreeable entente created between herself and her aunt by Catherine's defection? It must have been of pitiably flimsy stuff.

"He's not only disagreeable, he's poor!" Mrs. Fanning swept elegantly around the room emptying ashtrays, and with her pointed satin toe returned footstools to their wonted places. The tireder she was the straighter she held herself, her narrow elegant dress hung as if it enclosed a candle. "If he's so extraordinarily intelligent about the Middle Ages and Merovingian jewelry and *tools,* surely he could have learned by now what to do with his knife and fork."

"What about them?" Edith, who had been going to help Mrs. Fanning with a little light picking-up of the drawing room, reared up from an ashtray, stood stock still and scowled.

"Rude too, to be so silent. The knife and fork? Oh, you must have noticed—left all anyhow when he was finished and they nearly fell off the plate onto Mrs. Hildebrand when Anna came around to pick it up."

"So did the Provost!" Edith cried. "Didn't you see?" They paused in their quarrel long enough to visualize, with sharp horror, a rain of forks downflashing from the rims of plates to pierce, on one side, the solid flesh of Mrs. Hildebrand, that world-wide authority on Micronesian marriage ceremonies, on the other, Mrs. Warrington who

[162]

had been keeping the Provost very happy with her account of a trip to Asia Minor in 1910.

"Ah, well." This tolerant phrase meant nothing in itself, but served to conceal Mrs. Fanning's growing determination that Edith must not marry anyone so uncouth as Jacob Miller. If he ever became famous, that would be a different matter, of course. Uncouthness could then be labeled originality, but preferably this happened to people not in any way connected with the Fanning family; if he became *very* famous gaucherie would be metamorphosed into picturesque and lovable eccentricity. But becoming famous takes a long time, too long a time if one looks at things with an entirely practical eye. "Ah, well." Mrs. Fanning threw open a window to clear the air of cigarette smoke and Edith's rather tactless reference to the Provost's table manners. "The English have been through so much the last eight years, ten years, I suppose it's remarkable they've been able to retain any amenities at all. I presume we've really no idea of what they've been through." Even to her own ears this sounded like a lame explanation for the Provost's lighthearted way with cutlery and she veered away from the subject. "However, that's no excuse for that young boor. Now Sylvester *Wag*staff . . ." But Edith was gone. There was only the sound of her hurrying feet in the hall, on the mustard-colored stair carpet, and then from the upper hall the sound of her door clicking sharply shut.

The drawing room still smelled *used;* there was no other word for it; Mrs. Fanning opened another window, this one more slowly, because she was so tired, and her mind yielded up for her inspection the ranked and nagging grievances it had been obliging enough to cram down out of sight during the party—one, no cook; two, Edith ever-present but useless; three, Spring cleaning imminent but

[163]

Heavens, not until she got rid of the boys from Sharon; and, four, the boys from Sharon. She broke off the parade of grievances there, though there were others, five, six, seven and even eight, she could have thought of. It had seemed an easy enough thing to do, to offer to house two small boys for a week, easy and at the same time demonstrative of grace and generosity. "My dear, they will make *no* difference, no trouble," she had said, and had been pleased when her offer was accepted. Now she was tired of them, with four more days still to go. Since their coming to Evergreen Avenue there had been, she was beginning to admit though only to herself, a subtle change in rooms and people, in the air of the place. It was as if creatures from another world, more candid and more destructive, had come into her house. They did not mean to be naughty and in fact they were not naughty; they had not set the place on fire nor broken windows; they were not noisy; they were simply in the way, though she would have been hard put to describe how. It would have been better if they had never come, or if for some reason they had had to, it would be better if they were staying a long, long time, so she might go to work on them—on George's ears for instance. Lucius really ought to speak to George about those ears. Well, he hadn't, so she must speak to George. Or perhaps it would be more practical, the long run considered, to point them out to Lucius and suggest that no doubt their mother would appreciate his keeping track of them until such time in the future, as George was old enough to . . . oh, how very far ahead that day might be! But if only she had a long-time responsibility for the boys, instincts could be worked on, good ones fostered until they became habits, bad ones rooted out and tossed away— George's foolish stubbornness about tree-climbing for in-

[164]

stance—plucked out like weeds and held up for brief inspection educationally. "See, this horrid thing! *We* don't want it, do we!" and so tossed away forever. But they were there for such a short, short time. The habit of dropping socks and underwear on the floor was one thing; all she could do this week was remind Anna to pick them up every morning and rinse them out; but now, with Catherine gone, Anna couldn't because she would have to be in the kitchen most of her time. Edith couldn't cook; Edith had concentrated on history at her junior college. "It takes a historian not to be able to boil an egg," cried Mrs. Fanning, who was really tired.

She leaned one narrow arm on the mantel and stared down into a bed of silent red coals. The room hadn't needed a fire this Spring evening, but moving flames give life to a room so she had asked Forrest to light it. He hadn't been too alert about obeying her and that dreary young man had sprung forward and done it with a lighter from his pocket; ostentatious, she had felt. Now the room was empty, the fire no longer was required to leap and flicker decoratively and it had quickly sunk in on itself and now burned red and secret. Ten minutes ago the room had been almost oppressively full of Recusants, all of them cosily sated with shad, possessed of many hitherto unsuspected facts about early Welsh life—which of them, for instance, before this evening, had known how briskly goats had flourished in Wales in medieval times, only to be supplanted by sheep; goats, in fact, had all but disappeared—all kindly and chattering, chattering ever more quickly as going-home time approached. "But I said . . ." "But tell me now about Celia and her babies . . ." "But tell me how, if one assumes the capital to be Fourth Century we are to account for the total absence of entasis . . ." "But

[165]

Bergson says . . ." "But if you recall, Walpole never says . . ." *"I must leave this instant.* I have an eight o'clock class. It's been delightful. Oh, *don't try to stop me!"*

Now there was only the room that had contained the party; it was warm and luxurious, and to its owner, the present one of quite a long line of owners, it was a little strange, smelling of cigarettes and cigars and coffee and perhaps, too, a little of the breath on which the scraps of learned or friendly talk had flown from one Recusant to another. It was not late—eleven, getting on for eleven-fifteen. Mrs. Fanning lifted her tired eyes and consulted the clock on the mantel—twenty minutes past eleven. But she never went to bed as early as this. Even when she was tired, it would have been like ignominiously giving in to something, to go to bed. Though she had nearly exhausted herself making a pleasant evening for her guests, she could not go to bed. It *had* been pleasant, and tomorrow there would be an exhilarating tug-of-war with the domestic employment agency head in New York, and perhaps she could get back in time to go to the tea for the new master of Wolcott House and his wife; the meeting about D.P.'s wasn't until the following day; "discrimination against the Balts," she murmured, and frowned into the fire.

How fortunate it is that Mrs. Fanning is on the side of the angels. It is terrifying to imagine her with all her abounding capabilities, as a Hell's advocate—Mrs. Hitler-Fanning, immovable but watchful, merciless and omnipotent, sitting behind a monstrous desk fitted out with bells and buttons and neat little stacks of lists of the condemned. Oh, she would be powerful, and thorough, and terrifyingly silent; Mr. Howe would have no place in that room. What a lucky thing it is then, that even if it's for the wrong reason, she occupies herself with good rather than evil.

[166]

What was there left for her to accomplish now in this alien-seeming, exhausted room? The room wanted her out of it and time to recover. By tomorrow it would be its usual self, except of course if Anna had to stay in the kitchen all day it wouldn't be dusted, and smoothed and soothed. Oh, very tiresome. All because of the boys. Catherine never would have left if George and Lucius hadn't come. Mrs. Fanning, who had been told not a word about the menacing red-haired milliner and in any case would have been unable to credit Catherine as one leg of an eternal triangle, grasped the brass poker and scattered the fire into a garden of red, pulsing flowers, shut down and locked the windows, retrieved the gold evening bag which Mrs. Warrington could be counted on to send around for tomorrow, and snapped off all the lights with one majestic click of a switch.

Nellie and her sister dropped their coins in the glass cage and chose seats near the front of the trolley because their feet ached too much to carry them further back.

"So old, you practically have to chew for'm," Nellie said of one of the more distinguished Recusants.

"Yah," Delia replied, and surreptitiously undid the tight waistband of her black suit skirt. "Ah-h-h-h," she breathed, relieved.

"Well, how do you like working out?" Nellie inquired and Delia said she liked the five dollars all right. This reply disturbed Nellie; it was so mercenary. She herself went out working on these occasional evenings for a blend of reasons, not the most important of them being money. For one thing, she thoroughly enjoyed getting away for a few hours from her family. She would perch her hat over her nose, neatly and quickly wrap up her best apron in brown paper, and saying, "Ta, ta; expect me when you see me," to her husband and children, off she would prance to the corner and mount the bus or trolley that would take her to the big house where preparations for a party were about to begin. The work of waiting on the table at dinners was not hard; it was lively and temporary; she liked her reign even if it was brief over pantries with shelves and cupboards of china and drawers of silver and linen. "Though not for steady," she said, and eased off one shoe under the wicker trolley seat. "How about you, though?" she asked her sister. "There's a steady cook's job going begging in that house, now."

"Not me, money or not. There's too much fuss and feathers with them kind of people."

"Ah, I know. Trouble with them," Nellie explained, "they're so rich. So they don't *know* too much, and you can't expect it. *I* can twist 'em around me little finger, of course. Sometimes they sit gab-gabbing around the table after they're all through eating and I have to make 'em get a move on so I can get to me washing up. Well, so I go in and pour 'em all out some more wah-ter, slow. Course, they don't *need* no more wah-ter, but that's what I do, real slow, and usually they catch on."

Both sisters laughed in appreciation of this maneuver.

"*I'd* go in," Delia said with the boldness born of naïveté, "*I'd* just bang in and trow a couple of durty looks around."

"Holy Mother! You'd do no such thing! . . . Try taking your shoes off under the seat. It feels wonderful."

They shifted their stout bodies, settled them, folded their hands on the worn handbags in their laps, preparing for the long ride yet to come; in their folded, respectably gloved hands waited orange transfers. The trolley swayed along, brightly lighted and high and invincible through

[168]

the traffic of the town—a Trojan horse, carrying its occupants not forth to battle but, after the battle, home. The trolley-smell, like dry scorched paper, like the taste of electricity in the mouth, like no other smell in the world, sat pleasant and comfortable in their nostrils, because it was the going-home-after-work smell. The motorman tramped on his bell, dispelling crowds spilling from the jaws of movie theaters; he guided his rocking vehicle safely through the center of town, dangerous with pedestrians and traffic and winking traffic lights, and brought it in time out the other side of town along an interminably monotonous residential street of two-family houses and three-story apartment buildings. The trolley rushed faster than ever through this canyon, a Trojan horse scenting his stable.

Delia sucked reminiscently on her teeth. "I must remember to tell Dan about that sauce I made."

Nellie looked sideways at her; it wouldn't do to have her get the idea that just because she had worked out once in one of the big houses that she knew it all. "E-yeh?" she said. "You ought to see the fancy cooking some of my customers want done *some*times. Dumb though they are, they got their own standards, which are high. And I will say," she said, tolerantly, "they aren't any dumber than other rich people. You just got to expect it for them to be the way they are. They can't help it, you might say."

11

"Hand me that good brick over there, will you?"

"Not unless I can build too."

"Well, if you do exactly what I say."

A light, late-April, Friday morning breeze was lapping over the stable yard wall, lifting the pointed wisp of sandy hair on the crown of George's head, fluttering the young green crêpe leaves of trees. It was early morning and the sun which would beat warm at noon still came slanting into the courtyard and had to leave a wide band of blue shadow just under the wall, a perimeter of wet cobblestones it was chill to enter. The towers of Lucius' medieval brick cathedral rose higher and higher in the morning light, casting their own blue shadows. It was so early the pink bricks were still sparkling and wet. The boys moved about in the sun, working, wrangling, happy and absorbed.

Mrs. Fanning had gone to New York by the eight o'clock train to try to find a cook. The director of the agency she always went to for what she hoped would be permanent members of her staff was as erect and inflexible and uncompromising as herself; when they met the air positively crackled with mutual respect. Yesterday, by telephone, she had assured Mrs. Fanning, one of her favorite clients, that there were no cooks in New York worth having, no cooks at all, *not one;* so it would be quite futile, wouldn't it, for Mrs. Fanning to make the effort to come to town for interviews, but all along, while she held the instrument to the side of her head, she had known Mrs. Fanning would come, and her other hand had written "10 o'clock, Mrs. F. Bertha Spewack? Annie Casey? Oblowitz?" on her engagement pad. Only a hopelessly frivolous character would have placed a bet on the outcome of the imminent encounter in the agency office; it was a toss-up. . . . The front door on Evergreen Avenue had opened and shut that morning at exactly twenty minutes before eight, and now a lovely conjunction of Spring and laissez faire brooded over the establishment.

Little by little the cathedral was growing. "Let's make an upstairs piazza on it," George suggested.

"My God." Lucius voice was mild. "What you don't know about architecture." Fastidiously he set a brick where he planned the jutting out of a chapel. "Here, you go on and lay the foundation for the apse."

"Well, what's that? What's an apse?" George paused, skinny legs apart but ready to set off to do Lucius' bidding, narrow hands holding ready a particularly smooth and satisfactory brick. His sandy, questioning head tipped sideways, awaiting enlightenment.

"My God. Imagine not knowing what an apse is."

"I'm only eight!" George yelled, and dashed the brick to the cobbles where it broke in two.

"Oh good. Gimme; just what I needed for this corner."

They worked on, deeply absorbed. The sun slid upward,

the belt of cold wet blue shadow against the yard wall narrowed, narrowed, and disappeared and now the sun could see down into every cranny of the courtyard; only inside the cathedral itself was shadow left, and coolness and shadow would lurk all day under the vast hairy crumpled leaves of a rhubarb plant which flourished unreasonably— nobody had planted it—in a corner by the stable door. All at once George became very happy because in his mind he decided to become a tiny man, a little man just the size to walk in at the cathedral's front door. He began seeing everything from the point of view of this little man—the cobblestones became immense, immeasurably weighty gray boulders, squared-off by some giant; the match sticks scattered here and there by Tom's efforts to get his pipe going were lumber; George felt himself about to sweat under the exertion of heaving up a brick, staggering with it over to the rising edifice and getting it set in place. In fact, it couldn't be done, or wouldn't have been done but for the fact that the tiny man was supernaturally strong and willing. The floor of the cathedral, as Lucius was building it, was one horizontal brick in height. "That's a terribly high step for me," George objected, feeling in the muscles of his calves the effort necessary for the little church-going man to make; it was too much to expect. "What if we make a ramp, up?" But Lucius was so outraged at the suggestion that George had to tell him why.

"Good God." Lucius was contemptuous of the tiny man's trouble. "Let him jump. What can we put across the top of the windows?"

"You mean for window sills?"

"The *opposite* of window sills, stupid."

"Well, what do you call them?"

"I don't know. Go find me something."

[172]

They broke up an orange crate they found in the stable and managed lintels, but George continued to worry because he thought the proportions were wrong and that the windows were too far up the walls for the little man, for him, to look through without getting a crick in his neck. He could quite plainly see the small creature, in best Sunday suit and white collar, staring wistfully up toward the windows from his pew, and not being able to see out.

"Pews, Lucius! What'll we use for them?"

"Ah-h-h, forget pews."

The cathedral's creator saw it in the large, contentedly and calmly. He was working with steady movements, powered by the sun which was warm on the back of his neck between the jersey and his thick light hair to prodigies of engineering accomplishment. Bricks were wonderful, he thought. He loved their weight, which seemed to him to be exactly and honestly right for their size; he loved the orange-pink color and the surface which was at the same time gritty but clean. He balanced one in his hand and took a long time to decide where to put it. His wide gaze approved his handiwork.

Meanwhile Edith, who had availed herself of the reigning tranquillity and the almost-certainty of not being disturbed by her questioning aunt, was washing her hair for the second time that week.

"Forty-nine, fifty, fifty-one, fifty-two," she was counting aloud, standing by her open window in skirt and underwear, rubbing her head with a bath towel but at fifty-two she was transfixed by the sight of Jacob Miller walking across the lawn. "Oh!" she cried and darted back out of sight. What could he have come for at this hour of the morning? He must have come to see her. She rubbed wildly, and the hair tangled. He had looked very grim, striding over the grass. She ran to the mirror and tried, by wielding the big comb, to create order in a chaos of hair. Snarls sprang into being; such of the strands as were free from snags were wickedly elastic from being wet; they permitted the comb to pass through and then, treacherously, they fell heavy and dank. She caught up the towel again but now rubbing it made her hair fuzzy—oh, intolerable! If only she were the kind of young girl who is gay and little she could have run down to him still rubbing, appearing charming, peering up at him from under the towel and laughing. She started impulsively for the hall, the strength of her wish fooling her into believing she was that girl, but even before the doorway, she recoiled. "Oh, I *can't*. I'm *not*."

She could see from the window that he was out with the boys in the stable yard. While she watched, mesmerized and indecisive, she saw him thrust out a large arm and point downward with a long finger. What was he telling them?

She whirled back into the middle of the room. She must dress. He would go. He would go before she was dressed. Her hair was still too wet for her to put on a blouse; the collar would become soggy. Oh, how like a nightmare, that nightmare of being in the center of a wide, wide plain where legs wade through heavy sand, painfully, painfully, through sand too heavy for human legs to bear. She stamped with frustration; her legs *weren't* impeded but then the nightmare changed, easily, into the one of the closet full of dresses, a whole colored rackful, but when one by one they are snatched down and tried on, they won't *go* on; there is something hideously wrong with every one; maybe they have no buttons; maybe their necks

[174]

are sewed fast. But this wasn't nightmare; this was reality and reality was proving itself worse than the dream, because she cared more.

Of course he would wait—oh, but he wouldn't, he wouldn't. She did not know that if she had had other men friends she would not have felt so wild, up in her room, at the possible departure of this one even though this one was the one she loved. A little more experience would have distilled for her now, as she tweaked again at her recalcitrant hair, a little more courage and resourcefulness, a little more belief in her own ability now that she had caught his interest to retain it, even if she couldn't manage to get downstairs within the next five minutes.

A tooth snapped in the comb and she threw it across the room.

She ran to the bureau and pulled open the drawers, looking wildly for a blouse with no collar, for a perfectly beautiful sweater, for anything at all that she could put on in no time at all and appear before him tall and calm, well-dressed and gently smiling—smiling the sly, gay smile of the Venetian virgin.

Jacob Miller, his knees trembling and his mouth dry, was planning to get his whole future settled between ten and ten-thirty that morning. It ought to be perfectly simple, he told himself. Perhaps because he hadn't read enough novels, but largely esoteric tomes relevant to his work, it didn't occur to him that telling her of his existing marriage would surprise or shock Edith; it didn't shock him; it merely, at this late date, irritated him that he had, once, succumbed to a pretty face; she might be impatient with him, and annoyed, but he was so often impatient and annoyed at himself; he could explain he didn't know himself how it had happened; he had been lonely, and Selma was so pretty and eager, and childlike. Friendly too, and he hadn't had much of that. His uppermost feeling this morning aside from the feeling of drought in his mouth was that he must tell Edith in order to clear up the situation preliminary to saying he wanted to marry her as soon as he was free. Whether that would be before or after he went abroad to study, if he went, he did not know; Selma could probably arrange to get a divorce in a few weeks. He thought he would clear his way with Edith in much the way he was accustomed to go over, carefully but quickly, false conclusions drawn by early scholars, mistaken concepts, deductions drawn by the light of insufficient data, before he settled down to make sure he arrived at the truth.

At quarter of ten he appeared beside the brick cathedral and stood looking down on it. Nobody felt it necessary to say anything for a while, except for the ubiquitous "Hi," which has become the universal greeting throughout the civilized world, between child and child, shopping matron and friendly butcher, soldier and sailor, tinker and tailor and, who knows, probably bishop and bishop, if mutually well-disposed. The breeze was tossing itself around high up in the feathery part of the elms; George paused, looked up as though he had heard something, remembered something; he laid aside the brick he had been about to employ, got up off his haunches and ran from the courtyard around the corner, to listen and peer and assure himself that the harp, which he had not thought of since right after breakfast, was still there. He was prey to a recurrent nervous fear that some irresponsible cat, prowling about in the trees, might take a fancy to his lovely toy and unhook it with a nimble paw; warning Lentenor that this might

[176]

happen had partly calmed him; Lentenor would know what to do about cats, but it seemed to him now that the voice that came down to him was a reproachful whisper. "Never mind," he called up. "We'll be home day after day after day after tomorrow."

"She's gone to New York." Lucius offered Jacob this good news without looking up from his work.

"M-mn. I thought there was something different about Evergreen Avenue this morning." He pointed downward to the cathedral. "You know, your transept," he began, but faltered in the sudden beaming light of Lucius' raised face. Nothing was more obvious than that Lucius was perfectly satisfied with what he was doing. If anything in this world was irreproachable and lovely, it was his cathedral. So Jacob cleared his throat as though that were all he had meant to do anyway, and the hand with the long admonitory pedagogical pointing finger went back into the pocket of his dark jacket. "Where is *she?*" he asked and there was no need, this time either, to particularize. But Lucius couldn't say where she was. "In, maybe. Out. I don't know." Then he held his breath, setting a brick on the highest course of the northwest corner.

In the morning room Mr. Howe curried his gray goatee between thumb and finger, said, "Er-rumph," decisively, though there was no one by to attend to any words of wisdom he might be clearing the way for, and snapped open the morning paper with a fine free snap. Seldom enough did he have a chance at the paper so early in the day; usually his sister kept it beside her, folded, while she went over her mail, and not until that had been attended to to her entire satisfaction, would she change to a chair by the window and open the *Times;* and not until long after that was it Mr. Howe's turn. This morning she had left the

[177]

house even before the mailman had arrived; by now she must have bought and gone over a copy in the train with, this time, less attention to what Tito might be up to than the column "Household Situations Wanted—Female," and at this moment must be locked in equal combat with the director of the agency in New York.

Mr. Howe was glad to think that now, for once, he would be able to bring the full weight of his mind to bear on international affairs without disturbance, and, too, without the inhibition he felt most mornings—that Clara had already read all about them and digested their significance and in a way *tended to them,* so there wasn't much use for him to puzzle his mind. Clara, they both recognized, was a woman who, given a perfectly free hand, could easily and neatly have redded up in Europe. He hoped she would be able to prevail on the nearer-at-hand battlefield of an employment agency and obtain a cook. He snapped the paper once more, for pure pleasure. Then, before his still-straying attention had quite had time to flutter down and settle itself to the printed word, through the back window of the morning room he saw Jacob Miller coming up the path from the stable. Now what on earth was that young man doing here, so early in the morning? China was being rapidly overrun by Communists and Franco had just said something outrageous, but Franco must wait while Mr. Howe found out what on earth Jacob had come for. Clearing his throat again, "Er-rumph," like an aggrieved beaver whose valuable working time is being encroached on, he struggled up and went to the side door. Czech problems too must wait.

"Looking for something?" he inquired from the top step. The question sounded faintly unpleasant, more so than he had meant it to; Mr. Howe had not a large emotional range to his voice. But he did not regret what he believed to be his firmness with the wandering young man; he believed himself to be usefully engaged if he discouraged him from coming in, and now he was no longer a beaver but a trusty house-dog. He saw Jacob, not so much as his own possible son-in-law but rather as "that young man Clara seems to dislike so." In her absence, he defended the fort. Well, what *did* the young man think he was up to? There was no need to be too unpleasant; one might as well find out. "Not teaching?" he suggested, conversationally, making matters no better.

Jacob Miller, on the red pebble path, looked up. His reason refused to accept the fact that this thin pompous fellow, surely the last of God's creatures he had planned or wanted to encounter this pristine morning, could be any connection of Edith's. He made the mistake of attributing the growing weakness in his knees to a justifiable scorn. "It isn't like grade school, you know," he replied, rudely. "We don't teach from nine to three. I have one class today." He looked past Mr. Howe to the open door but there was no one there, no cap of smooth gold hair, no swinging blue or green skirt. After I marry Edith, he thought, we must arrange never to see this old man again.

"Nice work if you can get it." Poor Mr. Howe had somewhere heard or read this neat little comment and had been treasuring it up to use some likely moment, which the unfortunate fellow now supposed, wrongly, to have arrived. He expected Jacob to laugh and agree, but such a glance of contempt shot from the dark eyes that Mr. Howe pressed the *Times* defensively, with all its little black headlines upside down, close against his chest, and nervously he ejaculated, "Er-rumph?" as if he hadn't heard what he himself had said.

[179]

"On a barbarian helmet of the Fifth Century, now in the Metropolitan; copper, gilded," Jacob persisted, as if by being very explicit he could hurt Mr. Howe. . . . What do you know about the wonderful barbarians, or the Fifth Century or even the Twentieth Century, for that matter, or any other! He would have been furious if Mr. Howe had attempted to answer. "I want to see Edith." He was abrupt with concern.

"Oh." Mr. Howe turned and peered in at the open doorway. "But maybe she's gone out. Probably has."

"Would it be possible to find out?" Jacob shouldn't have have let his voice sound so impertinently polite; it further annoyed the beaver with the grievance who said sulkily that he didn't know *where* she was. They stood in a sun-drenched deadlock. Jacob would have done well to make an ally of Mr. Howe instead of an enemy; he might have been useful in many little ways, and it would have been such fun for him, who occasionally went so far as to mutter to himself, "Blamed bossy, though," right after having agreed with someone who had said what a wonderful woman his sister was, wonderful. . . . For Jacob on the red path, all the delight and the terror, which had been half-delight too, had fled from the morning. He hadn't known enough to be as apprehensive as he should have been about telling Edith of his marriage; he had looked forward to seeing her; the simple sight of her would have had a quieting, miraculous effect on him; her pleasure in being with him was always quite apparent to him, and it released his own pent-up gentleness, causing it to flow like a beneficent lava over all his angularities of spirit, his irritations and discords, covering them, melting them into nothing, into tranquillity. Oh, but this old man! . . . He

[180]

hated this old man who was so dull and obstructive. How could weak stubbornness prove so powerful? Why wouldn't the old fool *at least lean into the house and call her?* But he wouldn't; he wasn't going to. . . . It was like dealing with a man of soap.

In the house the sound of a telephone bell like a thin, dark, darting bird, flew through the hall. "Well, I'll just see to that," Mr. Howe said with brisk relief; on stiff quick legs he hurried in, shutting the door on Jacob, who cursed the telephone, that tool of modern tragedy. Lingering on the red path he thought, sadly, how, these days it is not the dagger nor the poisoned cup nor the treacherous blow, but in its effect partaking of the lethalness of all three today it is the telephone we must dread, or, equally, how it dispenses blessed relief in, "I am safe at home now, Mother. Good night," or "It's not pneumonia after all," or "I'll be at the house in ten minutes." There is no predicting the mood one will find the telephone in. Oh, he thought, the malevolence of one answered too soon, snatched up shrilling and shrilling like an unloved black canary and then, silence, snatched up before its first song was finished, and so it will not speak. . . . Nothing could have been of less significance than the message from a lending library that Mr. Howe was now taking, but the mere ringing had cut off Jacob from what little human contact he had with the house and had deprived him of what he felt to be his only chance to find Edith. He had wasted valuable minutes; he waited a few more; Mr. Howe did not reappear; Edith might never have been born.

Angrily he hurried back down the path to the stable yard. He would make one of the boys find her. What a household! Not content with their own manifest shortcomings what did they feel it reasonable to do but import two children, two boys of the most sorry ignorance, two boys who *did not even know which end of a cathedral to put the transept!* At least he could have the pleasure of disconcerting them by telling them of their ludicrous mistake. He strode into the courtyard—and both boys had gone. His eyes darted everywhere, but they were gone. The enchanting orange-pink cathedral waited in the sunshine for its roof and various other finishing touches. Nothing moved in the courtyard but a line of ants traveling up one side of a mountain of red sand and down the other. They tramped steadily; perhaps, in some unguessable way, they were at work, under contract to Lucius on some job connected with the building; their employer was away, but still they toiled faithfully; overtime, possibly.

Tom, the gardener, wheeled his barrow full of empty flower pots along the path from the greenhouse; he paused beside the pile of bricks.

"Some church," he said with admiration.

"An adumbration, certainly."

"Ha, ha. My, that's good," said Tom, who didn't get it. "Smart, ain't they?"

"Not so very smart." Jacob's voice was cold. He thrust a long finger downward. "If you will look at it," he suggested, "you will see they have built their transept at the wrong end." He might have had a pointer in his hand and be calling the attention of his class at the University to laughable blunders made by some inept restorer. He gave a short, unamused laugh that struck Tom as the epitome of sophistication.

"Well, my God, so they did!" He trundled away with his load. "Whatever a transept is," he amended, under his breath. "What difference, which end?" Then, with more

[182]

assurance, he spoke to his barrow. "Upsy-daisy!" He guided the front wheel up over the low wooden ridge at the edging of a path; it wouldn't do to break any more empty flower pots; Mrs. Fanning had been mad yesterday when he told her he'd need a couple of dozen new ones when he cleaned out the greenhouse for the Summer.

12

MRS. CANTY-MALLET swept to her place at the table and half-unfolding her napkin draped it across her lap, flung her fingers together in a laced-up peak and rested her elbows either side of her plate. "What fun!" she said. "*That's* new. When did you get that?" She detached a finger from the peak and waved it toward the Recusants' épergne, which the exigencies of the domestic situation had prevented anyone from removing to the pantry and swaddling in its maroon flannel bag.

Lucius peered around at her soberly from the other side of the table, from rather low down around the massive silver thing; so Mrs. Fanning's New York cousin thought it was a lark to visit in Evergreen Avenue, did she? Lucius could only suppose either that she had never been there before in all her life, or that she wasn't in for as long a stay as his had to be.

"There I was this afternoon at the glove counter at Bonwit's," Mrs. Canty-Mallet declared, almost as though her presence at that particular spot had been a supernatu-

ral occurrence over which she had had no control whatever, or as though she had turned up there while sleep-
walking, "and whom should I see but Clara!" This story
was directed toward the foot of the table, Mrs. Canty-
Mallet being the truly admirable type of woman whose
first tenet is: Amuse the men. She was very different from
her cousins; a stranger would scarcely have believed one
family tree could have ripened three such diverse characters. Mrs. Canty-Mallet's second tenet happened to be:
Why spare expense? and on this foundation she had established a splendid little interior decorating business. She
beamed at Mr. Howe over her laced-up fingers and waited
for him to express amusement, but he said only, ah yes,
well, because nothing prevented him from accepting the
bare facts of the described encounter—the glove counter,
the navy blue suède gloves emerging from their tissue
paper sheathes for Mrs. Canty-Mallet's inspection, the sudden realization of the two cousins, who had not seen each
other for months, or was it years, that they were standing
side by side. "Well," he said, "that was nice."

So he never heard about the delighted cries of recogni-
tion, the exclamations, the long course of persuasion ad-
ministered by Mrs. Fanning to Mrs. Canty-Mallet while
the glove clerk drooped and wilted behind the counter—
Mrs. Canty-Mallet had a two-button six and one-quarter
on her left hand which was elegantly if lifelessly suspended
in air by her left elbow resting on a round yellow velvet pad
and the clerk had thought she couldn't just walk off and
leave her—and he never learned how, in spite of a thousand reasons why it was impossible, Mrs. Canty-Mallet had
been persuaded to come back with her cousin for the night,
nor about the all-at-once total rejection of anything at all
that the clerk had to offer in navy blue suède, the return

to the Canty-Mallet apartment for an overnight case, the amusing note to Mr. Canty-Mallet left propped against his cocktail shaker, nor the fifty-mile ride up from New York on the train, during which Mrs. Fanning had urged her sister to try out Edith—why not?—in the vacancy now existing in her decorating shop.

"She's a rather *heavy* girl, you know," she had said. "If you know what I mean. Oh, but dependable, yes, I am sure, once she's interested. The trouble with her now is she's not interested in anything. Ella Wagstaff's boy—well, he's over thirty actually, I guess—he's been hanging around for years. He'll have all old Joe Wagstaff's money some day, but she won't look at him. It isn't as though I haven't tried to make her. But with you, I don't see why she wouldn't be quite useful. I don't see why you don't try her, at any rate. How long since you've seen her, actually?" And Mrs. Canty-Mallet had said, even before the train pulled away from Bridgeport, that she didn't see why she didn't either, though she actually hadn't seen her since before she was in college. What was there to be lost by trying, they had inquired of each other, reasonably.

"Well, so here I am!" was all Mrs. Canty-Mallet said, finally. Forrest hadn't changed much; she had almost forgotten how impervious he was to charm. Unlacing her fingers, darting a gay wasted smile at Mr. Howe and almost at the same instant a speculative glance at Edith, her possible future assistant, she picked up her soup spoon.

The cousins, though brought up together, were most unlike. Whereas Mrs. Fanning was as erect as a slender post Mrs. Canty-Mallet, pliant and accommodating, bent and swayed. Her clients always came away with the impression that they had had their own way. She wore becoming colors and was without any of Mrs. Fanning's conviction that she was, in any large, civic sense, her brother's keeper. Only a year and a half, from 1885 to 1887, had intervened between their arrival on this earth but perhaps even in long lawn dress and crocheted sacque the elder's character had been apparent and Providence, a trifle contrite at having ladled so much rectitude into one Howe had thought it best to equalize matters in the family by omitting it entirely from the future Mrs. Canty-Mallet. Not but what she wasn't kindness itself; indeed, that was what her friends always said: "Callie Canty-Mallet is kindness itself." "But I never could care terribly about quorums," she had once exasperated her elder cousin by saying.

"Guess who I saw in Sloane's yesterday," she said now, laying down her spoon and dodging the ponderous approach of Anna with a plate. *"Bessie* Bostwick. From my class at Farmington," she said for the benefit of Mr. Howe who, somehow, as ill luck would have it, had never managed to accumulate enough money to send Edith to boarding school.

"Oh, Bessie was in my class." Mrs. Fanning smiled across the table. "You've forgotten. She roomed right down the hall. Macauley is her name now."

"I know it's Macauley." Now they were both smiling; each adjusted herself, upward, within her expensive girdle, neither would ever capitulate. It was not that they both, nor indeed that either of them, cherished the memory of Bessie Bostwick as a girl; asked the color of her eyes, to avoid death at the stake, they couldn't have said, and during the forty-five years intervening between the sad, beautiful rites of daisies and ivies and farewell and the present she had led a blameless life in faraway Minneapolis unrecalled by either cousin. However, having renewed a claim in her by having encountered her buying bath mats in Sloane's, Mrs. Canty-Mallet felt she was hers—oh, not that it *mattered!* Heavens! . . . But Mrs. Fanning, fastidiously moving a salt celler a quarter of an inch to the south said, "I perfectly well remember all the trouble I had to get her to contribute to the collection for the Ladies' Aid. At the Congregational Church," she added, summoning up as a bulwark to her falsehood the vision of the white solid structure of the church building set immovable and eternal on its green sloping hill. But at that Mrs. Canty-Mallet pounced, triumphantly.

"Ha! That proves it, proves my point. You were picked to collect from the new girls because you were so *firm.* Don't you remember? You *terrified* them into giving."

Mrs. Fanning made a "tt-tt-tt" sound with her tongue and teeth, deprecating this tribute to her coercive powers. "Eat your rice, boys," she said. It might have surprised the cousins if an impartial statistician had been there to read them off the facts—that Bessie Bostwick had been a member of the class between the two Howe girls, that she had contributed more than generously to the Ladies' Aid at the instigation of her roommate and that her married name was Merriman; it might have surprised them or it might not. Both were so steeped in a belief of the worth of social amenities, both so nimble at leaping, verbally or in the mind, from bank to convenient bank over the little crystal rills of the simple truth, that they weren't surprised at much of anything any more. Any anecdote was true, to them, if it had artistic integrity; it didn't need to bear a too boringly close resemblance to fact.

"She's had rather an interesting life, Bessie," said Mrs. Fanning thoughtfully, for a parting shot; one would have said she had had a letter cosily packed with details from

[188]

her within the month, though the fact was that neither of them had heard one word nor thought one thought about Bessie Bostwick since the day, in response to thick white engraved summonses, they had clubbed together and sent a pierced silver tomato lifter to Minneapolis. "If you don't like it," she said suddenly, turning on George, "put butter on it."

"Did you get hold of a cook?" Mr. Howe asked.

"I did indeed." Mrs. Fanning reared her shoulders back even straighter, remembering the outcome of her morning's campaign. "I certainly did. I found out long ago you simply have to insist, with agencies."

"Oh—" Edith said in a small voice, but before she could continue George demanded to know when the new cook was coming, and if she were any pleasanter than Catherine, and Mr. Howe too looked up with interest, because if anyone had asked him point-blank he would have said he was very, very sorry but he was afraid he couldn't say much for tonight's dinner, Anna's cooking, not having observed that what he was eating were delicious specimens left over from the dinner party, left-overs, to be sure, but of such high quality as he seldom encountered fresh. So, knowing one can't expect good cooking from a chambermaid-waitress, he believed he wasn't having a very good dinner. His palate, if he had such a thing, hung useless and told him nothing. "Let's hope she comes soon," he said with a patient sigh.

Mrs. Fanning gathered up her mouth into a warning *moue* and glanced sideways at Lucius and George. She had thought it better, inconvenient and uncomfortable though it made matters, to delay the advent of the new cook until after they had gone on Tuesday. "Very soon," she said.

[189]

"Oh!" came from Edith again, more faintly, but then in a guilty rush, "Oh, I meant to tell you right away but I was busy." (You were thinking about Jacob, her heart reminded her.) "But *Catherine* called up and she said she wanted to come back."

"*All that way to New York for nothing!* . . . I shall have to consider . . . I am not at all sure I should want her back. . . . I am surprised, I must say!" Though Mrs. Fanning did not know it, her surprise was as nothing to the satisfaction and surprise of Catherine herself, who had routed the milliner by a bold frontal attack and was once more the only woman in the brakeman's heart.

"Well, not all that way for nothing *really*," Mrs. Canty-Mallet said amiably, paying no attention to her cousin's further diminuendo exclamations of uncertainty and amazement. "Edith, my dear, what would you think of coming to New York to help me in the shop? I shouldn't pay you a frightfully large amount to begin with, but enough to live on and you'd have fun. It's really tremendous fun," she said energetically. "Have you ever been to my little place?"

"No," Edith answered miserably. "No, I haven't, ever." But clear and sharp and three-dimensional before her inward eye the shop materialized—the bolts of white materials by the yard, expensively nubby, the *prie-dieu* made into a telephone table, the cobblers' benches turned into coffee tables with the ubiquitous interloper ivy flourishing in the nail wells, lamps ingeniously made out of old flower pots and flower pots made out of old lamps; not too much of any one thing, because this was a small, quite special shop; the old French wallpaper made into fans and the old French fans made into screens, the modest pewter lavabo that once had served a humble God-fearing family of Swiss peasants in the Engadine for washing their hands before supper now

[190]

destined to drip ferns and philodendron in some East 86th Street penthouse. She saw herself, one hip thrown out, holding up a bolt of white stuff for somebody to look at. How tired her feet would get, how bad for her figure to stand like that . . . but Mrs. Canty-Mallet was waiting, smiling at her over the épergne, holding a green grape in one hand and a triangle of Bel Paese cheese in the other.

"Well, think about it tonight. Let me know in the morning."

Mrs. Fanning said she hoped Edith realized what a wonderful opportunity this offer was and actually, wasn't it just what Edith had been waiting and hoping for *all these years?* But Edith, who wanted only to escape to her room upstairs, to be away from their startling plans for her and their shocking assumption that she would fall in with them —she wanted to be alone and not consider them, but have the evening to herself in order to train under the ends of her hair so it would look right tomorrow, Jacob having telephoned right after Catherine and asked her to accompany him to a lecture. She could say, only, "Oh, oh yes. It sounds wonderful. I don't know."

"Perhaps she's in love?" Mrs. Canty-Mallet asked charitably, when Edith had fled up the stairs. "She seems almost witless. Some local boy?"

"*Nobody.*" Mrs. Fanning was emphatic. She sent Lucius upstairs to bring Edith back, an exasperated arrow of a look between the shoulder blades of the retreating girl having failed to halt her.

When he got up to her room Lucius couldn't find her. She had gone down the back stairs to the kitchen to get vinegar with which to dampen the ends of her hair and train them under while crouching in her room before the hot copper sun of the electric heater. She could kill two

[191]

birds that evening, if left alone; she could give way once again to the terrible preoccupation with her hair of a young woman newly in love and she could read the published poems of the *avant-garde* poet who was tomorrow's lecturer. Jacob had sounded distraught over the telephone. "I want to talk to you," he had said, but surely he wouldn't talk while a poet read. She found the vinegar bottle in the brief moment Anna was in the pantry pouring coffee into the little pot, and she carried it back upstairs with her. Maybe Anna expected her to help with the dishes but why couldn't Tom's rather slovenly wife who shared with him the apartment upstairs in the stable have been persuaded to come in and help? With the sublime and almost impersonal and very necessary selfishness of her condition, Edith turned her back on Anna and sped off upstairs to spend the next hour on herself.

The two cousins linked arms and went along to the drawing room. Just as they got through the door Mrs. Canty-Mallet, remembering something, slid out her arm, drew back, and asked reproachfully, "Why on earth did you tell the Charlie Penroses you studied music in Brussels before you were married?"

"The Penroses? Sit there. It's more comfortable than it looks. Over here, Anna, please, with the coffee. Thank you." She returned her attention to the occupant of the ginger-brown satin slipper chair. "The Penroses?" she said again. "Sugar, or not?"

"Yes, please. Well, you did. I met Martha Penrose at the Cos Club one day last Winter and she told me all about what you'd told her about the Winter we spent in Belgium after boarding school and how a Dutch nobleman had threatened to jump in the Zuider Zee unless you married him. When he went home, I mean." She suspended her little spoon above her little cup and eyed her cousin indignantly. "That was *me*," she said.

"Oh, well," Mrs. Fanning carefully slid two lumps of sugar into Forrest Howe's cup. "Here you are, Forrest. Careful; don't spill. I don't remember telling the Penroses all that, though I did see them somewhere at dinner. I'm sure I must have said it happened to you. What does it matter!"

How party-broken they both were; this was not an unpleasantness, being by no means the first time one had taken the other to account for appropriating her own experiences to fill out a social moment. They had done that, blandly, all their lives. At times one had even lent the other support in public, if one of them launched on a story that rightly belonged to the other and, though suddenly becoming aware of what she was doing, had worked up too much momentum to stop. The only basis for subsequent criticism was when the story had not been well told. Quite firmly at boarding school, they had never lent each other clothes. Stockings and shirtwaists and jackets with soutache braid they kept a jealous guard over but the almost classic anecdote about what the stranger in a kilt said to Callie on a Fifth Avenue bus at dusk, the account of the walking trip in the rain in Italy, the story of the governess who would whip a corset bone from behind her skirt band to switch Clara, the story about the Italian inn-keeper who, when confronted with a fly in Callie's soup said, "It's good. Meat!" and "Ah, the end of the season!" when a phonograph needle turned up in her salad—all these were in the public domain and it is not surprising that now, sipping her coffee, Mrs. Fanning did not take Mrs. Canty-Mallet very seriously. "What was his name?" she asked.

"Whose?"

"That Dutchman, the one who was in love with me . . . you."

Then Mrs. Canty-Mallet had to stare far away across the room, and ponder. "Honestly," she said at last, "I can't for the life of me remember. Didn't I tell you at the time?"

"I'm not so sure you ever told me anything about him at all." Faint reproof floated in her voice, a shadow, an echo of a forty-year grievance she might have had at being kept in the dark.

"Must have. Would you have suddenly heard about him just lately, and told the Penroses?"

"Oh. Yes, I see. Well . . . possibly not. But I don't know that you ever told me his name. *Where is that child?*"

Whether it was Lucius she meant or Edith, neither of them appeared from the hall. How very, very stupid of Edith if she lost this chance at a perfectly good, an unusually good, job. Mrs. Fanning had no patience with Edith. Mrs. Fanning had been in her cousin's shop and in her mind's eye she saw it now, not at all unlike what Edith had seen, and she was easily able to visualize Edith there, Edith becomingly dressed in a pink linen smock coming forward to wait on the young man who, next month, next year, would enter, diffident, diffident but rich, to get a swatch of cherry-colored chintz for his mother. Or ball-fringe—oh, the possibilities were endless!

13

THE clippers whizzed upward on George's skinny neck, in and out of the artless groove that betrayed his extreme youth, and at their insane electric whine George's eyes grew bigger and bigger. Years ago, home in Sharon, their barber had fought a losing battle with their mother and now hid away the clippers in a cupboard the minute he saw her push open his door, but *this man . . . !* They're his favorite thing, George said to himself. His reflection, tiny, and conically white, had only his surprised head that was recognizable and even that to his increasingly concerned gaze was rapidly being transformed into the head of a stranger. Lucius was far away, three chairs down the row, so far away he might as well not have been there at all for all the help he was giving his brother, and from what George could see in the long mirror by rolling the eyes in his rigid face, Lucius too was being shorn within an inch of his life, but he was smiling. George thought with bitter accuracy, "He thinks he's going to look like Mr. Buongiorno." Lucius had always wanted a crew cut. Once, at home, he had confided to George during that very private and satisfactory hour at the end of the day when one of them parboiled slowly in the tub, playing with the soap, and the other, perched high and saintlike on the water-closet, dreamed and swung his legs, and neither took any thought for the morrow—"Oh, George," Lucius had then said in a confidential burst, "I wish I had black hair like the other guys and a long face." But probably Lucius would never have a long face; his wide square thoughtful brow precluded it and there wasn't much hope his straw-colored hair would ever be very dark; he'd be bald first, George had pointed out and Lucius had replied that nothing would please him more, the sooner the better—no more brushing.

Now, as near as George could tell, Lucius was getting the haircut of his life. Great haylike trusses on the floor ringed the chair where he sat but Mr. Howe, who had been pre-vailed on to walk the boys downtown and put them up, as it were, at his own barber's, was sunk behind the morning paper in a leather chair at the back of the shop and re-mained oblivious to what was happening to his charges. George sighed deeply. It wasn't that he objected to being made to look like an infant thug; he rather admired the effect, but the creeping, insistent clippers that sent a tremor like cold moth's feet all over him, kept rising and sinking in the perpetual question: *E-e-e-e-e what will your mother say when she-e-e-e-e sees you?*

He recalled the morning the previous Summer when the family had been visiting near New London and their mother had driven them to a barber shop in a hotel. Hastily, because there was no place to park, she had fished in her purse, given them money, and pushed them gently out the car door. "You go on in," she had said. "I'll be back as soon as I find a parking place. Remember, not

[196]

too short." They had started for the curb and she had leaned out, even while driving away, and called, "Not short at all!" Then she must have had a hard time finding somewhere to put the car because she hadn't reappeared for quite a while, but when she did come in at the door her eyes widened with horror and she swept up to the barber who was zealously exposing the very occipital bones of the hapless boy in the chair while enough light hair to stuff a mattress was falling steadily to the tiled floor. "No, no, *no!*" their mother had cried in anguish and in the same instant had met the calm mirrored gaze of a perfectly unknown little boy. George and Lucius, lightly trimmed, had long finished and were reading *Life* and *Time* in a corner. Lucius had laughed all the way home but George had been sorry for his mother, and he was again sorry for her, now, when he looked at his reflection.

Mr. Howe roused up when they got down from their chairs, inquired, incredibly, if they had both been tended to, thanked the barbers and tipped them in moderation. On a lower level the boys inspected each other, saying nothing. Lucius' head revealed itself to be even larger than his family had imagined and George's, all at once, to be far smaller. Horridly white skulls showed through the short hair, like plastic skulls, and there was a whiteness around all the edges that made the first tender Spring tan on their faces and necks look like a film of dirtiness.

"Jumping Jesus," Lucius whispered into George's all-at-once prominent ear, "you look like a pin."

Meanwhile Edith, that Saturday morning, was crouched in the mild copper glow of her electric heater and reading by its tawny light the poems she would, in Jacob's company, their shoulders touching, hear reread this afternoon

[197]

by their creator; with her free hand, delicately and precisely, she reversed nature, accomplishing that bending-under of the tips of her vinegar drenched hair from which she had been prevented by her aunt the previous evening. She tipped her head to receive the copper-colored warmth.

> ... nor our precarious tenderness let fall
> fall into winter in despite of this ...

Concentrating on the difficult poetry she was able to blot from her mind the memory of last evening—of Lucius having been sent to find her, of her caching the vinegar bottle in her medicine chest in case she could get back to her room in time to use it, of the inconclusive triangular conversation in the drawing room, one leg of it Mrs. Canty-Mallet's account of the joys and endeavors and rewards of an interior decorator's life, one leg the assurances by Mrs. Fanning that she had never heard of such a lucky girl as Edith and the remaining leg of the conversation Edith's own, a limp leg, all uncertainties and somewhat irritably expressed gratitude. Why *now?* Why this lovely week in April of all the other weeks of her life must she have to decide about going to work?

Somewhere far away from the domain established by the poem she was reading, the telephone rang; let someone else go, anyone else, someone who wasn't in love with Jacob Miller. She turned a page, not sure whether she would find over there more of the poem she was reading or whether she had finished it. It was hard to tell, with this poet; punctuation would have helped. Apparently there was another page to this one. The man seemed unable to end his works with any predictability. No one could have gone on writing after "the fall of death," but with this man there was never any assurance, no clue even, that the end was approaching. She turned back and started the poem again; obsessed with the belief she must wrest a meaning from it she attempted, by clotting the words together differently from the way she had first read them, by experimentally inserting commas here and there, to wring meaning from the proud ragged column of print. She gave it her whole mind, except for the part that speculated on what she would wear to the lecture, and how her hair was coming along . . . what if she sometime tried to make it fluffy like the Venetian bride? . . . and what if Mrs. Fanning had ordered salad for luncheon and the vinegar could not be found? Their shoulders would touch during the lecture, the olive-green tweed and the dark cloth, not all the time—sometimes—touch and then move apart and then deliciously touch again, as shoulders do at a time like that, without either owner having to admit, even to himself: I did it that time; that time I was the one who moved.

"fall into winter" ". . . fall"

she read again. How about a comma after the first "fall"? She tried it, scowling with zeal.

Anna came climbing up the front stairs and lumbered through the hall. She knew she should not have had to answer the telephone now she was doing Catherine's work as well as her own, but it did give her something to think about and occasionally, except with Mrs. Fanning, it could lead to a nice chat. She turned in at Edith's door. "Hello. Miller, he say he vurry sorry about this afternoon."

"What about it!" Edith stared up, stricken, one cheek in shadow, one burning in the rays of the copper sun. Anna, maintaining her V-shaped stance, was polite, but detached from the girl's fright; though herself a spinster she was unaware that the news she carried was tragic.

"He says, he can't go to the party this afternoon."

"Not a party, a lecture." Anxiety made her quibble and sharpened her voice.

"Vell. Votever." Anna ran a finger along her colorless lips and continued on to trap up, but casually, uselessly, the random ever-escaping strands of colorless hair above an ear.

"Why not?"

"Shange his mind, most likely." She gave a cackle of unconcerned laughter that cut a jagged slice into Edith's heart. "It might you go anyvay widdout'm." How the girl reacted to this practical advice it was impossible to tell because she dropped her eyes to the meaningless poem in her lap, to the silly, futile, antagonistic words marching so arrogantly on the white page. What she saw was the interior decorating shop, yawning wide for her.

"Did he sound sick?"

"Nott-a-bitt."

"I see."

All she would have to do was telephone Mrs. Canty-Mallet, a thirty-five cent call, and her future would be accounted for, wrapped up, tied up with ribbon, and thrown away. Did he believe she sat waiting in Evergreen Avenue without anything to do, waiting for him to take notice of her? This was so exactly the case it is wonderful she dared to look so haughty and so misused, kneeling there before her round light. She couldn't have looked any haughtier if she had had an actual grievance against him. She felt she must treat him as though she had. In her humiliation she didn't stop to ask herself whether going to work in a New York shop was the inevitable solution

[200]

but she supposed, sadly, because things so seldom turned out right for her, that it must be. Her hands lay inert on the closed book; what good was poetry?

"Vell." Anna turned slowly on her gunboat slippers; there wasn't going to be a nice chat after all. She trundled away. She climbed down the steep back stairs as though she were climbing down a mountain path, with stones and rocks and juniper alongside; at the landing halfway down she recalled that Miller's exact words; he had said to tell Miss Howe he was very, very sorry about the lecture, but something had come up, but would she meet him tomorrow outside the door of the closed Museum at five. The urgency in his voice she had not heard at all. "Vell, I did so tell her he was vurry sorry. . . . Soch steep stairs!" Anna said. Should she go back now, or later? She was far enough down to smell the cabbage that was beginning to stew when she had gone to answer the telephone. She stood a moment, one hand on the round rail, but then she decided, comfortably, not to go back up again. "It might he call again." She could hear cabbage bubbling by now, and indeed when she reached the stove the lid of the saucepan was hopping on one side and an irritable scum of froth was coming out the crack. "Yoost like a frawg," she said aloud, remembering Småland in Spring, and a pond, and herself a little girl in a blue dress standing on the edge. Her childhood was always quite near and un-clouded to Anna, and lovely to remember. "A big fine fat frawg, yoost like," she said, and bent a little and turned the gas flame lower.

Jacob sat motionless at the desk in the medieval cell watching the black crouching telephone as if it were a live treacherous little animal; his right hand was ready on the desk, longing in every muscle to fly out and subdue the animal the instant it gave evidence of life and spoke.

He had hurried downtown that morning from his boarding house, leaving breakfast only partly eaten, in order to get to the telephone in his office. He had wakened early with a jerk in the uncomfortable boarding-house bed, wide awake right away, and bitter with the sleep-brought question why he had not told Selma to answer his special delivery letter to her with a wire. He could not understand why he had not thought to tell her this; perhaps only five days ago, before he had written, his desire for an answer had been less urgent. Now it had become the most important problem in the world, dwarfing his uncertainty about his trip to Europe, with, it now appeared to him, the only solution to his cutting anxiety a direct talk with her by telephone, the urging of her to do his will. He had leapt up the shallow stone steps of the Museum to his office on the top floor, not even able to leap as fast as he wished, prey to the nightmare feeling that heavy, inimical hands were trying to hold him back. . . . The operator had reported that Mrs. Selma Miller was not at home. "Keep trying her every twenty minutes," he said, "but don't call me unless you get her."

Remembering her day-long expeditions that were composed of unpredictable strayings in and out of beauty parlors and hotel grilles, and pauses before counters where costume jewelry was sold, and soda fountains, he became frantic.

The little black beast screamed suddenly and he had pounced before it was through. Its interior voice was a cool, singing one. "On your call to Fort Way-in . . ."

"*Yes.*"

"They still do not *ans*-er."

"I told you! Don't call me unless you get her!"

[202]

"Very we-ull," the singing voice agreed, and just before cutting the connection he humbled himself to say, "But she might come in unexpectedly." Unexpectedly to whom, he wondered as he laid back the instrument—to Selma? But that could hardly be, though some of her comings and goings had often appeared random ones. To the operator? But who could have cared less? To him, probably. "She might, perfectly well," he said, and it was on some such miracle that he set himself to count. Zing-zinging along the wires his prayer ran, across the country, to sound from the bedside table in the never-seen room Selma shared with another young woman, zing back to his wide desk where he could not begin his day's work, zing out to Mrs. Fanning's morning room, where Edith was, perhaps.

The telephone rang.

"On your call to Fort Way-in . . ."

"*Yes?*"

"The party will probably not be in until the middle of the afternoon. Will you speak with anyone else?"

"No, no. But keep trying every twenty minutes."

So he telephoned the Fanning house and told Anna he could not take Miss Howe to the lecture that afternoon at three. "But tell her . . . tell her to please meet me outside the Museum tomorrow, Sunday, at five," he had added without knowing he was going to. He was glad the minute he had said the words. Perhaps he was better able to manage his life than he had for so long been fearing. Some of the tenseness around his mouth relaxed. He had been confident that Anna was noting down every word.

He got up and idled about the room. There was another hour before he had to give a lecture on mosaics. He scowled, trying not to hear in imagination the insistent,

[203]

unanswered ringing he had set going in Selma's bedroom; someone must have been there, a few minutes ago. But not Selma. For hours, while she sat at a beauty parlor table, gazing critically, maddeningly slowly, at the skim of red enamel on her finger nails—"I don't know that I *do* like Flamingo so very much. Could you take it off and try Pink Lotus?" she would say in her sweet uncertain voice, to the girl in the white uniform—or stood on one foot, one hip jutting out against plate glass—"Candied chocolate cherries, or jellied chocolate mints, oh which shall I get?"—all this time the bell in her room would be ringing. "Mints or cherries? Cherries or mints?"; he had heard the question posed a hundred times one Winter, or similar ones.

He set the door of his room ajar and prepared to go down the hall to the lecture room; with the door open he might hear the telephone. No, he couldn't possibly. He saw that the door across from his was open and the instructor whose room it was bent over his desk. Jacob, under unwonted stress, forced himself to ask a favor, cross the hall and say, "Look, I'm expecting an important out-of-town call but I've got this damned lecture on Ravenna. Could you possibly call me if it rings? I'm sorry." He didn't sound sorry, merely irritable.

"Sure, sure." The young instructor had never liked Jacob but he had just, all by himself, hit on a perfectly tenable hypothesis about how Egyptian buttons were fastened to the cloth—if they *were* buttons. He was fairly convinced they were. "Sure, sure," he said again, his voice warm.

"Thanks." Jacob turned away, but the warm voice went on, "Though I may have to go out in five minutes or so myself."

[204]

Jacob prowled the dais in the lecture room, repeatedly stepping down to open the door to the hall which members of the assembling class kept closing as they entered; they looked at him with surprise; ordinarily he demanded it closed. The only young men who took this course were the ones who had to. When he lectured he frowned, and he was brusque with the stupid; he had been known to shout at a thoughtless question. They did not know that the only reason he taught was because it was a required concomitant to his curatorship. He would have much preferred to have the whole Museum to himself, free of all students and all other professors, to be able to walk the empty corridors with his hands behind his back, to speak aloud only to statues, his only housekeeping the rearranging of his cases of brooches and buckles, and blue and red and pearl enameled pins. It had surprised him to realize that he would like Edith to share these pleasures with him. As he now saw it, a perfect life would be for him and Edith to set up married life in a private Museum closed to the public.

"Leave the door *open!*"

He began to lecture to the two rows of men sprawled in varnished, lobster-clawed chairs. The light seemed too bright to him and he walked to the wall switch by the door and tripped it, but a moment later a conscientious myopic boy peered reproachfully up from his notebook and asked if there please couldn't be a little light because he was trying to copy a plan. Jacob slammed back the switch. Today he spoke haltingly, leaving himself intervals of silence in one of which he prayed he might hear his telephone begin to ring; the young men to their profit, utilized these pauses to amplify their notes. Usually he spoke so negligently and arrogantly that they missed half of what he said.

". . . their severely plain exteriors belying all the color and richness of the mosaics within . . . destruction over the centuries . . . so, even with all we still have we cannot help regretting the churches lost through neglect, battles, restorations." He paused, and listened. There was no sound at all from down the hall. How could he make it ring? By wanting, harder and harder and harder? Oh, it was intolerable a man had so little control over his own fate. . . . How many, many centuries of other human beings there had been and how little one knows about them; maybe they had been able to manage better; how little one knows about one's self. How many millions of little human plans and intentions had, merely by the passing of time, come to their conclusion, either joyous or awry. What a long way it was, he thought, out to Fort Wayne, how many miles and miles of telephone wire stretched between his desk and the Western city, filament shining in the sun across country, unconcerned birds perched on it, their tiny beaks exploring, probing, beneath wings; like the wires, the filament of Jacob's understanding stretched backward, straight and strong across the years to Theodoric. "Now, as to Theodoric," he said, "four-ninety-three to five-twenty-six." He described the activity there must have been in the marshes and the pine wood near the sea, the builders, carpenters, plasterers, stone masons and workers in mosaic who must have swarmed about the town like bees. The young men in tweeds could see it all plainly; the lecture room walls dissolved and they became themselves those men and felt the hot Italian sun on the back of their heads, and smelled white dust in their nostrils.

". . . until it was captured by Pippin, the king of the Franks. That's all for today."

"Pippin, k. Franks," wrote each young man, and stirred, and blinked, and sighed, and closed the notebook on his wooden lobster claw.

"Next week at this time," Jacob said, ending the best lecture he would ever give.

Next week at this time what more would he have learned about himself and his own future that he did not know now? He thought: I will know everything, by then, if I can only reach Selma soon and tell her to go ahead and get a divorce. He walked back along the corridor to his silent cell, tired, and wondering, and nervous. Even looking forward to meeting Edith by the closed iron grille of the Museum tomorrow had no power to help him.

14

THE haircuts were not thought well of in Evergreen Avenue. At the sight of them Mrs. Fanning reared back in her chair and exclaimed aloud and Anna paused in her dusting to say, "My God, yoost like liddle vet shickens!" Mr. Howe came in for no censure at the time. Not from prudence but simply through a streak of good fortune he had sent the boys home alone while he continued on downtown to buy himself three sets of Summer underwear, so the boys arrived, convict-shorn, without even the scant support he might have provided while he, plucking thoughtfully at the glossy tip of his imperial, was far away, deep in negotiations that might well absorb the whole of the remainder of the morning, involving as they did a prolonged bout of practical eclectics—should he get one-piece pure white nainsook or light-weight ribbed cotton knit; there was also striped broadcloth to consider and now, how about the French seat, eh? It wasn't shortening the process of his choice any to be aware, as he and the clerk both were, that in the end he would pick the old, familiar kind, the kind he always wore, the one-piece job in nainsook. The disapprobation he would inevitably come in for at home might become somewhat diluted by the passage of two intervening hours, but it wasn't only ignorance of the existence of this disapprobation that let him linger so long over striped shorts, blue and white, navy and white, maroon and cream; he was honestly trying to screw himself up to the audacity of buying the maroon and cream, but in the end, he couldn't.

George scowled at Mrs. Fanning. "How could we help it?"

"Hair, hair," Anna murmured, ruminatively, while her duster flicked over miniatures laid out on a table, a millefiori paperweight, a book of poems. "Ever'body in this house thinking about their hair. Espessil Edith—" She broke off to laugh, and then remembered something. "You, Bill, be a good liddle boy roon upstairs'n tell Edith that Miller, he says to meet'm tomorra five o'clock."

"*Miss* Edith," Mrs. Fanning automatically corrected her as she had, unavailingly, for years. "Wait," she said to George who had started away, only too glad to have an excuse to remove his unsatisfactory haircut from woman's scrutiny. "Wait—" She sat, half-turned from them, at her desk with one hand motionless on the olive-green blotter. . . . Poor Mrs. Fanning, sitting there really alone, obliged to make yet another decision. It is really sad to contemplate her, her figure so erect and sure, but for once in her eyes a mist of uncertainty. . . . It is a terrible thing to know that one is always in the right, terrible to catch people at their mistakes, and yet, what is one to do? Surely not let them persevere on their mistaken course? . . . The momentary mist cleared from the sloe-dark eyes and she saw even clearer that there must be an end to all

[209]

this foolishness between Edith and Jacob Miller. If she couldn't manage to make her accept Callie Canty-Mallet's job, she would simply have to work up some other solution. "*I* will tell Miss Edith," she said to Anna, who was by now dusting the little gold French clock. "I am just going upstairs." She regarded the boys aimlessly dawdling before her. "Run out and play, boys. Play in the sun. I'll give the message to Edith, and as a matter of fact I do not want you to speak to her about it at all. Can you remember that? George? Lucius? Well, then, run along now and stay out until luncheon time."

She swept past them and up the stairs to her own room. She closed the door and going to the telephone beside her bed picked it up, and smiled into it, and invited Sylvester Wagstaff and his millions to tea on Sunday. "Oh, four-thirty, or perhaps a bit before," she said. "That will be nice. Oh, no. Not a party! No, no; just the family. Just ourselves."

Earlier that morning Tom, the gardener-chauffeur, got out of bed on the wrong side. In one glance across the breakfast table his wife recognized this and did her best to aggravate his bad temper, being herself a bored woman, of some spirit.

"Afraid it's going to rain today," she remarked, knowing he had planned to paint the porch chairs. She glanced out the window of their flat on the upper story of Mrs. Fanning's garage and nodded her head slowly. "Eh-yuh," she said, as if in reluctant confirmation of her prediction.

"Ga-ah!"

"Cats and dogs, it looks like. You want some more coffee?"

"That dishwater!"

She laughed pleasantly and, a little finger elegantly crooked, poured out for herself a second large cup.

"Still, if dishwater's all we got." He thrust his cup in her direction.

"Gone now," she said, and rising lightly set the empty pot in the sink and turned hot water into it; dark brown grounds fountained out and ran into the sink. "I *ast* you."

"Ga-ah!"

She beamed at him. "Old Joe Gloom, this morning." This was enough to set off a recital of grievances from deep within him, a recent dentistry bill, what she paid for groceries and the peculiarly poor use she made of these groceries, her brother's frequent visits, the price of her most recent pair of shoes, the nasty color of those shoes— green!—their shape too and the probable brevity of their life span, which he was convinced couldn't possibly be a day longer than two weeks. He could have painted a whole settee, perhaps even a wicker chair, in the time he lingered indoors, picking his teeth and berating his wife; it didn't help matters any when, turning away from her at last though she was still unrepentant, still maddeningly cheerful, he looked outdoors and saw a blaze of sunshine, and his paint not yet even stirred.

Vulnerable, and utterly unprepared, the boys back from the barber's encountered Tom in the cobbled courtyard. "Hi," they said, not having observed his face. They were ambling around with their hands in their pockets, trying to keep in the sun, which they had heard encouraged the growth of hair.

Tom halted. "How long're you going to leave that thing there in my way?" he demanded.

Lucius quickly took his hands from his pockets and went nearer to his masterpiece. "It's a cathedral."

[211]

Tom forced down his jaw in extravagant disbelief. "A *cat-edral!*"

"Yes, of course. A cathedral." But a flicker of anxiety appeared in his eyes; why hadn't Tom known it for what it was?

"With a transfer out in front? Go on! You're trying to fool me." He gave a snort of disagreeable laughter.

"Transept. Well . . . why not?" Lucius' doubt grew. "Why shouldn't it be? I mean, . . . aren't they?"

Beginning to feel better, and more like himself, Tom nudged the front of the building with the toe of his big shoe, not much, not enough to unsettle bricks, just enough to terrify Lucius. "I should've thought any dope would've known about transipts." His toe prodded again, and with more force, and bricks shifted.

"Don't do that, damn you!" Lucius cried and as he fell on his knees to protect his toppling masterpiece George hit the enemy full in the stomach.

"You leave alone our cathedral!" He hit out again, smack on the soft blue-demin stomach, beside himself with outrage and fraternal passion. He forgot, in a flash and forever, how Lucius had been high-handed in accepting his help and had scorned all his suggestions and had let him work only at insignificant parts, like paving. With his sneakered foot he lashed out at Tom's great thick leg; it hurt him severely. "Oh *you!*" he cried, impotent, too angry even for anathema. He bent and picked up a brick.

It was all over in less than a minute. Tom, roaring like a bull, jerked Lucius to his feet by the belt, slapped George across the face, and ran them both out of the courtyard. His exertions burst a button from his shirt and he roared again, pulled at the lacerated blue cotton cloth and made the boys look too. "Now see what you done!" Stumbling,

[212]

they looked over their shoulders briefly, and hurried away. Tom, swaggering, carried his repair work inside. "Them scrimey little twirps!" he said and his wife, all womanly sympathy and unexpected admiration, sewed on another button without even making him remove the shirt.

"Now what's the matter?" Mrs. Fanning looked at George's tear-ravaged face. Such an unattractive little boy, she thought, and was glad the week was so nearly up; under the cropped pale hair the face was small, insignificant and dirty. He looked like an unloved wet cat. "What is he crying for? Has he hurt himself?" she inquired of Lucius who was very near the bursting point from rage and frustration.

"We had to fight Tom." It did not occur to him that it had been only George who had visited physical reproof upon the gardener any more than it would have occurred to him, back in the courtyard, to have hit their tormentor—because what if he were right about transepts? George would have hit him anyway but Lucius, left alone with Tom, would have been more likely to get to the heart of the matter by talking it over, arguing, explaining, ultimately accepting correction, if absolutely necessary, though not without profanity. But events had moved too fast for him, mediation had been by-passed and in time to come he would always remember the battle in the courtyard as having been long, ferocious, bloody and superbly triangular.

"You had to fight Tom?"

She didn't listen to their simultaneous replies—"He kicked Lucius' cathedral!"—"He was laughing at my cathedral!" Nothing remained of her mouth but a thin line. She had Tom summoned to the house and she swept into

[213]

the morning room sucking the three male creatures in after her like a tall liner compelling reluctant rowboats to follow in her wake. She sat down and confronted them. *"Well?"* she inquired.

"I didn' kick his house," Tom protested, his voice as aggrieved as though he spoke the truth; then he speculated foxily whether it would set well with the old girl to give her the kind of smile one grownup gives another in the presence of childish foolishness; the adumbrations of this patronizing grimace began forming around his thick mouth, but he needn't have bothered; she was on his side anyway.

"Probably you were only fooling?" She moved her silver letter-opener three inches to the right and aligned it carefully with the edge of the blotter.

"Yeah, that's it. Sure, I was only fooling, like I was going to touch it, but I didn't really come anywheres near it."

George did not contradict but he stamped, once, and his eyes darted from one grownup to the other. Lucius, his head pressed back and his hands in his pockets, looked sideways at Tom; how anybody could lie like that and live! As the week had gone on and the boys had hardened up in self-defense they still had not forged themselves weapons against falsehood. Lucius by nature had a firmer hold on serenity than George, and he knew now that he wouldn't get anywhere if he tried to explain to Mrs. Fanning that what had really hurt him had been, not the menacing, blunt boot, but the cruel bit of news about transepts. He gazed reflectively at her face. The boys were quite accustomed to normal family exasperation but not to the dry subcutaneous kind they had encountered among the inhabitants of the Evergreen Avenue house. How mad and busy she is, all the time, he thought, kind of like a hornet, and then, his mind returning to his own problems, with a twinge of embarrassment he said to himself: As if I wouldn't have found out about transepts by myself, in time! He said nothing to Tom's explanations but George burned to have the simple truth made known, broke silence, and nodding solemnly, over and over, to punctuate his words he reminded Tom of what had actually taken place. "You said, 'Ho! It's all wrong!' and then you stuck out your big foot and bashed it and it began to shake—don't you remember!"

Tom gave a jovial false laugh. "Kids!" he said, and shook his head as though amused at their odd little ways. "Of course kids wouldn't know. Probably you can't expect it. But that Mr. Miller, I guess his name is, and me, yesterday, we was laughing because he seen the church what the boys call it, and he says how they got it built all wrong."

"*Mr. Miller!*" This was too much. So he had been to the house again and no one had told her. She closed her eyes like someone in prayer but when she opened them it was apparent she had not been engaged in supplication, nor in any exercise of piety, but in devising an all-encompassing revenge. "You will stay in your rooms all the rest of the morning," she said to the boys. "And you are not to talk to each other nor to anyone. I do not want to hear a sound out of you until luncheon. You ought to be ashamed of yourselves, causing all this commotion over nothing and I am sure if your mother knew she would be *mortified*." She turned to Tom. "I expect the porch furniture to be dry by tonight." All three felt that the heat of her annoyance would indeed be enough to dry out the essential oils by six.

Banished, George was rifling the guest-room desk and from the open window launched letter-paper darts toward the parasol tree. He could see gay glints of painted glass through the leaves which were today so much larger than they had been less than a week ago—that week a lifetime—when he first defied Mrs. Fanning by climbing up among them to hang his harp in a safe place. Not that it had proved to be such a very safe place after all. But he would always prefer to have it overcome, if that must sometimes happen, by a natural force like rain rather than by a human being, *much* rather than by Mrs. Fanning. "I keep my eye on you," he assured it. The monogrammed darts sped from his hand with the obvious intention of reaching an objective but once out in the air turned oddly idle, slipped sideways, feinted at the green screen of leaves surrounding the harp, turned aside and sidled down the air, down to the lawn. "Magic," George said with satisfaction; his harp was invulnerable, like truth. It winked and signaled its integrity to him through the green and the passing breeze played arpeggios on the prisms. "Oh boy," he said; day after day after tomorrow the hollow day would be over and they could go home. "And a good thing, too," he said aloud. Mrs. Fanning had called the boys back to her after dismissing Tom. She said she was afraid they did not quite realize the harm they had done; when people went visiting in other people's houses their major concern was to show an invariable consideration; she said that though Tom had been with her for only a few months she had found him quite satisfactory and now she was sorry—more than sorry, she had said, mystifying them somewhat—to have him upset. *What* a curious unpleasant habit of mind, the boys had thought, that assumes you know all about a subject and yet continues, relentlessly, telling you about it; reiteration is the cruelest of weapons. "So for the rest of the week you must keep out of the courtyard. He was only fooling with you. You should have been able to tell by the twinkle in his eyes."

"Pig's twinkle," George had murmured, making matters no better.

Now he launched an intricately folded envelope which went up, way up before it turned toward the ground; well, that was a pleasure. That could be done again. But he found there were no more envelopes in the cubbyhole and he looked around for other material for darts but there was nothing. "I guess I'll go to the bathroom, then," he said aloud. "She couldn't stop me from doing that, I should hope."

The door to Edith's room was part way open; he could see a slice of her, drooped on the floor before an electric heater. He silently slipped through the crack. "Hi," he whispered, and grinned. "S-sh. I'm being punished." She did not respond to his look or his words; her long hands lay on a closed book in her lap. "Because I beat up Tom."

"Oh, for Heaven's sake."

"*Well!* For Heaven's *sake!* I had to! I'll tell you about it." He sidled nearer and squatted down sociably but she turned her head away and said she didn't want to hear about it. George asked what was biting her and she burst out, "Oh, don't bother me. I'm furious, that's all. I was going to a wonderful lecture with Mr. Miller and now I'm not. That's all. It's nothing."

George nodded. "I see. Well, he probably had to go shopping with his wife, I guess."

"Jacob? He isn't married."

"He is, too."

"He isn't."

"He is, too. He told us, I and Lucius."

"When?"

"When was he married, do you mean?"

She leaned over and shook his jersey shoulder. "When did he *tell* you? I don't believe it." She was staring at him as though the force of her look would pull out information from him, or would force him to deny his own wicked words. "When?"

"When we took my harp to him, cross-patch. Now I'm going to the bathroom. That's where I'm on my way. I'm not supposed to talk to anybody," he finished virtuously, straightened up and slid back into the hall through her half-open door. Then he thrust his head back in. "Goodby, stinker," he hissed.

Lucius was furious. He sat in his room at a round table draped in curry-colored plush and cut angry jagged shapes out of paper from his well-stocked small suitcase that he had been supposed, and indeed had had every intention, to use that week for his homework. Sharp pointed towers he cut, unattached lengths of battlement with fierce machicolations, planes of war, tanks and frightful spears. He cut no cathedrals, rightly realizing that he was in no fit mood. As the scissors tore through the paper he hissed and whispered to himself the things he wished he had thought to say to Tom. "You great big fat bastard! You smelly stinker! Take away your big fat stinking foot from my cathedral or I'll kick it off. *How many times do I have to tell you!*" Why hadn't he said all these useful things in the courtyard? He should have, he should have. "You great dumb bastard!" They were so exactly right he *must* have said some of them; one or two? Probably he had. He cut a long, dashing, lopsided sword and began to make up the conversation that he might have had, that he had had, with

[218]

Tom. Perhaps conversation is not the exact word, considering Tom wasn't allowed to get a word in edgeways and Lucius never drew breath. His rage was blowing itself out, and now his mood swooped elegantly upward into flights of sarcasm.

"Actually, I have never met a man like you before," he murmured arrogantly, raising his blond eyebrows as far as they would go. "You surprise me. You actually don't seem to understand the simplest thing about architecture, do you?" The eyebrows climbed down, the eyes narrowed; "I am *mortified!*" said Lucius. He embroidered the theme of Tom's barbarian ignorance, adding graceful scallops of acrimony, flutings of disdain. "And how fat you are, just ghastly blubber, aren't you?" All the telling remarks he hadn't made and the little bon mots which would have been effortless to him and presumably so deadly to Tom turned into quite a fine thing before he was through. The beauty of this kind of conversation is twofold—there can be no reprisals, and it is never finished.

He cut slower and slower, more carefully. Presently a lovely little tower slipped away from his scissors and lay on the curry-colored plush. Lucius drew a deep breath that trembled at its end; his fit was over. "I'd have found out about transepts myself," he said, "sooner or later."

"But them boys may never come here again," Tom's wife said to him, standing in her kitchen. "They never been here before, as far as we know."

"Ga-ah. It ain't only them. I can't stand the old bag. She gives me enough work for three men and then she says 'Oh, To-om, the paint's gotta be dry by tonight.' How'm I gonna have it dry if I don't get no chance to begin?" He spread his thick hands wide and questioning, and his wife stood silent a moment longer, plucking thoughtfully at her under lip. From beneath a scowl she glanced around the kitchen she had thought so nice when they came, six months ago; she found she didn't care for it now, and the sight of a tousled bed in the little room beyond appeared to her to be something she definitely didn't need to put up with.

"Where'd we go?" She turned to her husband and a conspiratorial gleam started up in her little brown eyes.

"My folks. Your folks. Wherever we wanna."

"My folks."

"O.K."

"When're you gonna give nodiss?"

"I ain't gonna give her no nodiss." At once gay and complacent at having persuaded his wife to join him in striking a blow at the Evergreen Avenue establishment, he decided to go the limit. "What've we got that won't go in them two suitcases? Anyways I'll keep the key and come back some time, some night say, if we have to leave any stuff. . . . I *know* I won't get no reference." He hurriedly forestalled her. "I don't want no reference. Get busy."

So, quite unknown to the people in the house, a merry bustle began in the little apartment above the garage. Layers of possessions were built up in the two suitcases, a layer of Tom's shirts—"I'll have a good chance to sew on some buttons when I'm home doing nothing; Momma'll help me,"—a layer of heavy, pink, sliding rayon underwear, a layer of casually folded rayon dresses whose removal from the closet rack left, still, a stale smell hanging there. Shoes went in a paper bag. Bills and bottles and unloved hats were pitched toward the wastebasket.

"You gonna clean up the place?" There was a threatening note in his voice, and she laughed fondly and asked

[220]

what he took her for. He gave her an approving blow on the buttocks, she squawked extravagantly and jumped aside, they laughed, and sooner even than a confirmed optimist would have estimated, the two conspirators were ready to leave. They tiptoed down the stairs and let each other out by a seldom-used door that opened on a back street. Upstairs the sun shone full into the tumbled bed, flies swam around just under the ceiling—Tom hadn't been able to find time for the screens—hot water dripped and dripped all day from the faucet in the kitchen sink into the overflowing coffeepot.

Out in Fort Wayne Selma held out to the girl she roomed with an open fresh box of candy. "Look what I brought you. But I couldn't decide, cherries or mint," she confessed. "So I got mint."

"Mint I *love*," her friend assured her. "I love mint much better than cherries."

"I thought you would." Selma, who was not accustomed to give to others or to herself reasons for her actions and beliefs, gave no reason now for this example of prescience. She sat down on the edge of the bed and placidly worked at the catch of her handbag until she could persuade it to open, to get herself a cigarette. The contents of the bag surprised her. "Oh, look at this. I meant to show you. I got this letter yesterday from Jacob who now says *he* wants a divorce, if you can believe it, just when I've stopped caring whether I had one or not. And they tell me he's been calling up here all day. I got back just as he did, once."

The friend said *honestly,* just when everything was perfectly peaceful; and what had Selma said to him?

"Oh, well, I didn't want to go *into* it all, so I told the operator I wasn't me, I was away." She gave the pretty,

[221]

confiding, childlike laugh that once had charmed a younger Jacob.

The friend approved Selma's tactics. She urged her not to be in any hurry to oblige Jacob because, after all, what had he ever done for her? Married a whole year and then he hadn't given Selma a divorce when she wanted it. Spiteful, he must be.

Selma blew out her match and meticulously selected one particular candy from among thirty-six identical candies. "I don't know what to tell him," she said, giving way to that easy dreaminess that had enthralled him, enthralled and then, quite soon, maddened him. "What shall I tell him? He was *so* unbearable when *I* wanted one. His letter doesn't give any reason; it's probably just some idea he's got and I think I ought to think about it for a while, don't you?" The friend nodded. "Yes, well, that's why I said to the operator . . ." She bit into the candy and her eyes flew wide open with real amazement. "Cherries!"

"Oh, well, that's all right."

"But I said mint to the girl, I'm almost sure I did."

"Oh, that's all right, really. Let's have one. I love cherries *too*."

15

MRS. FANNING stood at an open window of the morning room looking out over the encircling dark green tufts of rhododendron to the avenue. The day was already very warm, unnatural sudden gusts blew in past her, and a gray sky hung close. The day is unsettled, she said to herself and then added, impatiently, but no more so than my own household. Ever since the moment those boys set foot in her house the beautiful neat fabric of domestic custom had been slowly warping—Catherine gone—Edith defiant, moody, inexplicable, and certainly unsuccessful at whatever projects she had in mind, she was *so* disagreeable— *Tom* gone! Only Anna was unaffected, singing and trumpeting all day, in her regrettable way. She couldn't understand how all this disintegration had come about, to her who was usually so impregnable, efficient, and nervously able. It was as though creatures from some sub-world, armed with invisible weapons had come among them.

"How does it look out?" Mr. Howe inquired from behind his May-June copy of *Bird-Watcher;* he flexed his knees comfortably, and turned two pages of *Bird-Watcher* and never knew the difference. Sundays were his favorite day because he had not even to glance toward the space on the mantel beside the gold clock for mail. Some old men are hebdomadally angry that there are no Sunday deliveries; not Mr. Howe; if the U. S. Post Office Department had amended its rules Mr. Howe might, almost, have written a letter to a newspaper about it.

"Nobody's carrying umbrellas that I can see, but it's black at the end of the avenue. It will rain." Mrs. Fanning bent slightly at the waist and looked up along the street of dark Greek façades toward the Chemistry Laboratory at the top. Churchgoers in the avenue moved slowly, a more-than-Sunday languor upon them. Though to all of them a storm seemed inevitable, something retarded their Sunday-clad limbs; they passed slowly by, their best clothes menaced. In the tops of the elms isolated little branches nodded affirmatively, once or twice, secretly informed by some breeze, by an airy intimation, that a storm was coming. Close-ranked tulips stood at the edges of lawns, shoulder to shoulder, ready to defy everyone's enemies, the rain and the wind; they glowed like enamels in the uneasy air. Summer must really be coming; two thunderstorms in one week! No doubt the same portentous weight of expected storm was resting on all the town, but Sundays Mrs. Fanning was always able, miraculously, to consider only Evergreen Avenue, eliminating from her mind all the widespread localities of her Monday through Friday enterprises; it was quite as though all those other streets of the town, those slums and settlement houses, and all the problem people who filled them to bursting obligingly went into a condition of trance for the week-end, and would not begin to move and breathe and fight and conceive

[224]

children and go about their troublesome ways again until the first drop of the gavel, Monday morning.

"I don't know that I feel so much like going to church," she said, one brown-spotted hand laid along her cheek, her dark, cylindrical figure motionless in the window frame.

"The boys leave this forenoon?" Mr. Howe asked.

"No, no, not until some time Tuesday. Why do you always say *forenoon?* They haven't been here quite a week yet, anyway."

"They *haven't?*" He said well, he was very much surprised to hear that. He did not actually dislike the boys, but he had been apprehensive that their being there would cause nameless inconveniences, and he had said as much, several times a day, to his sister. Actually, at their advent, he had retired beneath the integument of inattention most characteristic of him, so that of the occupants of the house their presence affected him the least. But the household would be more comfortable when they had gone; of all the occupants, only Anna loved them. "Seems like a month, doesn't it?" But there was no reply from Mrs. Fanning, it being part of her policy in philanthropic matters—and surely, having George and Lucius here was proving to be a case of the purest philanthropy—never to admit mistakes. This policy made her as good a basic platform as any other she could have devised for whirling on to yet other enterprises; for what would life *be* without committees to take up one's terrible free time? Intolerable.

Edith, not knowing what to do with herself for the rest of the morning until luncheon, nor indeed for the next fifty or sixty years, came lagging down the mustard-colored length of the carpeted wide stairs. Her legs and back ached from wondering why she had been betrayed, her

[225]

eyes felt dry and stiff from hours of staring into the darkness, lying tense, wondering about Jacob. He had not called again Saturday, as she had hoped he would. She had very little to go on. She lived over, in imagination, so many times that its virtue had worn thin, the scene on the sofa before the Recusants' dinner party, and it was becoming merely a scene, as in the theater, with herself for spectator; it no longer had the power to make her feel deliciously weak. By now there should have been between them further scenes, delicately more sensual, to replace it. . . . What did Jacob's wife look like? Pretty? All at once she had known, with a sick clarity at about twelve o'clock at night, just what she looked like—the Venetian virgin. Then what, she had asked herself the rest of the night, what had ever made her feel he loved her? She recalled the comment of the boy at the house party, long ago, and her bowed spirit acquiesced in his judgment.

"My dear," said Mrs. Fanning, sweeping into the hall so unexpectedly that Edith jumped, "I hope you've been thinking over your Cousin Callie's offer seriously, and expect to take it. You'll never get another such opportunity." She straightened the strip of damask under the silver card tray. If she could have accomplished a momentary transmogrification of minds with the unhappy girl, she would have, to insure her going. "Come into the morning room a moment, will you?"

Edith leaned against the side of an empty wing-chair. You think it's a chance to get me comfortably off your hands and out of this house, she thought, and I don't blame you for wanting this. I'm not your daughter. We do not love each other. Ever since the day I was forced, as a child, to leave my own home for the alien comfort of this big Evergreen Avenue house I have moved in a self-spun aura of resentment, because nothing here is mine, not even my life; or so it seems to me. I have said *Thank you* only when it has been impossible to avoid, but I have been without gratitude, and known myself to be thorny and näive and probably in your way. But if there ever has been any understanding between us, now is the time to draw on it because I don't want to go to New York. . . . But there has not been understanding, or love, either from you or Father, except perhaps, from him, a thin sort of "This is my daughter" pride, automatic and lifeless. So now I have no love to give you. What store of it I have managed to accumulate I was going to give Jacob. But now—where is Jacob?

As unconscious as ever of her need, as unwilling as ever to see responsibility and take it, Mr. Howe neatly flicked over a page of *Bird-Watcher* and brought his whole attention to bear on the nesting habits of Canada geese; fine birds, fine birds. "H'mn," he said, admiringly, "all the way down here from Labrador!"

"Father!"

"H'hmn? Yes, Edith?"

". . . nothing." She thrust her hands deep into the for-ever-empty slanting pockets of her skirt, and returned her attention to her aunt waiting in the window. It was hardly worth while, because she knew already what they were, to give Mrs. Fanning a chance to unleash all the good reasons she must be holding ready and she knew if she let her have her say she would yet retain under the strong gray hair, within her strong mind, unsaid but potent, a dozen other reasons for Edith's going. Mrs. Fanning would never say aloud, "If you marry Jacob Miller and continue to live in this town, Jacob Miller who hasn't a cent, just think of all the work I shall have, straightening problems out for you, and you will not be grateful to me. There will be babies and I shall insist on giving you presents for them you don't want and don't like; you will have to be asked for Sunday luncheon often; I can see us now—Jacob bored and rude, and I, bored and polite; I shall have to lend you Anna in emergencies. Your children will have colds and when I go to see you in your cheap flat I shall catch them, and be ill, and unable to attend committee meetings." Out loud she said, as nicely as though it had been true, "My cousin has always told me how much she liked you." When Edith had no reply to this she went on, "Life in a university town is pretty limited after all, isn't it? I'm sure you realize it, but think of all the opportunities you'd have in New York. Not that I want to force you in any way, but my cousin knows very interesting people." All this meandering affair with Jacob Miller had gone on too long! And what if in the course of it the job disappeared, as jobs have a way of doing? The tacit understanding had always been that Edith was to go to work after college when a good chance offered, but, on the other hand, no one would have opposed a perfectly suitable marriage.

Edith knew her face looked as though having to meet interesting people must be the ultimate woe, but she couldn't think of anything to say against it. After a sterile silence Mrs. Fanning must have felt that now she had, without question, the upper hand. She lightly but firmly lifted out and resettled in their classic folds the heavy citron-colored velvet curtains and with her face averted dared to say, "Mr. Miller had something come up yesterday that prevented his taking you to the lecture?"

Against this cruel unexpected stroke Edith had no ready nor adequate defense, neither for Jacob nor for herself; even her father looked up to see what she had to say. "We

[228]

missed connections," she lied quickly. "He's going to call." The big gray knot at the back of Mrs. Fanning's head looked skeptical but Mr. Howe accepting the lie that was nearer to the truth than any of them could know went back to reread a paragraph that advised the growing of one's own sunflower seeds in order to avoid disappointment, both for oneself and one's feathered friends, if one's hardware store ran short.

"Well, Cousin Callie can't keep the job open too long, I shouldn't suppose. Will you go tell Anna cucumber sandwiches for tea and that I'm having supper at the Faculty Club this evening but will she please leave a vegetable salad for the rest of you before she goes out, and fruit. In the icebox. French dressing."

Edith strayed right through Nicanor as she went aimlessly out into the yard after delivering the message to the kitchen, on around the corner of the house, and slumped down onto the wooden bench. It had never occurred to her that he could be married; married professors and instructors lived with their wives and usually children. Probably she was never meant, ever, to be happy, anywhere. He should have told her. . . . She tried to coat over the sharpness of the knowledge of Jacob-married with a layer of not-caring, as people coat over by eating bread disastrously sharp things they have made the mistake of swallowing. She ran her hand along the thickly painted wood; domed flakes, the roofs of ancient bubbles, crackled and broke. How sad, how strange; this was the same bench where he and she had conjured up happiness for themselves out of nothing, out of a handful of damp daffodils, months, years, ages ago . . . last Monday!

Lucius pulled Nicanor's long, dark-velvet ears through

[229]

his hands. "What'll we do," he murmured, idly. "Nothing happens here!"

"I know, I know," came in unusually deep tones from George; what else could one expect from a hollow day, he seemed to imply. Lucius had not asked a question; he had learned for himself there was nothing to do, or rather, that whatever they might think up in the Evergreen Avenue house would have no normal outcome. Whatever they did there somehow took a wrong turning, as if a malevolent magnet pulled, and then the result of their activities proved not to have been fun anyway. Even before breakfast that morning he and George had been scolded; the fact that he had kindly helped George to kneel up on the rim of the washbowl to inspect his haircut in the bathroom mirror—he had assured George he could take it as God's truth the hair hadn't grown a millimeter in the night, "not even the trillionth of an inch, George,"—should merely have showed how helpful he was to his brother and not, as Mrs. Fanning had implied, want of consideration for other people's property, George's foot having slipped as he frowningly contemplated his tonsure and sent a bottle of lavender bath salts crashing to the tiled floor. Shortly after this undeserved bit of ill fortune they had been sent to the garage to ask Tom to bring in some potted freesias from the greenhouse and when they had delightedly reported their discovery of the shambles in the abandoned apartment—the unmade bed, yesterday's cold coffee and warm butter—Mrs. Fanning had turned on them. "It's you, then, who made him go!"

"Us?" they cried, astounded. "*We* did?"

All morning they hung around under the parasol tree hoping for the thunderstorm. "Oh well, anyway, never

[230]

mind," Lucius would say vaguely, and then more energetically, "Remember, day after tomorrow!"

After a large Sunday luncheon they returned, to lie on the soft grass and digest and doze.

"If it rains I'm going right up this tree no matter what," George muttered from time to time; he was more concerned with one possible imminent trouble than the day-after-tomorrow release from all of them, still so far off. Day after tomorrow was a long way away. His harp, as he peered up, hung motionless in the ominous heavy air; he could see its enchanting colors but it had no voice for him. "It could get struck by lightning as easy as not." With a quick twinge in his stomach he knew exactly how it would look if a bolt searched it out, a million splintering red and green and crystal and lemon-yellow jewels flying irretrievably in all directions, a burst of splendor and then, no harp at all; just the string. Why he exempted the string from destruction may not be understandable, but he did and the picture of it hanging useless was pathetic, most affecting. "If she wasn't home I'd go right up the tree this minute. Why the heck doesn't she clear out and take a walk. She *ought* to take a walk before tea."

"Send Lentenor up," Lucius suggested, but then they both sighed, recognizing the foolishness of the suggestion, and that there are limitations to imaginary dogs, though who shall say what these limitations are? Only their creators. Both George and Lucius knew that Lentenor and Nicanor, lithe and dear and talented though they were, must not be asked to climb ornamental trees and bring down glass harps in their teeth. "Lie down, boys," Lucius said to them and watched them turn and turn and settle, and rest their long muzzles on their long paws.

"And stewed rhubarb for supper," said Cassandra-

George. "Pugh! All strings. I saw it in the kitchen when I came through." Lucius cried, "Hell's bells, *rhubarb?*" That *was* the last straw!

Mrs. Fanning, in the dining room, a little after four o'clock, swaddling the Recusants' épergne in its luxurious plum-colored flannel bag paused, expecting to hear Anna answer the ringing telephone at the kitchen extension, but without having informed her mistress of her decision Anna had made up her mind to answer no more bells of any kind until the advent of a cook, any cook, a new one from New York or Catherine *redivivus;* her feet couldn't take it. So Mrs. Fanning quickly tweaked the black silk cord that closed the bag and passed, rapid and erect, along the hall and into the morning room.

"Oh, she's napping—I rather think," she replied to Jacob's question, her voice purposefully vague. "Yes, I'm afraid so. No, she said nothing about meeting you today. I rather think she may be tired from packing." What an opportunity. Her eyes dropped to the rug to veil their intention, though no one was watching her.

"Packing?" repeated Jacob's startled voice.

"To go to her job in New York. She hadn't told you? Oh yes, it's one she's been intending to take for some time. . . . Yes, yes, I'll tell her to call you back, but of course she's quite busy." She hung up before he had a chance to speak and before she had put the instrument down it rang again. Western Union had a message for Lucius and George Langdon. "I'll take it. They are children visiting me. They're out. No, I don't know where they are at the moment. Yes, yes, of course I'll give it to them. They are out *playing* somewhere. . . . Yes, I have it. Thank you."

She swept through the hall again and out across the side

porch, ignoring Anna calling from the kitchen that she couldn't make French dressing without vinegar.

"George! What are you doing in that tree!"

"I'm not all the way up."

"We heard thunder," Lucius explained.

Edith, wan and big-eyed, came around the corner of the house as George climbed down, balked, resentful, and empty-handed. "Was that the telephone?" she asked. She was ready, she was all prepared, to flinch at a negative reply, but she couldn't help asking.

"Yes, it was," Mrs. Fanning said agreeably, and smiled on her audience of three. "Western Union for the boys. Your mother and father are coming home a day early, boys, and will be here to get you tomorrow instead of Tuesday."

"They *are?*" George's face flushed wholly with joy.

Edith said, doubtingly, "I thought I heard it ring twice . . . that is, as if it rang two times. Didn't it?"

Mrs. Fanning was searching the sky for weather signs. "H'hmn?" she murmured. "Oh, no. No, it does that sometimes, you know. Just a telegram from Bermuda." How calm and smooth is the voice of someone who knows best. "Though it would be a cablegram, I suppose, wouldn't it? So why don't you two go in and start in on your packing? You've got half an hour before tea."

"So I have to get my harp now."

"No, not now. Tomorrow will do and Tom will—oh no, not Tom! *Some*one will get it down for you. Think how your mother would feel if she came home after a nice rest and found you with a broken arm, or ankle." She thought it was quite remarkable she should be able to keep such a kind voice when she reflected that Tom would never have left but for the absurd fracas with these two. "You won't

[233]

need to change for supper tonight so you can put in your blue jackets, and toys. I'm going to be out for supper."

Lucius, in George's behalf, asked what if it rained pretty soon.

"It isn't going to rain. I've been saying to Mr. Howe all day, it isn't going to rain after all. Run along." She turned and trod firmly on Nicanor's tail as she started back for the house and Nicanor's great golden eyes rolled reproachfully up at her, but he never stirred.

"Good dog," said Lucius, proudly.

George, who often forgot to bear his grudges, forgot to again. Perhaps he would have clung to one now if he had remembered—so far, if temporarily, had his character deteriorated in a week—but as it was he thought, merely, as he regarded Edith: She hasn't got anything to do, any more than we have. Then, "Oh!" he exclaimed. "Hey! *Edith*— aren't you going to be late?"

"Late?"

George wagged his head. "You need a nurse," he said to her, as his mother in infrequent bursts of exasperation said to him. "Don't tell me you've forgotten all about meeting Jacob."

Corroboration came from Lucius. "At five o'clock, he told Anna. You'd better step on it."

But then the irrational girl horrified them by beginning to weep; they almost wished they hadn't told her; they wished they *hadn't* told her, except it ought to prove a way of getting rid of her. It took both of them a long time, and much repetition, not to speak of patience, to get across to her an essentially simple fact. "Mrs. Fanning must have forgotten," they said, seven or eight times, pleased, naturally, at this evidence of fallibility in their hostess; and in the end she never even thanked them but darted into

[234]

the house for her gloves and bag; they could hear her stumbling up the back stairs and right after that, the slamming of the front door. They swung around slowly and watched her running, running along beyond the low black iron railing, headed downtown. Her head was held up, her eyes straight ahead; she looked like the figurehead on a moving ship.

"She could at least wave," George pointed out irritably, unaware that he had just changed the whole course of her life, and Lucius nodded, and said in a voice whose profound solemnity was not necessarily at odds with a complete absence of meaning, "Sometimes I wonder."

16

DECEPTION was alien to George, whose gifts and instincts were all for the direct attack, and argument, endless argument, if necessary. That was why he had been surprised to have a roundabout solution occur to him for calming his worry about the harp being struck by lightning in the night. The thunderstorm built up all day, slowly, as if it did not want to profane the Sabbath, but surely, too, as if it couldn't be expected to contain itself forever. Lucius at the supper table said he could taste it coming in the stewed rhubarb and when he laid down his spoon after the first bite no one felt it worth while to exhort him to finish or to reason with him about vitamins or waste; he would be gone from Evergreen Avenue forever by that time to-morrow and it could never again concern anybody in that house whether or not he made good use of seasonal vegetable matter. Anyway, Mrs. Fanning was out, Mr. Howe wasn't noticing and Edith, who had arrived late and breathless, sliding into her chair with her cheeks flaming

[236]

and her eyes shining, was at that moment the last person in the world to care who ate rhubarb and who didn't.

George's good idea about what to do for the harp occurred to him as he poised his spoon above his dessert plate and he was so satisfied with it, instantly, that he ate the stringy greenish mess without a murmur; he knew he would have to be deft and quick about it, and unobtrusive, though considerably less so than if Mrs. Fanning were at home. He had hung around the halls all the late afternoon, waiting for her to be gone. He and Lucius had been required to come to the living room for tea with a plump young man named Wagstaff; the boys had been amused at his name but had found nothing to say to him, and they preserved a discreet silence when Mrs. Fanning said, not once but several times, "I *can't* think where Edith is! She was right here—and now where is she! Run up again, George dear, and take another look in her room." After the fat young man, casting reproachful glances into the corners of the hall, had early taken himself off, Mrs. Fanning was as restless as George and they kept encountering one another. She would say, "Ah, George," and pass on not telling him the thing in her mind, and he would say, "Hi," and nothing more, but he would revolve on one sneaker and watch her out of sight down a hall, or into the sewing room. If she had been less absorbed with knitting up reassurances inside herself she might have stopped and asked him why he wasn't out playing.

By six in the afternoon she had shut herself in her room to dress to go out to supper. Peace, peace, he had counseled himself; it won't be long now; something will occur to me. He had had need to adjure himself because the storm was rising up faster, like a great gray-black beast about to pounce, waiting only to decide where. He had watched and calculated. She came out sooner than he supposed she would; under the smart black hat with its *chou* of tulle her face looked troubled; she drew her black charcoal gloves through her fingers and looked to right and left. "George, *do* you know where Edith is?"

"Not exactly."

"Lucius, then? I'd like to have him give her a message after I've gone."

Oh, joy; she was going then. "*I'll* do it." If she would only go; the storm was creeping nearer; he had heard its chill breath streaming through the tree tops.

"I don't know," she said, doubtfully. "Lucius is older."

"But he forgets more. I'll tell her. What'll I tell her?"

But even then candor had escaped her. She could not say, simply, "Tell her Jacob Miller has been trying to see her. Tell her to call him." She had drawn her gloves on slowly, and stared over George's sandy head. "Tell her," she had said, choosing her words, "some man called today, earlier. I couldn't catch the name . . . *maybe* it was, I'm not sure really, it might have been that Mr. Miller. Tell her I'm sorry I forgot. . . . Oh, is that the doorbell? Then it's your supper time. Run right down. My taxi . . ."

"O.K., O.K." But now she had been as impatient to be gone as he was to have her go, and she did not linger to reprove him; by this time tomorrow he would be back in Sharon where he belonged and for all she cared he could say "O.K." the rest of his life. She had opened her purse for a quick look inside; just as she had thought, the secretary's notes for the annual meeting of the Sunday Night Supper Club were safe inside. The front doorbell had rung again. "I shall be at the Faculty Club," she had said and swept down her beautiful velvet stairs.

Supper had been silent and short, but enlivened pri-

[238]

vately for George by the birth of his happy idea. Not more than a minute after laying down his dessert spoon he was up in the parasol tree hooking the red string loop around his isolated teeth. Not a minute too soon, he thought, carefully backing down; already he heard a single great drop, and then another, falling on the parasol leaves; the leaves rustled and tossed themselves about in delighted anticipation; they spread themselves wide to receive the coming flood. George slipped into the pantry and it was but the work of an instant to decide where to put the harp; he bedded it down in comfort and utter safety in a soft drift of Quaker Oats and fitted back the cover. He carried the box out to the abandoned green wooden cupboard on the porch. There it could stay throughout the storm, no one the wiser, and when it was safe to do it, and only then, he would return and hang it back in the tree so that, tomorrow morning, when his parents came, there it would be, and Mrs. Fanning could superintend its removal.

Anna, who hadn't had anywhere to go on her evening off, was sitting in the kitchen when he came back a little later. She greeted him with delight. "Vell, hello, Bill!" She had been looking at a photograph in *Svea* of King Gustave and his embroidery. "Looket, Bill, soch a vunderful old man," she said, with love and admiration. "I'd yoost like to shake him by the hand vunce."

"Maybe you vill—will, I mean." George idled against the table where her elbows rested. "When you go back to Trekarten to have your little bakery, tell me about then."

But for once she did not launch into a contented bout of repetitiousness; perversely, this once she wouldn't. "No-o-o. I been thinking," she said. "I been remembering. Yes. . . . I been remembering about my brudder and I, how ve used to love to go and wisit our oncle. He had a

[239]

stuffed stork hung in his outdoor votter-closset. There he hang. I don't know vot he voss; ve called'm a stork." She drew the word out long, as long as the bird's long legs.

"Yes," George said. "Stork."

She laughed. "That's vot ve called'm," she said. "I don't know vot *you'd* call'm."

"Yes, so do we."

"Oh, you talk Svedish?" She teased him gently. "I didn't know. Pleased to meet you, Svedish boy!"

"We *do* say stork!"

"How could you?" inquired Anna, to whom the whole world of books was as though it did not exist. "You don't have'm in this country. Vell, there he hang for all the world to see, big as life. Hanged in my oncle's votter-closset. Oh, how ve loved to go there, my brudder and I, yoost to see'm."

Later that evening George lay stiff in his bed, trying not to sleep. The rain that had followed the thunderstorm was still heavy outdoors and though Mrs. Fanning had come home perhaps she was not yet asleep, and he had to stay awake until such time as he could safely rehang the harp where it must be on Monday morning; he couldn't risk having his father and mother hear one of her absurd tirades about tree-climbing and broken legs; she might even tell them he had been naughty and obstinate; *he* obstinate! He drowsed off occasionally, and then would jerk awake. He woke once to hear the clock strike eleven and rearing up, listened further; no rain fell; there was no sound in the house; everyone must be sleeping.

So now up the dark tree whose top was silvered with sudden moonlight he carefully climbed. For the last time he hooked the string loop back over the knob and, sighing with relief, made his silent way back down the wet trunk—relief because this must be, positively, the last time in his visit that it would be necessary to disobey; there was almost no remaining hollow day to disobey in. Bright moonlight flooded the wet world. The grass was moongreen, soaked and brilliant; the house was a block of coal, the nearby greenhouse a huge dripping faceted jewel; through its tilted windows came the scent of plants waiting to be set outdoors for the Summer; Tom hadn't managed to find the time; who would do it now? George, feeling incredibly wide-awake, dropped to the lawn. The greenhouse plants were awake too; he could see the faces of geraniums and fuchsias staring out at him. "Geraniums never sleep," he said.

He looked up at the sky. A few small clouds sped across the moon.

This was the last time he would ever hang his singing harp in this tree. He stood quiet a moment. His hands and wrists and his skimpy seersucker pajamas were covered with black marks from the bark of the tree. Slowly he moved one foot over the shorn grass and cold wet washed his small bare instep. He fetched a trembling deep sigh, now that there was nothing left to bother him. The hollow day was almost over and there was nothing now—there wasn't, was there? *Was* there— There could be nothing else he should have seen to. A fragmentary, nagging doubt, a shred of uncertainty, chased around under his pale crest of hair, but for the life of him he couldn't think what it was. *Had* she told him something he must do; when she left to go out to supper at the Faculty Club had she said something—oh, that she was sorry about the telephone call and he must tell Edith so. Yes, that was it; that was all; he sighed again in relief. Oh, well! Hours and hours ago that had been and anyway grownups ought to have learned by their time of life to manage their own affairs, which were not ever as important as they seemed to think. The westward flight of time must have divested her message of its urgency, and it couldn't matter now. The only thing that did matter was that, throughout a week of stress and menace, he had managed to preserve his harp from harm, from rain and trouble and strange inimical people. A light breeze stirred in the parasol tree, a breeze that felt almost like dawn chilled the skin under the wet patches of his pajamas and set the harp whispering merrily among the leaves and twigs. But he knew that really it would be a long time until morning; there was a long time yet for him to sleep and the breeze to play with the delicate, colored prisms.

Up the porch steps he went and into the hall. He remembered to turn and bolt the door after himself and this caused him to whisper, "Yea, George, mission completed," approvingly, and then, as silently as nobody at all, he mounted the wide shallow stairs where moonlight from a hall window, down the mustard-colored velvet, dripped in a still cascade.